How Marcus Whitman Saved

Oliver W. Nixon

PREFACE.

This little volume is not intended to be a history of Oregon missions or even a complete biography of Dr. Whitman. Its aim is simply to bring out, prominently, in a series of sketches, the heroism and Christian patriotism of the man who rendered great and distinguished service to his country, which has never been fully appreciated or recognized.

In my historical facts I have tried to be correct and to give credit to authorities where I could. I expect some of my critics will ask, as they have in the past: "Who is your authority for this fact and that?" I only answer, I don't know unless I am authority. In 1850 and 1851 I was a teacher of the young men and maidens, and bright-eyed boys and girls of the old pioneers of Oregon.

Many years ago I told the story of that school to Hezekiah Butterworth, who made it famous in his idyllic romance, "The Log School House on the Columbia." It was a time when history was being made. The great tragedy at Waiilatpui was fresh in the minds of the people. With such surroundings one comes in touch with the spirit of history.

Later on, I was purser upon the Lot Whitcomb, the first steamer ever built in Oregon, and came in contact with all classes of people. If I have failed to interpret the history correctly, it is because I failed to understand it. The sketches have been written in hours snatched from pressing duties, and no claim is made of high literary excellence. But if they aid the public, even in a small degree, to better understand and appreciate the grand man whose remains rest in his martyr's grave at Waiilatpui, unhonored by any monument, I shall be amply compensated.

O. W. N.

INTRODUCTION

BY

REV. FRANK W. GUNSAULUS, D.D.,

Pastor of Plymouth Church, and President of Armour Institute, Chicago.

Among the efforts at description which will associate themselves with either our ignorance or our intelligence as to our own country, the following words by our greatest orator, will always have their place:

"What do we want with the vast, worthless area, this region of savages and wild beasts, of deserts, of shifting sands and whirlwinds of dust, of cactus and prairie dogs? To what use could we ever hope to put these great deserts, or these endless mountain ranges, impenetrable, and covered to their base with eternal snow? What can we ever hope to do with the Western coast, a coast of three thousand miles, rock-bound, cheerless, and uninviting, and not a harbor on it? What use have we for such a country? Mr. President, I will never vote one cent from the public treasury to place the Pacific coast one inch nearer to Boston than it is now."

Perhaps no words uttered in the United States Senate were ever more certainly wide of their mark than these of Daniel Webster. In their presence, the name of Marcus Whitman is a bright streak of light penetrating a vague cloud-land. Washington, with finer prevision, had said: "I shall not be contented until I have explored the Western country." Even the Father of his Country did not understand the vast realm to which he referred, nor had his mind any boundaries sufficiently great to inclose that portion of the country which Marcus Whitman preserved to the United States.

An interesting series of splendid happenings has united the ages of

4

history in heroic deeds, and this volume is a fitting testimonial of the immense significance of one heroic deed in one heroic life. The conservatism, which is always respectable and respected, had its utterance in the copious eloquence of Daniel Webster; the radicalism, which always goes to the root of every question, had its expression in the answer which Whitman made to the great New Englander.

Even Daniel Webster, at a moment like this, seems less grand of proportion than does the plain and poor missionary, with "a half pint of seed wheat" in his hand, and words upon his lips which are an enduring part of our history. Only a really illumined man, at that hour, could fitly answer Senator McDuffie, when he said: "Do you think your honest farmers in Pennsylvania, New York, or even Ohio and Missouri, would abandon their farms and go upon any such enterprise as this?" Whitman made answer by breaking the barrier of the Rockies with his own courage and faith.

It may well be hoped that such a memorial as this may be adopted in home and public library as a chapter in Americanism and its advance, worthy to minister to the imagination and idealism of our whole people. The heroism of the days to come, which we need, must grow out of the heroism of the days that have been. The impulse to do and dare noble things to-morrow, will grow strong from contemplating the memory of such yesterdays.

This volume has suggested such a picture as will sometime be made as a tribute to genius and the embodiment of highest art by some great painter. The picture will represent the room in which the old heroic missionary, having traveled over mountains and through deserts until his clothing of fur was well-nigh worn from him, and his frame bowed by anxiety and exposure, at that instant when the great Secretary and orator said to him: "There cannot be made a wagon road over the mountains; Sir George Simpson says so," whereat the intrepid pioneer replied: "There is a wagon road, for I have made it."

What could be a more fitting memorial for such a man as this than a Christian college called Whitman College? He was more to the ulterior

Northwest than John Harvard has ever been to the Northeast of our common country. Nothing but such an institution may represent all the ideas and inspirations which were the wealth of such a man's brain and heart and his gift to the Republic. He was an *avant courier* of the truths on which alone republics and democracies may endure.

Whitman not only conducted the expedition of men and wagons to Oregon, after President Tyler had made his promise that the bargain, which Daniel Webster proposed, should not be made, but he led an expedition of ideas and sentiments which have made the names Oregon, Washington and Idaho synonymous with human progress, good government and civilization. When the soldier-statesman of the Civil War, Col. Baker, mentioned the name and memory of Marcus Whitman to Abraham Lincoln, he did it with the utmost reverence for one of the founders of that civilization which, in the far Northwest, has spread its influence over so vast a territory to make the mines of California the resources of freedom, and to bind the forests and plains with the destiny of the Union.

When Thomas Starr King was most eloquent in his efforts to keep California true to liberty and union, in that struggle of debate before the Civil War opened, he worked upon the basis, made larger and sounder by the fearless ambassador of Christian civilization. In an hour when the mind of progress grows tired of the perpetual presence of Napoleon, again clad in all his theatrical glamour before the eyes of youth, we may well be grateful for this sketch of a sober far-seeing man of loyal devotion to the great public ends; whose unselfishness made him seem, even then, a startling figure at the nation's capital; whose noble bearing, great faith, supreme courage, and vision of the future, mark him as a genuine and typical American.

These hopes and inspirations are all enshrined in the educational enterprise known as Whitman College. Every student of history must be glad to recognize the fact that the history of which this book is the chronicle, is also a prophecy, and that whatever may be the fate of men's names or men's schemes in the flight of time, this college will be a beacon, shining with the light of Marcus Whitman's heroism and devotion.

CHAPTER I.

THE TITLE OF THE UNITED STATES TO OREGON—THE HUDSON BAY COMPANY—THE LOUISIANA PURCHASE

The home of civilization was originally in the far East, but its journeys have forever been westward. The history of the world is a great panorama, with its pictures constantly shifting and changing. The desire for change and new fields early asserted itself. The human family divided up under the law of selection and affinities, shaped themselves into bands and nationalities, and started upon their journey to people the world.

Two branches of the original stock remained as fixtures in Asia, while half a dozen branches deployed and reached out for the then distant and unexplored lands of the West. They reached Europe. The Gaul and the Celt, the Teuton and Slav, ever onward in their march, reached and were checked by the Atlantic that washed the present English, German and Spanish coasts. The Latin, Greek and Illyrian were alike checked by the Mediterranean. For a long period it seemed as if their journey westward was ended; that they had reached their Ultima Thule; that the western limit had been found.

For many centuries the millions rested in that belief, until the great discoveries of 1492 awakened them to new dreams of western possibilities. At once and under new incentives the westward march began again. The States of the Atlantic were settled and the wilderness subdued. No sooner was this but partially accomplished than the same spirit, "the western fever," seized upon the people.

It seems to have been engrafted in the nature of man, as it is in the nature of birds, to migrate. In caravan after caravan they pushed their way over the Allegheny Mountains, invaded the rich valleys, floated down the great rivers, gave battle to the savage inhabitants and in perils many, and with discouragements sufficient to defeat less heroic characters, they took possession of the now great States of the Middle West. The country to be

7

settled was so vast as to seem to our fathers limitless. They had but little desire as a nation for further expansion.

Up to the date of 1792, the Far West was an unexplored region. The United States made no claim to any lands bordering upon the Pacific, and the discovery made in the year 1792 was more accidental than intentional, as far as the nation was concerned.

Captain Robert Gray, who made the discovery, was born in Tiverton, R. I., 1755, and died at Charleston, S. C., in 1806. He was a famous sailor, and was the first citizen who ever carried the American flag around the globe. His vessel, The Columbia, was fitted out by a syndicate of Boston merchants, with articles for barter for the natives in Pacific ports. In his second great voyage in 1792 he discovered the mouth of the Columbia river. There had been rumors of such a great river through Spanish sources, and the old American captain probably, mainly for the sake of barter and to get fresh supplies, had his nautical eyes open.

Men see through a glass darkly and a wiser, higher power than man may have guided the old explorer in safety over the dangerous bar, into the great river he discovered and named. He was struck by the grandeur and magnificence of the river as well as by the beauty of the country. He at once christened it "The Columbia," the name of his good ship which had already carried the American flag around the globe. He sailed several miles up the river, landed and took possession in the name of the United States.

It is a singular coincidence that both Spain and England had vessels just at this time on this coast, hunting for the same river, and so near together as to be in hailing distance of each other. Captain Gray only a few days before had met Captain Vancouver, the Englishman, and had spoken to him. Captain Vancouver had sailed over the very ground passed over soon after by Gray, but failed to find the river. He had noted, too, a change in the color of the waters, but it did not sufficiently impress him to cause an investigation.

After Captain Gray had finished his exploration and gone to sea, he again fell in with Vancouver and reported the result of his discoveries. Vancouver immediately turned about, found the mouth of the river, sailed up the Columbia to the rapids and up the Willamette to near the falls.

In the conference between the English and Americans in 1827, which resulted in the renewal of the treaty of 1818, while the British commissioners acknowledged that Gray was first to discover and enter the Columbia river, yet they demanded that "he should equally share the honor with Captain Vancouver." They claimed that while Gray discovered the mouth of the river, he only sailed up it a few miles, while "Captain Vancouver made a full and complete discovery." One of the authorities stated concisely that, "Captain Gray's claim is limited to the mouth of the river."

This limit was in plain violation of the rules regulating all such events, and no country knew it better than England. Besides, it was Captain Gray's discovery, told to the English commander Vancouver, which made him turn back on his course to rediscover the same river. The claim that the English made, that "Captain Gray made but a single step in the progress of discovery," in the light of these facts, marks their claims as remarkably weak. The right of discovery was then the first claim made by the United States upon Oregon.

The second was by the Louisiana purchase from France in 1803. This was the same territory ceded from France to Spain in 1762 and returned to France in 1800, and sold to the United States for $15,000,000 in 1803, "with all its rights and appurtenances, as fully and in the same manner as they were acquired by the French Republic."

There has always been a dispute as to how far into the region of the northwest this claim of the French extended. In the sale no parallels were given; but it was claimed that their rights reached to the Pacific Ocean. Dr. Barrows says, "If, however, the claims of France failed to reach the Pacific on the parallel of 49 degrees, it must have been because they encountered the old claims of Spain, that preceded the Nootka treaty and were tacitly conceded by England. Between the French claims and the Spanish claims

9

there was left no territory for England to base a claim on. If the United States did not acquire through to the Pacific in the Louisiana purchase, it was because Spain was owner of the territory prior to the first, second and third transfers. It is difficult to perceive standing ground for the English in either of the claims mentioned.

The claim of England that the Nootka treaty of 1790 abrogated the rights of Spain to the territory of Oregon, which she then held, is untenable, from the fact that no right of sovereignty or jurisdiction was conveyed by that treaty. Whatever right Spain had prior to that treaty was not disturbed, and all legal rights vested in Spain were still in force when she ceded the territory to France in 1800, and also when France ceded the same to the United States in 1803.

The third claim of the United States was by the commission sent out by Jefferson in 1803, when Lewis and Clarke and their fellow voyagers struck the headwaters of the Columbia and followed it to its mouth and up its tributary rivers.

The fourth was the actual settlement of the Astor Fur Company at Astoria in 1811. True it was a private enterprise, but was given the sanction of the United States and a U. S. naval officer was allowed to command the leading vessel in Astor's enterprise, thus placing the seal of nationality upon it. True the town was captured and the effects confiscated in 1812 by the British squadron of the Pacific, commanded by Captain Hillyar, but the fact of actual settlement by Americans at Astoria, even for a short time, had its value in the later argument. In the treaty of Ghent with England in 1814, Astoria, with all its rights, was ordered to be restored to its original owners, but even this was not consummated until 1846.

America's fifth claim was in her treaty with Spain in 1818, when Spain relinquished any and all claims to the territory in dispute to the United States.

The sixth and last claim was from Mexico, by a treaty in 1828, by which the United States acquired all interest Mexico claimed, formerly in common with Spain, but now under her own government.

Such is a brief statement, but I trust a sufficient one, for an intelligent understanding of the questions of ownership.

It will be seen that the United States was vested in all the rights held over Oregon by every other power except one, that of Great Britain. Her claim rested, as we have seen, in the fact that "Captain Gray only discovered the mouth of the river," but did not survey it to the extent that the English Captain Vancouver did, after being told by Gray of his discovery. They also made claims of settlement by their Fur Company, just as the United States did by the settlement made by Astor and others. As the Hudson Bay Company and the Northwest Fur Company of Montreal figure so extensively in the contest for English ownership of Oregon, it is well to have a clear idea of their origin and power.

The Hudson Bay Company was organized in 1670 by Charles II., with Prince Rupert, the King's cousin, at its head, with other favorites of his Court. They were invested with remarkable powers, such as had never before, nor have since, been granted to a corporation. They were granted absolute proprietorship, with subordinate sovereignty, over all that country known by name of "Rupert's Land" including all regions "discovered or undiscovered within the entrance to Hudson Strait." It was by far the largest of all English dependencies at that time.

For more than a century the company confined its active operations to a coast traffic.

The original stock of this company was $50,820. During the first fifty years the capital stock was increased to $457,000 wholly out of the profits, besides paying dividends.

During the last half of the 17th century the Northwest Fur Company became a formidable opponent to the Hudson Bay Company, and the rivalry and great wealth of both companies served to stimulate them to reach out

11

toward the Rocky Mountains and the Pacific Ocean.

After Canada had become an English dependency and the competition had grown into such proportions as to interfere with the great monopoly, in the year 1821, there was a coalition between the Northwest and the Hudson Bay Companies on a basis of equal value, and the consolidated stock was marked at $1,916,000, every dollar of which was profits, as was shown at the time, except the original stock of both companies, which amounted to about $135,000. And yet during all this period there had been made an unusual dividend to stockholders of 10 per cent.

Single vessels from headquarters carried furs to London valued at from three to four hundred thousand dollars. It is not at all strange that a company which was so rolling in wealth and which was in supreme control of a territory reaching through seventy-five degrees of longitude, from Davis Strait to Mt. Saint Elias, and through twenty-eight degrees of latitude, from the mouth of the Mackenzie to the California border, should hold tenaciously to its privileges.

It was a grand monopoly, but it must be said of it that no kingly power ever ruled over savage subjects with such wisdom and discretion. Of necessity, they treated their savage workmen kindly, but they managed to make them fill the coffers of the Hudson Bay Company with a wealth of riches, as the years came and went. Their lives and safety and profits all depended upon keeping their dependents in a good humor and binding them to themselves. The leading men of the company were men of great business tact and shrewdness, and one of their chief requisites was to thoroughly understand Indian character.

They managed year by year so to gain control of the savage tribes that the factor of a trading post had more power over a fractious band, than could have been exerted by an army of men with guns and bayonets. If, now and then, a chief grew sullen and belligerent, he was at once quietly bought up by a judicious present, and the company got it all back many times over from the tribe, when their furs were marketed.

12

It was the refusal of the missionaries of Oregon to condone crime and wink at savage methods, as the Hudson Bay Company did, which first brought about misunderstanding and unpleasantness, as we shall see in another place.

It was this power and controlling influence which met the pioneer fur traders and missionaries, upon entering Oregon. They controlled the savage life and the white men there were wholly dependent upon them.

In 1811 an American fur company at Astoria undertook to open business upon what they regarded as American soil. They had scarcely settled down to work when the war of 1812 began and they were speedily routed.

In 1818 a treaty was made, which said, "It is agreed that any country that may be claimed by either party on the Northwest coast of America westward of the Stony Mountains shall, together with its harbors, bays, creeks and the navigation of all rivers within the same, be free and open for ten years from the date of the signature of the present convention, to the vessels, citizens, and subjects of the two powers; it being well understood that the agreement is not to be construed to the prejudice of any claim which either of the two high contracting parties may have to any part of said country; nor shall it be taken to affect the claims of any other power or state to any of said country; the only object of the high contracting parties in that respect being to prevent disputes and differences among themselves."

That looked fair and friendly enough. But how did the Hudson Bay Company carry it out? They went on just as they had done before, governing to suit their own selfish interests. They froze out and starved out every American fur company that dared to settle in any portion of their territory. They fixed the price of every commodity, and had such a hold on the various tribes that a foreign company had no chance to live and prosper.

It so continued until the ten-year limit was nearly up, when in 1827 the commission representing the two powers met and re-enacted the treaty of

1818, which went into effect in 1828. It was a giant monopoly, but dealing as it did with savage life, and gathering its wealth from sources which had never before contributed to the world's commerce, it was allowed to run its course until it came in contact with the advancing civilization of the United States, and was worsted in the conflict.

With the adoption of the Ashburton treaty the Hudson Bay Company was shorn of much of its kingly power and old time grandeur. But it remained a money-making organization. Under the terms of the treaty the great corporation was fully protected. This Ashburton treaty was written in England and from English standpoints, and every property and possessory right of this powerful company was strictly guarded. The interests of the company were made English interests.

Under this treaty the United States agreed to pay all valuations upon Hudson Bay Company property south of forty-nine degrees; while England was to make a settlement for all above that line. The company promptly sent in a bill to the United States for $3,882,036.27, while their dependent company, the Puget Sound Agricultural Company, sent in a more modest demand for $1,168,000. These bills were in a state of liquidation until 1864, when the United States made a final settlement, and paid the Hudson Bay Company $450,000 and the Puget Sound Company $200,000.

They also, at the time of presenting bills to the United States, presented one to England for $4,990,036.07. In 1869 the English government settled the claim by paying $1,500,000. This amount was paid from the treasury of the Dominion of Canada, and all the vast territory north of 49 degrees came under the government of the Dominion. It was, however, stipulated and agreed that the company should retain all its forts, with ten acres of ground surrounding each, together with one-twentieth of all the land from the Red river to the Rocky Mountains, besides valuable blocks of land to which it laid special claim.

The company goes on trading as of old; its organization is still complete; it still makes large dividends of about $400,000 per year, and has

14

untold prospective wealth in its lands, which are the best in the Dominion.

Among the most interesting facts connected with our title to Oregon are those in connection with the Louisiana purchase by the United States from France in 1803. Many readers of current history have overlooked the fact, that it was wholly due to England, and her overweening ambition, that the United States was enabled to buy this great domain. Letters, which have recently been published, written by those closest to the high contracting parties, have revealed the romance, and the inside facts of this great deal, perhaps the most important the United States ever made, and made so speedily as to dazzle the Nation.

Few take in the fact that the "Louisiana Purchase" meant not only the rich state at the mouth of our great river, but also, Arkansas, Missouri, Iowa, Nebraska, Colorado, Wyoming, Montana, Idaho, Oregon, with probably the two Dakotas. Roughly estimated it was a claim by a foreign power upon our continent to territory of over 900,000 square miles.

At the time, but little was thought of its value save and except the getting possession of the rich soil of Louisiana for the purposes of the Southern planter, and being able to own and control the mouth of our great river upon which, at that time, all the states of the North and West were wholly dependent for their commerce.

While Napoleon and the French Government were upon the most friendly terms with the United States, and conceded to our commerce the widest facilities, yet there was a lurking fear that such conditions might at any time change. The desirability of obtaining such possession had often been canvassed, with scarcely a ray of hope for its consummation. The United States was poor, and while the South and the West were deeply interested, the East, which held the balance of power, was determinedly set against it. The same narrow statesmanship existed then, which later on undervalued all our possessions beyond the Stony Mountains, and was willing and even anxious that they should pass into the possession of a foreign power.

France acquired this vast property from Spain in 1800. In March, 1802, there was a great treaty entered into between France on one side and Great Britain, Spain and the Batavian Republic on the other. It was known as "The Amiens Treaty." It was a short-lived treaty which was hopelessly ruptured in 1803.

England, foreseeing the rupture, had not delayed to get ready for the event. Then as now, she was, "Mistress upon the high seas," and set about arranging to seize everything afloat that carried the French flag. Her policy was soon made plain, and that was to first make war upon all French dependencies.

No man knew better than Napoleon how powerless he would be to make any successful defense. His treasury was well-nigh bankrupt and he must have money for home defense as soon as the victorious army of the enemy should return from the Mississippi campaign, which he foresaw. While the treaty of Amiens was not really abrogated until May, 1803, yet upon January 1, 1803, the whole matter was well understood by Napoleon and his advisers.

Early in that month the government received disquieting news from Admiral Villeneuve who was in command of the French fleet in West India waters. It plainly stated that it was undoubtedly the fact that the first blow of the English would be made at New Orleans.

This knowledge was promptly conveyed to the American Minister Monroe, well knowing that the United States was almost as much interested in the matter as France was, as it would stop all traffic from all the States along the Ohio and Mississippi rivers, and be a death blow to American prosperity for an indefinite period. The recently published letters, already referred to, say of the conference between Minister Monroe and Bonaparte:

"Unfortunately Mr. Monroe at this time did not understand the French language well enough to follow a speaker who talked as rapidly as did Bonaparte, and the intervention of an interpreter was necessary. 'We are not

16

able alone to defend the colony of Louisiana,' the First Consul began. 'Your new regions of the southwest are nearly as deeply interested in its remaining in friendly hands as we are in holding it. Our fleet is not equal to the needs of the French Nation. Can you not help us to defend the mouth of the Mississippi river?'

"'We could not take such a step without a treaty, offensive and defensive,' the American answered. 'Our Senate really is the treaty-making power. It is against us. The President, Mr. Jefferson, is my friend, as well as my superior officer. Tell me, General, what you have in your mind.'

"Bonaparte walked the room, a small private consulting cabinet adjoining the Salles des Ambassadeurs. He had his hands clasped behind him, his head bent forward—his usual position when in deep thought. 'I acquired the great territory to which the Mississippi mouth is the entrance,' he finally began, 'and I have the right to dispose of my own. France is not able now to hold it. Rather than see it in England's hands, I donate it to America. Why will your country not buy it from France?' There Bonaparte stopped. Mr. Monroe's face was like a flame. What a diplomatic feat it would be for him! What a triumph for the administration of Jefferson to add such a territory to the national domain!

"No man living was a better judge of his fellows than Bonaparte. He read the thoughts of the man before him as though they were on a written scroll. He saw the emotions of his soul. 'Well, what do you think of it?' said General Bonaparte.

"'The matter is so vast in its direct relations to my country and what may result from it, that it dazes me,' the American answered. 'But the idea is magnificent. It deserves to emanate from a mind like yours.' The First Consul bowed low. Monroe never flattered, and the look of truth was in his eyes, its ring in his voice. 'I must send a special communication at once touching this matter to President Jefferson. My messenger must take the first safe passage to America.'

17

"'The Blonde, the fastest ship in our navy, leaves Brest at once with orders for the West Indian fleet, I will detain her thirty-six hours, till your dispatches are ready,' the First Consul said. 'Your messenger shall go on our ship.'

"'How much shall I say the territory will cost us?' The great Corsican—who was just ending the audience, which had been full two hours long—came up to the American Minister. After a moment he spoke again. 'Between nations who are really friends there need be no chaffering. Could I defend this territory, not all the gold in the world would buy it. But I am giving to a friend what I am unable to keep. I need 100,000,000 francs in coin or its equivalent. Whatever action we take must be speedy. Above all, let there be absolute silence and secrecy,' and Bonaparte bowed our minister out. The audience was ended. The protracted audience between Napoleon and the American Minister was such as to arouse gossip, but the secret was safe in the hands of the two men, both of whom were statesmen and diplomats who knew the value of secrecy in such an emergency.

"The profoundly astonishing dispatches reached President Jefferson promptly. He kept it a secret until he could sound a majority of the Senators and be assured of the standing of such a proposition.

"The main difficulty that was found would be in raising the 75,000,000 francs it was proposed to give. In those days, with a depleted treasury, it was a large sum of money. The United States had millions of unoccupied acres, but had few millions in cash in its treasury. But our statesmen, to their great honor, proved equal to the emergency. Through the agency of Stephen Girard as financier in chief, the loan necessary was negotiated through the Dutch House of Hapes in Amsterdam, and the money paid to France, and the United States entered into possession of the vast estate."

FALLS OF THE WILLAMETTE.

This much of the well-nigh forgotten history we have thought appropriate to note in this connection; first, because of the new light given to it from the recent disclosures made; and, second, to call attention to the fact that a second time, forty-three years later, it served a valiant purpose in thwarting English ambition and serving America's highest interests.

Estimated from the standpoint of money and material values, it was a great transaction, especially notable in view of existing conditions, but from the standpoint of State and National grandeur, carrying with it peace and hope and happiness to millions, and continuous rule of the Republic from ocean to ocean, it assumes a greatness never surpassed in a single transaction, and not easily over-estimated, and never in the history of the English people did a single transaction, with dates so widely separated, arise, and so effectually check their imperious demands.

The American Republic may well remember with deep gratitude President Jefferson, and the far-seeing statesmen who rallied to his call and consummated the grand work. They can at the same time see the foresight and wisdom of Jefferson in, at once, the very next year, sending the expedition of Lewis and Clarke to the headwaters of the Columbia River, and causing a complete survey to be made to its mouth. It was a complete refutation of the claim of the English Commissioners, in 1837, that while "Captain Gray only discovered the mouth of the river, Captain Vancouver made a complete survey." The American mistake was, not in the purchase and active work then done, but the lassitude and inexcusable neglect in the forty subsequent years which imperiled every interest the Republic held in the territory beyond the Rocky Mountains.

When the treaty of 1846 was signed, it was hoped that the questions at issue were settled forever; but the Hudson Bay Company was slow to surrender its grasp on any of the territory it could hold, and especially one so rich in all materials that constituted its wealth and power.

19

The treaty of 1846 between the United States and Great Britain read:

"From the point on the 49th parallel to the middle of the channel which separates the continent from Vancouver's Island and thence southerly through the middle of said channel and of the Fuca Straits, to the Pacific Ocean, provided, however, that the navigation of such channel and straits south of the latitude 49 degrees remain free and open to both parties."

This led to after trouble and much ill feeling. The passage referred to in the treaty is about seven miles wide, between the archipelago and Vancouver Island. The archipelago is made up of half a dozen principal islands, and many smaller ones. The largest island, San Juan, contained about 50,000 acres, and the Hudson Bay Company, knowing something of its value, had taken possession, and proposed to hold it. The legislature of Oregon, however, included it in Island County by an act of 1852, which passed to the Territory of Washington in 1853 by the division of Oregon. In 1854 the Collector of Customs for the Puget Sound came in conflict with the Hudson Bay authorities and a lively row was raised.

The Hudson Bay Company raised the English flag and the collector as promptly landed and raised the Stars and Stripes. There was a constant contention between the United States and State authorities, and the Hudson Bay people, in which the latter were worsted, until in 1856-7, after much correspondence, both governments appointed a commission to settle the difficulty. Then followed years of discussion which grew from time to time warlike, but there was no settlement of the points in dispute.

In December, 1860, the British Government tired of the contest, proposed arbitration by one of the European powers and named either the Swiss Republic, Denmark or Belgium. Then followed the war of the Rebellion and America had no time to reach the case until 1868-9, when the whole matter was referred to two commissioners from each government and the boundary to be determined by the President of the General Council of the Swiss Republic.

This proposition was defeated and afterward in 1871 the whole matter was left to the decision of the Emperor of Germany. He made the award to the United States on all points of dispute in October, 1872, and thus ended the long contest over the boundary line between the two countries, after more than half a century's bickering.

CHAPTER II.

ENGLISH AND AMERICAN OPINION OF THE VALUE OF THE NORTHWEST TERRITORY—THE NEGLECT OF AMERICAN STATESMEN.

The history briefly recited in the previous chapter, fully reveals the status of the United States as to ownership of Oregon. Prior to the date to which our story more specifically relates, the United States had gone on perfecting her titles by the various means already described. For the Nation's interest, it was a great good fortune at this early period that a broad-minded, far-seeing man like Thomas Jefferson was President. It was his wisdom and discretion and statesmanship that enabled the country to overcome all difficulties and to make the Louisiana purchase.

Looking deeper into the years of the future than his contemporaries, he organized the expedition of Lewis and Clarke and surveyed the Columbia River from its source to its mouth. It was regarded by many at the time as a needless and unjustifiable expense; and their report did not create a ripple of applause, and it was an even nine years after the completion of the expedition, and after the death of one of the explorers, before the report was printed and given to the public.

But no reader of history will fail to see how important the expedition was as a link in our chain of evidence. The great misfortune of that time was, that there were not more Jeffersons. True, it did not people Oregon, nor was it followed by any legislation protecting any interest the United States held in the great territory.

There were Congressmen and Senators, who, from time to time, made efforts to second the work of Jefferson. Floyd, of Virginia, as early as 1820, made an eloquent plea for the occupation of the territory and a formal recognition of our rights as rulers. In 1824 a bill passed the lower house of Congress embodying the idea of Floyd stated four years previously, but upon reaching the Senate it fell on dull ears. When the question was before the Senate in 1828, renewing the treaty of 1818 with England, Floyd again attempted to have a bill passed to give land to actual settlers who would emigrate to Oregon, and as usual, failed.

In February, 1838, Senator Linn, of Missouri, always the friend of Oregon, introduced a bill with the main features of the House bill which passed that body in 1824, but again failed in the Senate. The Government, however, was moved to send a special commissioner to Oregon to discover its real conditions and report. But nothing practical resulted.

It is not a pleasant thing to turn the pages of history made by American statesmen during the first third of the century, and even nearly to the end of its first half. There is a lack of wisdom and foresight and broad-mindedness, which shatters our ideals of the mental grandeur of the builders of the Republic.

Diplomatically they had laid strong claim to the now known grand country beyond "the Stony Mountains." They had never lost an opportunity by treaty to hold their interests; and yet from year to year and from decade to decade, they had seen a foreign power, led by a great corporation, ruling all the territory with a mailed hand. While they made but feeble protest in the way we have mentioned, they did even worse, they turned their shafts of oratory and wit and denunciation loose against the country itself and all its interests.

MAP SHOWING OREGON IN 1842, WHITMAN'S RIDE, THE RETURN TRIP TO OREGON, THE SPANISH POSSESSIONS AND THE LOUISIANA PURCHASE.
View larger image.

Turn for a brief review of the political record of that period. Among the ablest men of that day was Senator Benton. He, in his speech of 1825, said, that "The ridge of the Rocky Mountains may be named as a convenient, natural and everlasting boundary. Along this ridge the western limits of the Republic should be drawn, and the statue of the fabled God Terminus should be erected on its highest peak, never to be thrown down." In quoting Senator Benton of 1825, it is always but fair to say he had long before the day of Whitman's arrival in Washington greatly modified his views.

But Senators equally intelligent and influential—such as Winthrop, of Massachusetts, as late as 1844, quoted this sentence from Benton and commended its wisdom and statesmanship. It was in this discussion and while the treaty adopted in 1846 was being considered, that General Jackson is on record as saying, that, "Our safety lay in a compact government."

One of the remarkable speeches in the discussion of the Ashburton-Webster Treaty was that made by Senator McDuffie. Nothing could better show the educating power of the Hudson Bay Company in the United States, and the ignorance of our statesmen, as to extent and value of the territory.

McDuffie said: "What is the character of this country?" (referring to Oregon). "As I understand it there are seven hundred miles this side of the Rocky Mountains that are uninhabitable; where rain never falls; mountains wholly impassable, except through gaps and depressions, to be reached only by going hundreds of miles out of the direct course. Well, now, what are you going to do in such a case? How are you going to apply steam? Have you made an estimate of the cost of a railroad to the mouth of the Columbia? Why the wealth of the Indies would be insufficient. Of what use would it be for agricultural purposes? I would not, for that purpose, give a pinch of snuff for the whole territory. I wish the Rocky Mountains were an impassable barrier. If there was an embankment of even five feet to be removed I would not consent to expend five dollars to remove it and enable our population to go there. I thank God for his mercy in placing the Rocky Mountains there."

Will the reader please take notice that the speech was delivered on the 25th day of January, 1843, just about the time that Whitman, in the ever-memorable ride, was floundering through the snow drifts of the

24

Wasatch and Uintah Mountains, deserted by his guide and surrounded by discouragements that would have appalled any man not inspired by heroic purpose.

It was at this same session of 1843, prior to the visit of Whitman, that Linn, of Missouri, had offered a bill which made specific legal provisions for Oregon, and he succeeded in passing the bill, which went to the House and as usual was defeated. The prevailing idea was that which was expressed by General Jackson to President Monroe, and before referred to, in which Jackson says, "It should be our policy to concentrate our population and confine our frontier to proper limits until our country, in those limits, is filled with a dense population. It is the denseness of our population that gives strength and security to our frontier." That "interminable desert," those "arid plains," those "impassable mountains," and "the impossibility of a wagon road from the United States," were the burdens of many speeches from the statesmen of that time. And then they emphasized the whole with the clincher that, after overcoming these terrible obstacles that intervened, we reached a land that was "worthless," not even worth a "pinch of snuff."

Senator Dayton, of New Jersey, in 1844, in the discussion of the Oregon boundary question, said: "With the exception of land along the Willamette and strips along other water courses, the whole country is as irreclaimable and barren a waste as the Desert of Sahara. Nor is this the worst; the climate is so unfriendly to human life that the native population has dwindled away under the ravages of malaria."

The National Intelligencer, about the same date, republished from the Louisville Journal and sanctioned the sentiments, as follows:

"Of all the countries upon the face of the earth Oregon is one of the least favored by heaven. It is the mere riddlings of creation. It is almost as barren as Sahara and quite as unhealthy as the Campagna of Italy. Russia has her Siberia and England has her Botany Bay and if the United States should ever need a country to which to banish her rogues and scoundrels, the utility of such a region as Oregon would be demonstrated. Until then, we are

25

perfectly willing to leave this magnificent country to the Indians, trappers and buffalo hunters that roam over its sand banks."

In furtherance of the Jackson sentiment of "a dense population," Senator Dayton said: "I have no faith in the unlimited extensions of this government. We have already conflicting interests, more than enough, and God forbid that the time should ever come when a state on the shores of the Pacific, with its interests and tendencies of trade all looking toward Asiatic nations of the east, shall add its jarring claims to our already distracted and over-burdened confederacy. We are nearer to the remote nations of Europe than to Oregon."

The Hudson Bay Company had done its educating work well. If they had graduated American statesmen in a full course of Hudson Bay training and argument and literature, they could not have made them more efficient. Our statesmen did not doubt that the honest title of the property was vested in the United States; for they had gone on from time to time perfecting this title; yet they had no idea of its value and seemed to hold it only for diplomatic purposes or for prospective barter.

The United States had no contestant for the property except England, but in 1818 she was not ready to make any assertion of her rights. In 1828 she still postponed making any demand and renewed the treaty, well knowing that the little island many thousands of miles across the Atlantic, was the supreme ruler of all the vast territory.

Again, when the Ashburton Treaty was at issue, and the question of boundary which had been for forty-eight years a bone of contention, the government again ignored Oregon, and was satisfied with settling the boundaries between a few farms up in Maine.

But it requires no argument in view of this long continued series of acts, to reach the conclusion that American interests in Oregon were endangered most of all from the apathy and ignorance of our own statesmen.

That loyal old pioneer, Rev. Jason Lee, the chief of the Methodist Mission in Oregon, visited Washington in 1838 and presented the conditions of the country and its dangers forcibly. With funds contributed by generous friends he succeeded in taking back with him quite a delegation of actual settlers for Oregon. But neither Congress nor the people were aroused.

For all practical purposes Oregon was treated as a "foreign land." There was not even a show of a protectorate over the few American immigrants who had gathered there. The "American Board," which sent missionaries only to foreign lands, had charge of the mission fields, and carefully secured passports for their missionaries before starting them upon their long journey. The Rev. Myron Eells in his interesting volume entitled "Father Eells," gives a copy of the passport issued to his father. It records—

"The Rev. Cushing Eells, Missionary and Teacher of the American Board of Commissioners for Foreign Missions to the tribes west of the Rocky Mountains, having signified to this department his desire to pass through the Indian Country to the Columbia River, and requested the permission required by law to enable him so to do, such permission is hereby granted; and he is commended to the friendly attention of civil and military agents and officers and of citizens, if at any time it shall be necessary to his protection. Given under my hand and the seal of the War Department this 27th day of February, 1838.

"J. R. POINSETT,
"Secretary of War."

It is a truth so plain as to need no argument, that during all these earlier years the whole effort of the fur traders had been to deceive all nationalities as to the value of the Northwestern country. In their selfishness they had deceived England as well as America. Their idea and hope was to keep out emigration. But England had been better informed than the United States, for the reason that all the commerce was with England, and English

27

capitalists who had large interests in the Hudson Bay Company, very naturally were better informed, but even they were not anxious for English colonization and an interference with their bonanza.

They controlled the English press, and so late as 1840 we read in the "British and Foreign Review," that "upon the whole, therefore, the Oregon country holds out no great promise as an agricultural field."

The London Examiner in 1843 wonders that "Ignorant Americans" were "disposed to quarrel over a country, the whole in dispute not being worth to either party twenty thousand pounds."

The Edinburgh Review, generally fair, said: "Only a very small portion of the land is capable of cultivation. It is a case in which the American people have been misled as to climate and soil. In a few years all that gives life to the country, both the hunter and his prey will be extinct, and their places will be supplied by a thin white and half-breed population scattered along the fertile valleys supported by pastures instead of the chase, and gradually degenerating into barbarism, far more offensive than backwoodsmen." Our English friends, it may be observed, had long had a poor opinion of "backwoodsmen."

The Edinburgh Review, in 1843, says: "However the political question between England and the United States as to their claim on Oregon shall be determined, Oregon will never be colonized overland from the United States. The world must assume a new phase before the American wagons make a plain road to the Columbia River."

In this educating work of the English press, we can easily understand how public opinion was molded, and how our statesmen were misinformed and misdirected. It was, no doubt, largely due to the shrewd work of the great monopoly in Oregon backed up by the English Government. Its first object was to keep it unsettled as long as possible, for on that depended the millions for the Hudson Bay Company's treasury, but beyond that, the government plainly depended upon the powerful organization to hold all the land as a

British possession.

In the war of 1812, one of the first moves was to dispatch a fleet to the Columbia, with orders, as the record shows, "to take and destroy everything American on the northwest coast."

The prosperous people of Oregon, Washington and Idaho are in a position now to enjoy such prophetic fulminations, but they can easily see the dangers that were escaped. It was a double danger, danger from abroad and at home, and of the latter most of all. The Nation had been deceived. It must be undeceived.

The outlook was not hopeful. The year 1843 had been ushered in. The long-looked-for and talked-of treaty had been signed, and Oregon again ignored. There was scarcely a shadow cast of coming events to give hope to the friends of far-away Oregon.

Suppose some watchman from the dome of the Capitol casting his eyes westward in 1843, could have seen that little caravan winding through valleys and over the hills and hurrying eastward, but who would dream that its leader was "a man of destiny," bearing messages to a nation soon to be aroused? Of how little or how much importance was this messenger or his message, turn to "The Ride to Save Oregon" and judge. But certain it is, a great change, bordering on revolution, was portending.

CHAPTER III.

THE ROMANCE OF THE OREGON MISSION.

These pages are mainly designed to show in brief the historical and political environments of Oregon in pioneer days, and the patriotic services rendered the nation by Dr. Marcus Whitman. But to attempt to picture this life and omit the missionary, would be like reciting the play of Hamlet and omitting Hamlet.

The mission work to the Oregon Indians began in a romance and ended in a great tragedy. The city of St. Louis in that day was so near the border of civilization that it was accustomed to see much of the rugged and wild life of the plains; yet in 1832 the people beheld even to them the odd sight of four Flathead Indians in Indian dress and equipment parading their principal streets.

General Clarke, who commanded the military post of that city, was promptly notified and took the strangers in charge. He had been an Indian commissioner for many years in the far West, knew the tribe well and could easily communicate with them. With it all he was a good friend to the Indians and at once made arrangements at the fort to make them comfortable. They informed him that they were all chiefs of the tribe and had spent the entire Summer and Fall upon their long journey. Their wearied manner and wasted appearance told the fact impressively, even had the general not known the locality where they belonged.

For a while they were reticent regarding their mission, as is usual with Indians; but in due time their story was fully revealed. They had heard of "The White Man's Book of Life," and had come "to hunt for it" and "to ask for teachers to be sent" to their tribe.

To Gen. Clarke this was a novel proposition to come in that way from wild Indians. Gen. Clarke was a devoted Catholic and treated his guests as a humane and hospitable man. After they were rested up he piloted them to every place which he thought would entertain and interest them. Frequent visits were made to Catholic churches, and to theaters and shows of every kind. And so they spent the balance of the Winter.

During this time, two of the Indians, from the long journey and possibly from over-eating rich food, to which they were unaccustomed, were taken sick and died, and were given honored burial by the soldiers. When the early Spring sun began to shine, the two remaining Indians commenced their preparations for return home.

Gen. Clarke proposed to give them a banquet upon the last evening of their sojourn, and start them upon their way loaded with all the comforts he could give. At this banquet one of the Indians made a speech. It was that speech, brimming over with Indian eloquence, which fired the Christian hearts of the Nation into a new life. The speech was translated into English and thus doubtless loses much of its charm.

The chief said: "I come to you over the trail of many moons from the setting sun. You were the friends of my fathers, who have all gone the long way. I came with an eye partly open for my people, who sit in darkness. I go back with both eyes closed. How can I go back blind, to my blind people? I made my way to you with strong arms through many enemies and strange lands that I might carry back much to them. I go back with both arms broken and empty. Two fathers came with us, they were the braves of many winters and wars. We leave them asleep here by your great water and wigwams. They were tired in many moons and their moccasins wore out.

"My people sent me to get the "White Man's Book of Heaven." You took me to where you allow your women to dance as we do not ours, and the book was not there. You took me to where they worship the Great Spirit with candles and the book was not there. You showed me images of the good spirits and the pictures of the good land beyond, but the book was not among them to tell us the way. I am going back the long and sad trail to my people in the dark land. You make my feet heavy with gifts and my

31

moccasins will grow old in carrying them, yet the book is not among them. When I tell my poor blind people after one more snow, in the big council, that I did not bring the book, no word will be spoken by our old men or by our young braves. One by one they will rise up and go out in silence. My people will die in darkness, and they will go a long path to other hunting grounds. No white man will go with them, and no White Man's Book to make the way plain. I have no more words."

When this speech was translated and sent East it was published in the Christian Advocate in March, 1833, with a ringing editorial from President Fisk of Wilbraham College. "Who will respond to go beyond the Rocky Mountains and carry the Book of Heaven?" It made a profound impression. It was a Macedonian cry of "Come over and help us," not to be resisted. Old men and women who read this call, and attended the meetings at that time, are still living, and can attest to its power. It stirred the church as it has seldom been stirred into activity.

This incident of the appearance in St. Louis and demand of the four Flathead Indians has been so fully verified in history as to need no additional proof to silence modern sceptics who have ridiculed it. All the earlier histories such as "Gray's History of Oregon," "Reed's Mission of the Methodist Church," Governor Simpson's narrative, Barrow's "Oregon," Parkman's "Oregon Trail," with the correspondence of the Lees, verified the truth of the occurrence.

Bancroft, in his thirty-eight-volume history, in volume 1, page 579, says, "Hearing of the Christians and how heaven favors them, four Flathead Indian chiefs, in 1832, went to St. Louis and asked for teachers," etc. As this latter testimony is from a source which discredited missionary work, as we shall show in another chapter, it is good testimony upon the point. Some modern doubters have also ridiculed the speech reported to have been made by the Indian chief. Those who know Indians best will bear testimony to its genuineness.

Almost every tribe of Indians has its orator and story-teller, and some of them as famous in their way as the Beechers and Phillipses and Depews, among the whites, or the Douglasses and Langstons among the negroes.

In 1851 the writer of this book was purser upon the steamer Lot Whitcomb, which ran between Milwaukee and Astoria, Oregon. One beautiful morning I wandered a mile or more down the beach and was seated upon the sand, watching the great combers as they rolled in from the Pacific, which, after a storm, is an especially grand sight; when suddenly, as if he had arisen from the ground, an Indian appeared near by and accosted me. He was a fine specimen of a savage, clean and well dressed. He evidently knew who I was and my position on the steamer and had followed me to make his plea. With a toss of his arm and a motion of his body he threw the fold of his blanket across his left shoulder as gracefully as a Roman Senator could have done, and began his speech. "Hy-iu hyas kloshe Boston, Boston hy-iu steamboat hy-iu cuitan. Indian halo steamboat, halo cuitan." It was a rare mixture of English words with the Chinook, which I easily understood.

The burthen of his speech was, the greatness and richness and goodness of white men; (they called all white men Boston men); they owned all the steamboats and horses; that the Indians were very poor; that his squaw and pappoose were away up the Willamette river, so far away that his moccasins would be worn out before he could reach their wigwam; that he had no money and wanted to ride.

I have heard the great orators of the nation in the pulpit and halls of legislation, but I never listened to a more eloquent plea, or saw gestures more graceful than were those of that wild Wasco Indian, of which I alone was the audience.

Another interesting historical scrap of the romantic history of these Flathead chiefs is furnished in the fact that the celebrated Indian artist, George Catlin, was on one of his tours in the West taking sketches in the spring of 1833. Soon after their leaving St. Louis he dropped in with the two Indians on their return journey and traveled with them for some days, taking pictures of both, and they are now numbers 207 and 208 in his great

33

collection.

Upon his return east he read the Indian speech, and of the excitement it had caused, and not having been told by the Indians of the cause of their journey, and wishing to be assured that he had accidentally struck a great historic prize in securing the pictures, he sat down and wrote Gen. Clarke at St. Louis, asking him if the speech was true and the story correct. Gen. Clarke promptly replied, "The story is true; that was the only object of their visit." Taken in connection with the after history, no two pictures in any collection have a deeper or grander significance.

THE LOT WHITCOMB.
The first Steamboat built in Oregon.

We may add here that within a month after leaving St. Louis, one of the Indians was taken sick and died, and but one reached his home in safety.

When I reached Oregon in 1850, the first tribe of Indians I visited in their home was the Flatheads. But whether the story is true in all its minutiae or not, it matters but little. It was believed true, and produced grand results. It can hardly be said, from the standpoint of the Christian missionary, that the work in Oregon was a grand success. And yet, never were missionaries more heroic, or that labored in any field with greater fidelity for the true interests of the Indian savages to whom they were sent.

They were great, warm-hearted, intelligent, educated, earnest men and women, who endured privation, isolation and discomfort with cheerfulness, that they might teach Christianity and save souls. There was no failure from any incompetency of the teachers, but from complications and surroundings hopelessly beyond their power to change.

They brought with them over their long, weary journey the Bible, Christianity and civilization, and the school. They were met at first with a cordial reception by the Indians, but a great corporation, dependent upon the steel trap and continuous savage life, soon showed its hand. It was a foreign un-American opposition. It had met every American company that had attempted to share in the business promoted by savage life, and routed them. The missionaries were wide-awake men and were quick to see the drift of affairs.

Dr. Whitman early foresaw what was to happen. He saw the possibilities of the country and that the first battle was between the schoolhouse and civilization, and the tepee and savagery. He resolved to do everything possible for the Indian before it began. In a letter to his father-in-law, dated May 16, 1844, from Waiilatpui, he says:

"It does not concern me so much what is to become of any particular set of Indians, as to give them the offer of salvation through the Gospel, and the opportunity of civilization, and then I am content to do good to all men as I have opportunity. I have no doubt our greatest work is to be to aid the white settlement of this country and help to found its religious institutions. Providence has its full share in all those events. Although the Indians have made, and are making rapid advance in religious knowledge and civilization, yet it cannot be hoped that time will be allowed to mature the work of Christianization or civilization before white settlers will demand the soil and the removal both of the Indians and the Missions.

"What Americans desire of this kind they always effect, and it is useless to oppose or desire it otherwise. To guide as far as can be done, and direct these tendencies for the best, is evidently the part of wisdom. Indeed, I am fully convinced that when people refuse or neglect to fill the design of Providence, they ought not to complain at the results, and so it is equally useless for Christians to be over-anxious on their account.

"The Indians have in no case obeyed the command to multiply and replenish the earth, and they cannot stand in the way of others doing so. A place will be left them to do this as fully as their ability to obey will permit, and the more we do for them the more fully will this be realized. No exclusiveness can be asked for any portion of the human family. The exercise

35

of his rights are all that can be desired. In order for this to be understood to its proper extent, in regard to the Indians, it is necessary that they seek to preserve their rights by peaceable means only. Any violation of this rule will be visited with only evil results to themselves."

This letter from Dr. Whitman to his wife's father, dated about seven months after his return from his memorable "Ride to Save Oregon," is for the first time made public in the published transactions of the State Historical Society of Oregon in 1893. It is important from the fact that it gives a complete key to the life and acts of this silent man and his motives for the part he took in the great historic drama, in which the statesmen of the two nations were to be the actors, with millions of people the interested audience.

In another place we will show how Whitman has been misrepresented by modern historians, and an attempt made to deprive him of all honor, and call attention to the above record, all the more valuable because never intended for the public eye when written.

In the same letter Whitman says, "As I hold the settlement of this country by Americans, rather than by English colonists, most important, I am happy to have been the means of landing so large an immigration on the shores of the Columbia with their wagons, families and stock, all in safety."

Such sentiments reveal only the broad-minded, far-seeing Christian man, who, though many thousand miles away from its protecting influence, still loved "The banner of beauty and glory." He had gone to Oregon with only a desire to teach savages Christianity; but saw in the near future the inevitable, and, without lessening his interest in his savage pupils, he entered the broader field.

Who can doubt that both were calls from a power higher than man? Or who can point to an instance upon historic pages where the great work assigned was prosecuted with greater fidelity? Having accomplished a feat unparalleled for its heroism and without a break in its grand success, he makes no report of it to any state or national organization, but while he

36

talked freely with his friends of his work it is only now, after he has rested for forty-seven and more years, that this modest letter written to his wife's father at the time, strongly reveals his motives.

Having accomplished his great undertaking, he was still the missionary and friend of the Indians, and at once dropped back to his work, and the drudgery of his Indian mission.

Again we find him enlarging his field of work, teaching his savage friends, not only Christianity, but how to sow, and plant, and reap, and build houses, and prepare for civilization. He took no part in the new political life which he had made possible. He was a stranger to all things except those which concerned the work he was called to do. In his letter he speaks of earnestly desiring to return East and bring out the second company of immigrants the coming Spring, but the needs of his mission, his wasted fields, and his mill burned during his absence, seemed to demand his presence at home.

The world speaks of this event and that, as "It so happened." They will refer to the advent of the Flathead Indians in St. Louis in 1832, as "It so happened." The more thoughtful readers of history find fewer things "accidental." In this great historic romance the Flathead Indians were not an accident. The American Board, the Methodist Board, Dr. Whitman and Jason Lee, and their co-workers, were not accidents. They were all men inspired to a specific work, and having entered upon it, the field widened into dimensions of unforeseen grandeur, whose benefits the Nation has never yet befittingly acknowledged.

CHAPTER IV.

THE WEDDING JOURNEY ACROSS THE PLAINS.

The romance of the Oregon Mission did not end with the call of the Flathead Indians. This was savage romance, that of civilization followed.

The Methodists sent the Lees in 1834, and the American Board tried to get the right men for the work to accompany them, but failed. But in 1835 they sent Dr. Marcus Whitman and the Rev. Samuel Parker to Oregon upon a trip of discovery, to find out the real conditions, present and prospective.

They got an early start in 1835 and reached Green River, where they met large bodies of Indians and Indian traders, and were made fully acquainted with the situation. The Indians gave large promises, and the field seemed wide and inviting. Upon consultation it was agreed that Dr. Whitman should return to the States and report to the American Board, while Dr. Parker should go on to the Columbia. Two Indian boys from the Pacific Coast, Richard and John, volunteered to return with Dr. Whitman and come back with him the following year.

The Doctor and his Indian boys reached his home in Rushville, New York, late on Saturday night in November, and not making known the event to his family, astonished the congregation in his church by walking up the aisle with his Indians, and calling out an audible exclamation from his good old mother, "Well, there is Marcus Whitman."

Upon the report of Dr. Whitman the American Board resolved to at once occupy the field. Dr. Whitman had long been engaged to be married to Miss Narcissa Prentice, the daughter of Judge Prentice, of Prattsburg, New York, who was as much of an enthusiast in the Oregon Indian Mission work as the Doctor himself. The American Board thought it unwise to send the young couple alone on so distant a journey, and at once began the search for company. The wedding day, which had been fixed, was postponed, and valuable time was passing, and no suitable parties would volunteer for the work, when its trials and dangers were explained.

The Board had received word that the Rev. H. H. Spalding, who had recently married, was then with his wife on his way to the Osage Mission to enter upon a new field of work. It was in January and Whitman took to the road in his sleigh in pursuit of the traveling missionaries. He overtook them near the village of Hudson and hailed them in his cheery way:

"Ship ahoy, you are wanted for the Oregon Mission."

After a short colloquy they drove on to the hotel of the little village. There the subject was canvassed and none of its dangers hidden. Mr. Spalding promptly made up his mind, and said:

"My dear, I do not think it your duty to go, but we will leave it to you after we have prayed."

Mrs. Spalding asked to be left alone, and in ten minutes she appeared with a beaming face and said: "I have made up my mind to go."

"But your health, my dear?"

"I like the command just as it stands," says Mrs. Spalding, "Go ye into all the world and preach the Gospel, with no exceptions for poor health."

Others referred to the hardships and dangers and terrors of the journey, but Dr. Spalding says: "They all did not move her an iota."

Such was the party for the wedding journey. It did look like a dangerous journey for a woman who had been many months an invalid, but events proved Mrs. Spalding a real heroine, with a courage and pluck scarcely equaled, and under the circumstances never excelled. Having turned her face toward Oregon she never looked back and never was heard to murmur or regret her decision.

This difficulty being removed, the day was again set for the marriage of Dr. Whitman and Miss Prentice, which took place in February, 1836. All authorities mark Narcissa Prentice as a woman of great force of character.

She was the adored daughter of a refined Christian home and had the love of a wide circle of friends. She was the soprano singer in the choir of the village church of which she and her family were members.

In the volume of the magazine of American History for 1884, the editor, the late Miss Martha J. Lamb, says:

"The voice of Miss Prentice was of remarkable sweetness. She was a graceful blonde, stately and dignified in her bearing, without a particle of affectation." Says Miss Lamb: "When preparing to leave for Oregon the church held a farewell service and the minister gave out the well-known hymn:

'Yes, my native land I love thee,
All thy scenes I love them well;
Friends, connection, happy country,
Can I bid you all farewell?'

"The whole congregation joined heartily in the singing, but before the hymn was half through, one by one they ceased singing and audible sobs were heard in every part of the great audience. The last stanza was sung by the sweet voice of Mrs. Whitman alone, clear, musical and unwavering."

One of the pleasant things since it was announced that these sketches would be written, is the number of people, that before were unknown, who have volunteered charming personal sketches of Dr. and Mrs. Whitman.

A venerable friend who often, he fears, attended church more for the songs of Miss Prentice than for the sermons, was also at their wedding. The venerable J. S. Seeley, of Aurora, Illinois, writes: "It was just fifty-nine years ago this March since I drove Dr. and Mrs. Whitman from Elmira, N. Y., to Hollidaysburg, Pa., in my sleigh. This place was at the foot of the Allegheny Mountains (east side) on the Pennsylvania canal. The canal boats were built in two sections and were taken over the mountains on a railroad.

"They expected to find the canal open on the west side and thus reach the Ohio River on the way to Oregon. I was with them some seven days. Dr. Whitman impressed me as a man of strong sterling character and lots of push, but he was not a great talker. Mrs. Whitman was of medium size and impressed me as a woman of great resolution."

A younger sister of the bride, Mrs. H. P. Jackson, of Oberlin, Ohio, writes: "Mrs. Whitman was the mentor of her younger sisters in the home. She joined the church when eleven years old, and from her early years expressed a desire to be a missionary. The wedding occurred in the church at Angelica, N. Y., to which place my father had removed, and the ceremony was performed by the Rev. Everett Hull. I recollect how deeply interested the two Indian boys were in the ceremony, and how their faces brightened when the doctor told them that Mrs. Whitman would go back with them to Oregon. We all had the greatest faith and trust in Dr. Whitman, and in all our letters from our dear sister there was never a word of regret or repining at the life she had chosen."

The two Indian boys were placed in school and learned to read and speak English during the Winter.

The journey down the Ohio and up the Mississippi and Missouri Rivers was tedious, but uneventful.

Those who navigated the Missouri River, fifty years ago, have not forgotten its snags and sand bars, which caused a constant chattering of the bells in the engineer's room from morning until evening, and all through the night, unless the prudent captain tied up to the shore. The man and his "lead line" was constantly on the prow singing out "twelve feet," "quarter past

41

twain," then suddenly "six feet," when the bells would ring out as the boat's nose would bury in the concealed sandbar.

But the party safely reached its destination, and was landed with all its effects, wagons, stock and outfit.

The company was made up of Dr. and Mrs. Whitman, Rev. Mr. and Mrs. Spalding, H. H. Gray, two teamsters and the two Indian boys.

The American Fur Company, which was sending out a convoy to their port in Oregon, had promised to start from Council Bluffs upon a given date, and make them welcome members of the company. It was a large company made up of two hundred men and six hundred animals. On the journey in from Oregon, in 1835, cholera had attacked the company, and Dr. Whitman had rendered such faithful and efficient service that they felt under obligations to him. But they had heard there were to be women along and the old mountaineers did not want to be bothered with women upon such a journey, and they moved out promptly without waiting for the doctor's party, which had been delayed.

When Dr. Whitman reached Council Bluffs and found them gone, he was greatly disturbed. There was nothing to do but make forced marches and catch the train before it reached the more dangerous Indian country. Dr. Spalding would have liked to have found it an excuse to return home, but Mrs. Spalding remarked: "I have started to the Rocky Mountains and I expect to go there."

Spalding in a dressing gown in his study, or in a city pulpit, would have been in his element, but he was not especially marked for an Indian missionary. Early in the campaign a Missouri cow kicked him off the ferryboat into the river. The ague racked every bone in his body, and a Kansas tornado at one time lifted both his tent and his blanket and left him helpless. He seemed to catch every disaster that came along. A man may have excellent points in his make-up, as Dr. Spalding had, and yet not be a good pioneer.

42

He and his noble wife made a grand success, however, when they got into the field of work. It was Mrs. Spalding who first translated Bible truths and Christian songs into the Indian dialect.

It seemed a discouraging start for the little company when compelled to pull out upon the boundless plains alone. But led by Whitman, they persevered and caught the convoy late in May.

The doctor's boys now proved of good service. They were patient and untiring and at home on the trail. They took charge of all the loose stock. The cows they were taking along would be of great value upon reaching their destination, and they proved to be of value along the journey as well, as milk suppliers for the little party.

The first part of the journey Mrs. Whitman rode mainly in the wagon with Mrs. Spalding, who was not strong enough for horseback riding. But soon she took to her pony and liked it so much better, that she rode nearly all the way on horseback. They were soon initiated into the trials and dangers of the journey.

On May 9th Mrs. Whitman writes in her diary: "We had great difficulty to-day. Husband became so completely exhausted with swimming the river, that it was with difficulty he made the shore the last time. We had but one canoe, made of skins, and that was partly eaten by the dogs the night before."

She speaks of "meeting large bodies of Pawnee Indians," and says:

"They seemed very much surprised and pleased to see white women. They were noble looking Indians.

"We attempted, by a hard march, to reach Loup Fork. The wagons got there at eleven at night, but husband and I rode with the Indian boys until nine o'clock, when Richard proposed that we go on and they would stay with the loose cattle upon the prairie, and drive them in early in the morning. We did not like to leave them and concluded to stay. Husband had a cup tied to his saddle, and in this he milked what we wanted to drink; this was our supper. Our saddle-blankets with our rubber-cloaks were our beds. Having offered thanksgiving for the blessings of the day, and seeking protection for the night, we committed ourselves to rest. We awoke refreshed and rode into camp before breakfast."

Here they caught up with the Fur Company caravan, after nearly a month's traveling. These brave women, with their kindness and tact, soon won the good-will and friendship of the old plainsmen, and every vestige of opposition to having women in the train disappeared and every possible civility and courtesy was extended to them. One far-seeing old American trader, who had felt the iron heel of the English Company beyond the Stony Mountains, pointing to the little missionary band, prophetically remarked: "There is something that the Honorable Hudson Bay Company cannot drive out of Oregon."

In her diary of the journey, Mrs. Whitman never expresses a fear, and yet remembering my own sensations upon the same journey, I can scarcely conceive that two delicately nurtured women would not be subjected to great anxieties.

The Platte River, in that day, was but little understood and looked much worse than it really was. Where forded it was a mile wide, and not often more than breast deep to the horses. Two men, on the best horses, rode fifty yards in advance of the wagons, zig-zagging up and down, while the head-driver kept an eye open for the shallowest water and kept upon the bar. In doing this a train would sometimes have to travel nearly twice the distance of the width of the river to get across. The bed of the river is made of shifting sand, and a team is not allowed to stop for a moment, or it will steadily settle down and go out of sight.

DR. MARCUS WHITMAN.
At the time of his marriage.

A balky team or a break in the harness requires prompt relief or all will be lost. But after all the Platte River is remembered by all old plainsmen with a blessing. For three hundred miles it administered to the comfort of the pioneers.

It is even doubtful whether they could have gone the journey had it not been for the Platte, as it rolls its sands down into the Missouri. The water is turbid with sand at all times, as the winds in their wide sweep across sandy plains perpetually add to its supply. But the water when dipped up over night and the sand allowed to settle, is clear and pure and refreshing.

The pioneers, however, took the Platte water as it ran, often remarking: "In this country a fellow needs sand and the Platte was built to furnish it." In June Mrs. Whitman writes: "We are now in the buffalo country and my husband and I relish it; he has a different way of cooking every part of the animal."

Mrs. Whitman makes the following entry in her diary, for the benefit of her young sisters:

"Now, H. and E., you must not think it very hard to have to get up so early after sleeping on the soft ground, when you find it hard work to open your eyes at seven o'clock. Just think of me every morning. At the word 'Arise!' we all spring. While the horses are feeding we get breakfast in a hurry and eat it. By that time the words 'Catch up, catch up,' ring throughout the camp for moving. We are ready to start usually at six, travel until eleven, encamp, rest and feed, and start again at two and travel till six and if we come to a good tavern, camp for the night."

A certain number of men were set apart for hunters each day and they were expected to bring in four mule loads of meat to supply the daily demands. While in the buffalo country this was an easy task; when it came to deer, antelope and birds, it was much more difficult work.

The antelope is a great delicacy, but he is the fleetest footed runner upon the plains and has to be captured, generally, by strategy. He has an inordinate curiosity. The hunter lies down and waves a red handkerchief on the end of his ramrod and the whole herd seems to have the greatest desire to know what it is. They gallop around, trot high and snort and keep coming nearer, until within gun shot they pay dearly for their curiosity.

To avoid danger and failure of meat supplies before leaving the buffalo country, the company stopped and laid in a good supply of jerked buffalo meat. It was well they did, for it was about all they had for a long distance. As Mrs. Whitman says in her diary:

"Dried buffalo meat and tea for breakfast, and tea and dried buffalo meat for supper," but jokingly adds: "The doctor gives it variety by cooking every part of the animal in a different way." But after all it was a novel menu for a bridal trip.

By a strange miscalculation they ran out of flour before the journey was half ended. But, says Mrs. Whitman, "My health continues good, but sister Spalding has been made sick by the diet."

On July 22d, she writes:

"Had a tedious ride until four p. m. I thought of my mother's bread as a child would, but did not find it. I should relish it extremely well. But we feel that the good Father has blessed us beyond our most sanguine expectations. It is good to feel that He is all I want and if I had ten thousand lives I would give them all to Him."

The road discovered by the pioneers through the South Pass seems to have been made by nature on purpose to unite the Pacific with the Atlantic slope by an easy wagon road. The Wind River and Rocky Mountains appear

46

to have run out of material, or spread out to make it an easy climb. So gentle is the ascent the bulk of the way that the traveler is scarcely aware of the fact that he is climbing the great "Stony Mountains."

Fremont discovered the pass in 1842 and went through it again in 1843, and Stanbury in 1849, but it is well to remember that upon this notable bridal tour, these Christian ladies passed over the same route six years before "The Pathfinder," or the engineer corps of the United States, ever saw it.

It is always an object of interest to know when the top has been reached and to see the famous spring from which the water divides and runs both ways. Our missionary band, accustomed to have regular worship on the plains, when they reached the dividing of the waters held an especially interesting service. The Rev. Dr. Jonathan Edwards graphically describes it. He says:

"There is a scene connected with their journey which demands extraordinary attention in view of its great significance. It is one that arouses all that is good within us, and has been pronounced as hardly paralleled in American records for historic grandeur and far-reaching consequence. It is sublimely beautiful and inspiring in its effects, and would baffle the genius of a true poet to describe it with adequate fitness. They were yet high on the Rocky Mountains, with the great expanse of the Pacific slope opening before them like a magnificent panorama. Their hearts were profoundly moved as they witnessed the landscape unfolding its delightful scenes, and as they viewed the vast empire given them to win for King Emanuel.

"There we find the little group of five missionaries, and the two Nez Perces boys that Whitman took with him to New York selecting a spot where the bunch grass grows high and thick. Their hearts go out to God in joyful adoration for His protecting care over them thus far, especially so, because they felt the greatest difficulties had been overcome and they now entered the country for the people of which they had devoted their lives. The sky is bright above them, the sun shines serenely and the atmosphere is light and invigorating. The sun continues his course and illuminates the western

47

horizon like a flame of fire, as if striving to give them a temporary glimpse of the vast domain between them and the Pacific Ocean. They spread their blankets carefully on the grass, and lifted the American flag to wave gracefully in the breeze, and with the Bible in the center, they knelt, and with prayer and praise on their lips, they take possession of the western side of the American continent in His name who proclaimed "Peace on earth and good will toward men." How strongly it evidences their faith in their mission and the conquering power of the King of Peace. What a soul-inspiring scene."

Continuing her diary, Mrs. Whitman says: "I have been in a peaceful state of mind all day."

July 25th she writes: "The ride has been very mountainous, paths only winding along the sides of steep mountains, in many places so narrow that the animal would scarcely find room to place his foot."

It is upon this date that she again mourns over the doctor's persistence in hauling along his historic wagon. Even the good wife in full sympathy with her husband failed to see it as he did; it was the pioneer chariot, loaded with a richness that no wagon before or since contained.

On July 25th: "Husband has had a tedious time with the wagon to-day. It got stuck in the creek, and on the mountain side, so steep that the horses could scarcely climb, it was upset twice. It was a wonder that it was not turning somersaults continually. It is not grateful to my feelings to see him wearing himself out with excessive fatigue. All the most difficult portions of the way he has walked, in a laborious attempt to take the wagon." Those who have gone over the same road and remember the hard pulls at the end of long ropes, where there was plenty of help, will wonder most that he succeeded.

The company arrived at Fort Hall on August 1st. Here they succeeded in buying a little rice, which was regarded a valuable addition to their slender stock of eatables. They had gone beyond the buffalo range and had to live upon the dried meat, venison and wild ducks or fish, all of which

48

were scarce and in limited supply.

Speaking of crossing Snake River Mrs. Whitman says: "We put the packs on the tallest horses, the highest being selected for Mrs. Spalding and myself.

"The river where we crossed is divided into three branches, by islands. The last branch is half a mile wide and so deep as to come up to the horses' sides, and a very strong current. The wagon turned upside down in the current, and the mules were entangled in the harness. I once thought of the terrors of the rivers, but now I cross the most difficult streams without a fear."

Among the novel ferries she speaks of was a dried elk skin with two ropes attached. The party to be ferried lies flat down on the skin and two Indian women swimming, holding the ropes in their mouths, pull it across the stream.

One of the notable qualities of Dr. Whitman was his observance of the small things in every-day life. Many a man who reaches after grand results overlooks and neglects the little events. Mrs. Whitman says:

"For weeks and weeks our camping places have been upon open plains with not a tree in sight, but even here we find rest and comfort. My husband, the best the world ever produced, is always ready to provide a comfortable shade from the noonday sun when we stop. With one of our saddle-blankets stretched across the sage brush or upheld by sticks, our saddle blankets and fishamores placed on the ground, our resting is delightful."

Among the notable events of the journey was when the party reached Green River, the place of annual meeting of the Indians and the traders. It was this place that Dr. Whitman had reached the year previous. The Green is one of the large branches of the Colorado, which heads among the snow banks of Fremont's Peak, a thousand miles away. In its picturesque rugged beauty few sections excel the scenery along the river, and now the whole scene, alive with frontier and savage life, was one to impress itself indelibly upon the memories of our travelers.

There were about two hundred traders and two thousand Indians, representatives of tribes located many hundreds of miles distant. The Cayuse and Nez Perces, who expected Dr. Whitman and his delegation, were present to honor the occasion, and meet the boys, John and Richard, who had accompanied the doctor from this place the year before. The Indians expressed great delight over the successful journey; but most of all they were delighted with the noble white squaws who had come over the long trail. They were demonstrative and scoured the mountains for delicacies in game from the woods and brought trout from the river, and seemed constantly to fear that they were neglecting some courtesy expected of them.

They finally got up a war tournament, and six hundred armed and mounted Indians, in their war paint, with savage yells bore down toward the tents of the ladies, and it was almost too realistic of savage life to be enjoyed.

Here the brides were permitted to rest for ten days, and until their tired animals could recuperate. The scenery along the last three hundred miles was most charming, and almost made the travelers forget the precipitous climbs and the steep descents. The days sped past, and the wagon being left behind to be sent for later on, the wedding party marched more rapidly. They reached Walla Walla River, eight miles from the fort, the last day of August, and on September 1st they made an early start and galloped into the fort. The party was hospitably received.

Says Mrs. Whitman: "They were just eating breakfast when we arrived, and soon we were seated at the table and treated to fresh salmon, potatoes, tea, bread and butter. What a variety, thought I. You cannot imagine what an appetite these rides in the mountains give a person."

We have preferred to let Mrs. Whitman tell in her own way the story of this memorable wedding journey. The reader will look in vain for any

50

mourning or disquietude. Two noble women started in to be the helpmeets of two good men, and what a grand success they made of it. There is nowhere any spirit of grumbling, but on the contrary, a joyousness and exhilaration. True womanhood of all time is honored in the lives of such women. It was but the coming of the first white women who ever crossed the Rocky Mountains and notable as an heroic wedding journey, but to the world it was not only exalted heroism, but a great historic event, the building of an empire whose wide-reaching good cannot easily be overestimated.

It was an event unparalleled in real or romantic literature, and so pure and exalted in its motives, and prosecuted so unostentatiously, as to honor true womanhood for all time to come.

CHAPTER V.

MISSION LIFE IN WAIILATPUI.

Most writers speak of the Mission at Waiilatpui, as "The Presbyterian Mission." While it does not much matter whether it was Presbyterian or Congregational, it is well to have the history correct. The two great churches at that time were united in their foreign missionary work, and their missionaries were taken from both denominations. A year or more ago I asked the late Professor Marcus Whitman Montgomery, of the Chicago Theological Seminary (a namesake of Dr. Whitman), to go over Dr. Whitman's church record while in Boston. He sends me the following, which may be regarded as authentic:

Ravenswood, Chicago, Jan. 5, 1894.

Dr. O. W. Nixon:

Dear Sir—The record of Dr. Whitman's church membership is as follows: Converted during a revival in the Congregational Church at Plainfield, Mass., in 1819, Rev. Moses Hallock, pastor. His first joining of a church was at Rushville, Yates County, N. Y., where he joined the Congregational Church in 1824, Rev. David Page, pastor. He was a member of this church for nine years, then he removed to Wheeler Center, Steuben County, N. Y. There being no Congregational Church there he joined the Presbyterian Church of Wheeler Center, Rev. James T. Hotchkiss, pastor. He was a member of this Presbyterian Church for three years, then he went to the Pacific Coast. This mission church was Presbyterian in name and Congregational in practice, while Whitman and the other missionaries were supported by the American Board. The American Board was always Congregational, but, at that time, the Presbyterians were co-operating with the American Board.

These are the bottom facts as I have every reason to believe. Very truly yours,

MARCUS WHITMAN MONTGOMERY.

The Rev. H. H. Spalding was a Presbyterian, and the Mission Church was Presbyterian in name, but was Congregational in practice, and had a confession of faith and covenant of its own. While the record shows Whitman to have been a Congregationalist, it also shows that he united with the Presbyterian Church when he settled at Wheeler Center, N. Y., where there was no Congregational Church. But the fact remains that his memory and the acts of his grand life are amply sufficient to interest both these great denominations.

Mrs. Whitman joined the Presbyterian Church when a young girl of eleven.

Dr. Whitman was born at Rushville, N. Y., September 4, 1802, and was thirty-three years old when he entered upon his work in Oregon. When first converted he resolved to study for the ministry, but a chain of circumstances changed his plans and he studied medicine. The early hardships and privations educated him into an admirable fitness for the chosen work of his life.

Picture that little missionary band as they stood together at Fort Walla Walla in September, 1836, and consulted about the great problems to solve. It was all new. There were no precedents to guide them. They easily understood that the first thing to do was to consult the ruling powers of Oregon—the Hudson Bay Company officials at Fort Vancouver. This would require another journey of three hundred miles, but as it could be made in boats, and the Indians were capital oarsmen, they resolved to take their wives with them, and thus complete the wedding journey.

The gallant Dr. McLoughlin, Chief Factor of the Hudson Bay Company, was a keen judge of human nature, and read men and women as scholars read books, and he was captivated with the open, manly ways of Dr.

Whitman and the womanly accomplishments of the fair young wife, who had braved the perils of an overland journey with wholly unselfish purposes. Whitman soon developed to Dr. McLoughlin all his plans and his hopes. Perhaps there was a professional free masonry between the men that brought them closer together, but, by nature, they were both men endowed richly with the best manly characters.

Dr. McLoughlin resolved to do the best thing possible for them, while he still protected the interests of his great monopoly. Dr. Whitman's idea, was to build one mission at the Dalles so as to be convenient to shipping; McLoughlin at once saw it would not do. He had already pushed the Methodist Mission far up the Willamette out of the way of the fort and its work, and argued with Whitman that it would be best for him to go to the Walla Walla country, three hundred miles away, and Spalding, one hundred and twenty-five miles farther on.

He argued that the river Indians were far less hopeful subjects to deal with, and that the bunch grass Indians, the Cayuse and Nez Perces, had expressed a great anxiety for teachers. This arrangement had been partially agreed to by Mr. Parker the year before. After a full canvass of the entire subject, Dr. McLoughlin promised all the aid in his power to give them a comfortable start.

At his earnest petition, Mrs. Whitman and Mrs. Spalding remained at Vancouver while their husbands went back to erect houses that would shelter them from the coming winter. To make Mrs. Whitman feel at ease, and that she was not taxing the generosity of their new friends, Dr. McLoughlin placed his daughter under her instruction, both in her class work and music. Every effort was made to interest and entertain the guests; the afternoons were given to excursions on the water, or on horseback, or in rambles through the great fir forests, still as wild as nature made them.

There is a grandeur in the great forest beyond the Stony Mountains unequaled in any portion of the world. In our Northern latitudes the undergrowth is so thick as to make comfortable traveling impossible, but in

54

the fir woods and in the pine and redwood forests of Oregon, there are comparatively few of such obstructions. The great giants ten or twelve feet in diameter, two hundred and seventy feet high, and one hundred feet without a limb, hide the sun, and upon a summer day make jaunts through the forest delightful to a lover of nature.

It was a grand rest and a pleasing finale to the hardships of the wedding journey for these heroic women, and Mrs. Whitman, in her diary, never a day neglects to remember her kind benefactors. They rested here for about one and a half months, when Mr. Spalding came after them and reported the houses so far advanced as to give them shelter. We read the following note in Mrs. Whitman's diary, 1836:

"December 26th. Where are we now, and who are we, that we should be thus blessed of the Lord? I can scarcely realize that we are thus comfortably fixed and keeping house so soon after our marriage, when considering what was then before us.

"We arrived here on the 10th, distance twenty-five miles from Fort Walla Walla. Found a house reared and the lean-to enclosed, a good chimney and fireplace and the floor laid. No windows or doors, except blankets. My heart truly leaped for joy as I lighted from my horse, entered and seated myself before a pleasant fire (for it was now night). It occurred to me that my dear parents had made a similar beginning and perhaps a more difficult one than ours.

"We had neither straw, bedstead or table, nor anything to make them of except green cottonwood. All our boards are sawed by hand. Here my husband and his laborers (two Owyhees from Vancouver, and a man who crossed the mountains with us), and Mr. Gray had been encamped in a tent since the 19th of October, toiling excessively hard to accomplish this much for our comfortable residence during the remainder of the winter.

"It is, indeed, a lovely situation. We are on a beautiful level peninsula formed by the branches of the Walla Walla River, upon the base of which our house stands, on the southeast corner, near the shore of the main river. To run a fence across to the opposite river on the north from our house—this, with the river, would enclose three hundred acres of good land for cultivation, all directly under the eye.

"The rivers are barely skirted with timber. This is all the woodland we can see. Beyond them, as far as the eye can reach, plains and mountains appear. On the east, a few rods from the house, is a range of small hills covered with bunch grass, very excellent food for animals and upon which they subsist during winter, even digging it from under the snow."

MISSION STATION AT WAIILATPUI.

This section is now reported as among the most fertile and beautiful places in Washington. Looking away in a southeasterly direction, the scenic beauty is grandly impressive. The Indians named the place Wai-i-lat-pui (the place of rye grass). For twenty miles there is a level reach of fertile soil through which flows like a silver thread the Walla Walla River, while in the distance loom up toward the clouds as a background the picturesque Blue Mountains. The greatest drawback was the long distance to any timber suitable for making boards, and the almost entire lack of helpers.

The Cayuse Indians seemed delighted with the prospect of a Mission church and school, but they thought it disgraceful for them to work. The doctor had to go from nine to fifteen miles to get his timber for boards, and then hew or saw them out by hand. It was not, therefore, strange, as Mrs. Whitman writes in her diary, December 26th: "No doors or windows." From the day he entered upon his work, Dr. Whitman was well-nigh an incessant toiler. Every year he built an addition to his house.

T. J. Furnham, who wrote a book of "Travels Across the Great Western Prairies and Rocky Mountains," visited the Whitman Mission in September, 1839. He says: "I found 250 acres enclosed and 200 acres under good cultivation. I found forty or fifty Indian children between the ages of

56

seven and eighteen years in school, and Mrs. Whitman an indefatigable instructor. One building was in course of construction and a small grist mill in running order."

He says again: "It appeared to me quite remarkable that the doctor could have made so many improvements since the year 1836; but the industry which crowded every hour of the day, his untiring energy of character, and the very efficient aid of his wife in relieving him in a great degree from the labors of the school, enabled him, without funds for such purposes, and without other aid than that of a fellow missionary for short intervals, to fence, plow, build, plant an orchard, and do all the other laborious acts of opening a plantation on the face of that distant wilderness, learn an Indian language, and do the duties, meanwhile, of a physician to the associate stations on the Clearwater and Spokane."

People who give their money for missionary work can easily see that in the case in hand they received faithful service. This is no prejudiced report, but facts based upon the knowledge of a stranger, who had no reason to misrepresent or exaggerate.

One of the first efforts of Dr. Whitman was to induce his Indians to build permanent homes, to plow, plant and sow. This the Hudson Bay Company had always discouraged. They wanted their savage aids as nomads and hunters, ready to move hundreds and hundreds of miles away in search of furs. They had never been encouraged to raise either grain or fruit, cattle or sheep.

Dr. Jonathan Edwards says, in speaking of The Whitman Mission in 1842: "The Indians were cultivating from one-fourth to four acres of land, had seventy head of cattle, and some of them a few sheep." The same author gives a graphic description of the painstaking work of Dr. and Mrs. Whitman, not only in the school room, but in the Indian home, to show them the comforts and benefits of civilization. Every Indian who will plant is furnished the seed.

He also describes the orderly Sunday at the Mission. Up to the year 1838 the principal meat used as food by the Mission was horse flesh. The cattle were too few to be sacrificed in that way. In 1837 Mrs. Whitman writes in her diary: "We have had but little venison furnished by the Indians, but to supply our men and visitors we have bought of the Indians and eaten ten wild horses."

In 1841 their stock of hogs and cattle had so increased that they were able to make a partial change of diet.

Another witness to the value of Dr. Whitman's missionary work is Joseph Drayton, of Commodore Wilkes' exploring expedition of 1841.

He says of the Mission: "All the premises looked comfortable, the garden especially fine, vegetables and melons in great variety. The wheat in the fields was seven feet high and nearly ripe, and the corn nine feet in the tassel." He marks the drawbacks of the Mission: "The roving of the Indians, rarely staying at home more than three months at a time." "They are off after buffalo," and "again off after the salmon," and "not more than fifty or sixty remain during the winter."

These Cayuse Indians were not a numerous band, but they were born traders, were wealthy, and had a great influence over other tribes. Their wealth consisted mainly in horses; a single Indian Chief owned two thousand head. One of their good qualities Mrs. Whitman speaks of, is, "there are no thieves among them." She has to keep nothing locked out of fear from thieves; but they had one trying habit of which Mrs. Whitman had great trouble to break them—that was, they thought they had a right to go into every room in the house, and seemed to think that something was wrong when deprived of visiting the bedrooms of the family.

In June, 1839, a great sorrow came to Dr. and Mrs. Whitman. They had but one child, a little girl of two years and three months old. In their isolated condition one can easily imagine what a large place a bright and attractive child would have in the heart of father and mother in such a home.

In the pursuance of his duties the doctor was absent night after night, and some of his more distant patients occupied him frequently many days.

It was at such times that Mrs. Whitman found great comfort and happiness in her little daughter. The child had learned the Indian language and spoke it fluently, to the delight of the Indians, and had learned all the songs sung in the Nez Perces dialect, having inherited the musical talent of her mother. It was in September, 1839, that she was accidentally drowned in the Walla Walla River. In her diary Mrs. Whitman writes to her mother:

"I cannot describe what our feelings were when night came and our dear child a corpse in the next room. We went to bed, but not to sleep, for sleep had departed from our eyes. The morning came, we arose, but our child slept on. I prepared a shroud for her during the day; we kept her four days; it was a great blessing and comfort to me so long as she looked natural and was so sweet I could caress her. But when her visage began to change I felt it a great privilege that I could put her in so safe a resting place as the grave, to see her no more until the resurrection morning.

"Although her grave is in sight every time I step out of the door, my thoughts seldom wander there to find her. I look above with unspeakable delight, and contemplate her as enjoying the full delights of that bright world where her joys are perfect."

One seldom reads a more pathetic story than this recorded by Mrs. Whitman, and yet, the almost heartbroken mother in her anguish never murmurs or rebels. On the morning of the day she was drowned, Mrs. Whitman writes, the little daughter was permitted to select a hymn for the family worship. She made a selection of the old-time favorite:

"ROCK OF AGES."

"While I draw this fleeting breath,
When my eyelids close in death;
When I rise to worlds unknown,

59

And behold Thee on Thy Throne;
Rock of ages cleft for me,
Let me hide myself in Thee."

When the Indians came in for the afternoon service Dr. Whitman turned to the same hymn and the baby girl again with her sweet voice joined in the singing. Says Mrs. Whitman:

"This was the last we heard her sing. Little did we think that her young life was so fleeting or that those sparkling eyes would so soon be closed in death, and her spirit rise to worlds unknown to behold on His Throne of glory Him who said: 'I will be a God to thee and thy seed after thee.'"

They got water for the household use from the running river, and the two little tin cups were found on the edge of the water. An old Indian dived in and soon brought out the body, but life was extinct.

The profoundly Christian character of the mother is revealed in every note of the sad event.

She writes: "Lord, it is right; it is right. She is not mine, but thine; she was only lent to me to comfort me for a little season, and now, dear Savior, Thou hast the best right to her. Thy will, not mine, be done." Perils and hardships had long been theirs, but this was their great sorrow. But it only seemed to excite them to greater achievements in the work before them. Not a single interest was neglected.

The sudden death of "The Little White Cayuse," as the Indians called her, seemed to estrange the Indians from the Mission. They almost worshiped her, and came almost daily to see her and hear her sing the Cayuse songs. The old Chief had many times said: "When I die I give everything I have to the 'Little White Cayuse.'" From this time on the Indians frequently showed a bad spirit. They saw the flocks and herds of the Mission increasing, and the fields of waving grain, and began to grow jealous and make demands that would have overtaxed and caused fear in almost any other man than a Whitman.

Both before and after his memorable ride to Washington, his good friend, Dr. McLoughlin, many times begged him to leave the Mission for a while, until the Indians got in a better frame of mind. No man knew the Indians so well as McLoughlin, and he saw the impending danger; but no entreaties moved Whitman. Here was his life work and here he would remain.

In these sketches there is no effort to tell the complete Oregon Mission story, but only so much of it as will make clear the heroic and patriotic services of Dr. and Mrs. Whitman. The reader will find a most careful study of the whole broad field of pioneer mission work upon the Pacific Coast in the Rev. Myron Eells' two books, the "History of Indian Missions," and the "Biography of Rev. Cushing Eells."

How much or how little the work of the Oregon Missionaries benefited the Indians eternity alone will reveal. They simply obeyed the call "to preach the gospel to every creature."

A train of circumstances, a series of evolutions in national history which they neither originated nor could stop, were portending. But that the Missionaries first of all saw the drift of coming events, and wisely guided them to the peace and lasting good of the nation is as plain as any page of written history.

With the light of that time, with the terrible massacre at Waiilatpui in sight, it is not strange that good people felt that there had been great sacrifice with small good results. All the years since have been correcting such false estimates. The American Board and the Christian people of the land have made their greatest mistake in not rallying to the defense of their martyr heroes.

No "forty thousand dollars" ever spent by that organization before or since has been so prolific in good. The argument to sustain this assertion will be found in other sketches.

The United States Government could well afford to give a million dollars every year to the American Board for fifty years to come, and to endow Whitman College magnificently, and then not pay a moiety for the benefit it has received as a nation, and never acknowledged.

The best possible answer of the church and of the friends of missions to those who sneeringly ask, What good has resulted to the world for all the millions spent on missions? is to point to that neglected grave at Waiilatpui, and recite the story of heroism and patriotism of Dr. Marcus Whitman.

CHAPTER VI.

THE RIDE TO SAVE OREGON.

The world loves a hero, and the pioneer history of our several States furnishes as interesting characters as are anywhere recorded. In view of the facts and conditions already recited, the old Missionaries were anxious and restless, and yet felt in a measure powerless to avert the danger threatened. They believed fully that under the terms of the treaty of 1818, re-affirmed in 1828, whichever nationality settled and organized the territory, that nation would hold it.

This was not directly affirmed in the terms of that treaty, but was so interpreted by the Americans and English in Oregon, and was greatly strengthened by the fact that leading statesmen in Congress had for nearly half a century wholly neglected Oregon, and time and again gone upon record as declaring it worthless and undesirable. In their conferences the Missionaries from time to time had gone over the whole question, and did everything in their power to encourage immigration.

Their glowing accounts of the fertility of the soil, the balmy climate, the towering forests, the indications of richness in minerals, had each year induced a limited number of more daring Americans to immigrate.

In this work of the Missionaries Jason Lee, the chief of the Methodist Missions, was, up to the date of the incident we are to narrate, the most successful of all. He was a man of great strength of character. Like Whitman, he was also a man of great physical strength, fearless, and, with it all, wise and brainy. No other man among the pioneers, for his untiring energy in courting immigration, can be so nearly classed with Whitman.

They were all men, who, though in Oregon to convert Indian savages to Christianity, yet were intensely American. They thought it no abuse of their Christianity to carry the banner of the Cross in one hand and the banner of their country in the other. Missionaries as they were, thousands of miles from home, neglected by the Government, yet the love of country seemed to shine with constantly increasing luster.

In addition to the Missionaries, at the time of which we write, there was quite a population of agriculturists and traders in the near vicinity of each mission. These heartily coöperated with the Missionaries and shared their anxieties. In 1840-'41 many of them met and canvassed the subject whether they should make an attempt to organize a government under the Stars and Stripes; but they easily saw that they were outnumbered by the English, who were already organized and were the real autocrats of the country.

So the time passed until the fall of 1842, when Elijah White, an Indian agent for the Government in the Northwest, brought a party of Americans, men, women and children, numbering one hundred and twenty, safely through to Waiilatpui. In this company was a more than usually intelligent, well-informed Christian gentleman, destined to fill an important place in our story, General Amos L. Lovejoy. He was thoroughly posted in national affairs, and gave Dr. Whitman his first intimation of the probability that the Ashburton Treaty would likely come to a crisis before Congress adjourned in March, 1843. This related, as it was supposed, to the entire boundary between the United States and the English possessions.

The question had been raised in 1794, "Where is 'the angle of Nova Scotia,' and where are the 'highlands between the angle and the northwest head of the Connecticut River?'" Time and again it had been before commissioners, and diplomats had many times grown eloquent in explaining, but heretofore nothing had come of it. Much was made of it, and yet it was only a dispute as to who owned some twelve thousand and twenty acres of land, much of which was of little value.

Looking back now one wonders at the shortsightedness of statesmen who quarreled for forty-eight years over this garden patch of rocky land in Maine, when three great states were quietly slipping away with scarcely a protest. But this arrival of recruits, and this knowledge of the political situation revealed by General Lovejoy, at once settled Dr. Whitman upon his line of duty.

To Mrs. Whitman he at once explained the situation, and said he felt impelled to go to Washington. She was a missionary's wife, a courageous, true-hearted, patriotic woman, who loved and believed in her husband, and at once consented. Under the rules the local members of the Mission had to be consulted, and runners were at once dispatched to the several stations, and all responded promptly, as the demand was for their immediate presence.

There was a second rule governing such cases of leave of absence, and that was the sanction, from headquarters, of the American Board in Boston. But in this emergency Dr. Whitman preferred to take all the responsibility and cut the red tape. Dr. Eells, one of the noblest of the old Missionaries, writes an account of that conference, and it is all the more valuable from the fact that he was opposed to the enterprise.

Dr. Eells says: "The purpose of Dr. Whitman was fixed. In his estimation the saving of Oregon to the United Spates was of paramount importance, and he would make the attempt to do so, even if he had to withdraw from the Mission in order to accomplish his purpose. In reply to considerations intended to hold Dr. Whitman to his assigned work, he said: 'I am not expatriated by becoming a missionary.'

"The idea of his withdrawal could not be entertained. Therefore, to retain him in the Mission, a vote to approve of his making this perilous endeavor prevailed."

In addition to this the Doctor undoubtedly intended to visit the American Board and explain the mission work and its needs, and protest against some of its orders. But in this there was no need of such haste as to cause the mid-winter journey. In this note of Dr. Eells the explanation is doubtless correct.

Dr. Spalding says: "Dr. Whitman's last remarks were, as he mounted his horse for the long journey: 'If the Board dismisses me, I will do what I can to save Oregon to the country. My life is of but little worth if I can save this country to the American people.'"

They all regarded it a most perilous undertaking. They knew well of the hardships of such a journey in the summer season, when grass could be found to feed the stock, and men live in comfort in the open air. But to all their pleadings and specifications of danger, Dr. Whitman had but one reply, "I must go." As Dr. Eells says:—"They finally all yielded when he said, 'I will go, even if I have to break my connection with the American Board.'" They all loved him, and he was too valuable a man for them to allow that.

Besides, they became thoroughly convinced that the man and the missionary had received a call from a higher source than an earthly one, and a missionary board should not stand in the way. It was resolved that he must not be allowed to make such a journey alone. A call was at once made, "Who will volunteer to go with him?" Again the unseen power was experienced when General Lovejoy said: "I will go with Dr. Whitman."

The man seems to have been sent for just such a purpose. Aside from the fact that he was tired out with the long five months' ride upon the plains, and had not been fully rested, no better man could have been chosen. He was an educated, Christian gentleman, full of cheerfulness, brave, cautious, and a true friend.

MRS. NARCISSA PRENTICE WHITMAN.

Mrs. Whitman, in her diary, dwells upon this with loving thoughtfulness, and her soul breaks forth in thanksgiving to the good Father above, who has sent so good and true a companion for the long and dangerous journey. She refers to it again and again that he will have a friend in his hours of peril and danger, and not have to depend entirely upon the savages for his society.

66

The conference passed a resolution, as stated, giving leave of absence and fixed the time for his starting in "five days" from that day. It was not often they had such an opportunity for letter-carriers, and each began a voluminous correspondence.

The Doctor set about his active preparations, arranging his outfit and seeing that everything was in order. The next day he had a call to see a sick man at old Fort Walla Walla, and as he needed many articles for his journey which could be had there, he went with this double purpose. He found at the Fort a score or more of traders, clerks and leading men of the Hudson Bay Company, assembled there. They were nearly all Englishmen, and the discussion soon turned upon the treaty, and the outlook, and as might be inferred, was not cheering to Whitman. But his object was to gain information and not to argue.

The dinner was soon announced and the Doctor sat down to a royal banquet with his jovial English friends. For no man was more highly esteemed by all than was Whitman. The chief factor at Vancouver, Dr. McLoughlin, from the very outset of their acquaintance, took a liking to both the Doctor and Mrs. Whitman, and in hundreds of cases showed them marked and fatherly kindness. Mrs. Whitman, in her diary, recently published in the proceedings of the Oregon State Historical Society, mainly in the years 1891 and 1893, often refers to the fatherly kindness of the good old man whose home she shared for weeks and months, and he begged her when first reaching Oregon to stop all winter and wait until her own humble home could be made comfortable.

But while the company were enjoying their repast, an express messenger of the company arrived from Fort Colville, three hundred and fifty miles up the Columbia, and electrified his audience by the announcement that a colony of one hundred and forty Englishmen and Canadians were on the road.

In such a company it is easy to see such an announcement was exciting news. One young priest threw his cap in the air and shouted,

"Hurrah for Oregon—America is too late, we have got the country."

Dr. Whitman carefully concealed all his intentions—in fact, this was enjoined upon all the missionary band, as publicity would likely defeat any hope of good results. Those who will take the pains to read Mrs. Whitman's diary will notice how she avoids saying anything to excite comment regarding the purposes of his winter visit to Washington. In her letter to her father and mother she simply says: "I expect my dear husband will be so full of his great work that he will forget to tell you of our life in Oregon. He can explain what it is," etc.

It is said "Women cannot keep a secret," but here is an instance of one that did. In his absence she visited Fort Vancouver, Astoria, Oregon City, and other points. She is painstaking in keeping a regular record of every-day events. But the secret of his mission to the States was perfectly safe with the good wife.

As soon as the Doctor could with politeness excuse himself, he mounted his pony and galloped away home, pondering the news he had received. By the time he reached Waiilatpui he resolved there must be no tarrying for "five days." On the morning of the third day after the conference the spirit was upon him, and he took such messages as were ready, and on October 3d, 1842, bade a long good-bye to his wife and home, and the two men, their guide, and three pack mules, began that ever memorable journey—escorted for a long distance by many Cayuse braves.

Intelligent readers of all classes can easily mark the heroism of such an undertaking under such circumstances, but the old plainsman and the mountaineer who know the terrors of the journey, will point to it as without a parallel in all history. It was surmised by most that it was "A ride down to the valley of the shadow of death."

It is comforting and assuring of that power which sustains a believing soul, to turn the pages of the diary of Mrs. Whitman, as day by day she follows the little caravan with thought and prayer, and see with what confidence she expresses the belief that an Almighty Arm is guiding her loved one in safety through all perils.

It is easy to surmise the feelings of the Missionary band when they sent in their letters and messages and learned that the Doctor was far on his journey and had not waited the required limit of "five days."

The echo of dissatisfaction was heard even for years after, very much to the disturbance of the good wife. And she in her diary expresses profound thankfulness when, years after, the last vestige of criticism ceased and the old cordiality was restored.

As for Dr. Whitman, with his whole being impressed with the importance of his work and the need for haste, it is doubtful whether he even remembered the "five days" limit.

The great thought with him was, I must reach Washington before Congress adjourns, or all may be lost. The after disclosures convinced the aggrieved Missionaries that Whitman was right, and they deeply regretted some of the sharp criticisms they made and wrote East.

With horses fresh, the little company made a rapid ride, reaching Fort Hall in eleven days. The road thus far was plain and familiar to every member of the party. Prior to leaving home there had been rumors that the Blackfoot Indians had suddenly grown hostile, and would make the journey dangerous along the regular line of travel.

Upon reaching Fort Hall, Captain Grant, who seems to have been placed at that point solely to discourage and defeat immigration, set about his task in the usual way. Without knowing, he shrewdly suspected that the old Missionary had business of importance on hand which it would be well to thwart. He had before had many a tilt with Whitman and knew something of his determination. It was Grant who had almost compelled every incoming settler to forsake his wagon at Fort Hall, sacrifice his goods, and force women and children to ride on horseback or go on foot the balance of the journey.

Six years before he had plead with Whitman to do this, and had failed, and Whitman had thus taken the first wagon into Oregon that ever crossed the Rockies. Now he set about to defeat his journey to the States. He told of the hopelessness of a journey over the Rocky Mountains, with snow already twenty feet deep. He also informed him that from recent advices the Sioux and Pawnee Indians were at war, and it would be almost certain death to the party to undertake to pass through their country.

This, all told for a single purpose, was partly true and partly false. The writer, a few years after, when war broke out between the Cheyennes and the Pawnees, passed entirely through the Cheyenne country and was treated with the utmost courtesy and kindness by the Cheyenne braves.

But Captain Grant's argument had more effect upon Whitman than upon a former occasion. The Captain even began to hope that he had effectually blocked the way. But he was dealing with a man of great grit, not easily discouraged, and, we may say it reverently, an inspired man. He had started to go to the States and he would continue his journey.

Captain Grant was at his wits' end. He had no authority to stop Whitman and his party; he carried with him a permit signed by "Lewis Cass, Secretary of War," commanding all in authority to protect, aid, etc.

The American Board was as careful in having all Oregon missionaries armed with such credentials as if sending them to a foreign land, and, in fact, there was no vestige of American government in Oregon in that day. The Hudson Bay Company, wholly English, ruled over everything, whether whites or Indians.

Much to Captain Grant's chagrin, Whitman, instead of turning backward, set out southeast to discover a new route to the States. He knew in a general way the lay of the mountain ranges, but he had never heard that a white man's foot had passed that way. First east and south from Fort Hall, in

70

the direction of the now present site of Salt Lake City, from thence to Fort Uintah and Fort Uncompahgra, then to Taos, Santa Fe, to Bent's Fort, and St. Louis. This course led them over some very rough mountainous country.

In his diary Gen. Lovejoy says: "From Fort Hall to Fort Uintah we met with terribly severe weather. The deep snow caused us to lose much time. Here we took a new guide to Fort Uncompahgra on Grand River in Spanish country, which we safely reached and employed a new guide there. Passing over a high mountain on our way to Taos we encountered a terrible snow storm, which compelled us to seek shelter in a dark defile, and although we made several attempts to press on, we were detained some ten days. When we got upon the mountain again we met with another violent snow storm, which almost blinded man and beast. The pelting snow and cold made the dumb brutes well-nigh unmanageable."

Finally the guide stopped and acknowledged he was lost and would go no farther, and they resolved to return to their camp in the sheltered ravine. But the drifting snow had obliterated every sign of the path by which they had come, and the guide acknowledged that he could not direct the way. In this dire dilemma, says Gen. Lovejoy, "Dr. Whitman dismounted and upon his knees in the snow commended himself, his distant wife, his missionary companions and work, and his Oregon, to the Infinite One for guidance and protection.

"The lead mule left to himself by the guide, turning his long ears this way and that, finally started plunging through the snow drifts, his Mexican guide and all the party following instead of guiding, the old guide remarking: 'This mule will find the camp if he can live long enough to reach it.' And he did." As woodsmen well know this knowledge of directions in dumb brutes is far superior often to the wisest judgment of men.

The writer well remembers a terrible experience when lost in the great forests of Arkansas, covered with the back water from the Mississippi River, which was rapidly rising. Two of us rode for hours. The water would grow deeper in one direction; we would try another and find it no better; we were hopelessly lost. My companion was an experienced woodsman and claimed that he was going in the right direction, so I followed until in despair I called to him, and showed him the high water mark upon the trees ten feet above our heads as we sat upon our horses.

I remarked: "I have followed you; now you follow me. I am going to let my old horse find the way out." I gave him the rein; he seemed to understand it. He raised his head, took an observation, turned at right angles from the way we had insisted was our course, wound around logs and past marshes, and in two hours brought us safely to camp.

This incident of Dr. Whitman's mule, as well as all such, educates one in kindness to all dumb animal life.

Reaching camp the guide at once announced that, "I will go no farther; the way is impossible." "This," says Gen. Lovejoy, "was a terrible blow to Dr. Whitman. He had already lost more than ten days of valuable time." But it would be impossible to move without a guide. Whitman was a man who knew no such word as fail. His order was: "I must go on."

There was but one thing to do. He said to Gen. Lovejoy: "You stay in camp and recuperate and feed the stock, and I will return with the guide to Fort Uncompahgra, and get a new man."

And so Lovejoy began "recuperation," and recuperated his dumb animals by collecting the brush and inner bark of the willows upon which they fed. It is astonishing how a mule or horse on the plains can find food enough to live on, under such conditions.

The writer had a pet mule in one of his journeys over the great plains, which he would tie to a sage bush near the tent when not a vestige of grass was anywhere in sight, and yet waking up in the night at any hour I would hear Ben pawing and chewing. He would paw up the tender roots of the sage and in the morning look as plump and full as if he had feasted on good No. 2 corn.

72

"The doctor," says Lovejoy, "was gone just one week, when he again reached our camp in the ravine with a new guide."

The storm abated and they passed over the mountain and made good progress toward Taos.

Their most severe experience was on reaching Grand River. People who know, mark this as one of the most dangerous and treacherous rivers in the West. Its rapid, deep, cold current, even in the Summer, is very much dreaded. Hundreds of people have lost their lives in it. Where they struck the Grand it was about six hundred feet wide. Two hundred feet upon each shore was solid ice, while a rushing torrent two hundred feet wide was between.

The guide studied it, and said: "It is too dangerous to attempt to cross." "We must cross, and at once," said Whitman. He got down from his horse, cut a willow pole eight feet long, put it upon his shoulder, and after remounting, said: "Now you shove me off." Lovejoy and the guide did as ordered, and the General says: "Both horse and rider temporarily went out of sight, but soon appeared, swimming. The horse struck the rocky bottom and waded toward the shore where the doctor, dismounting, broke the ice with his pole and helped his horse out. Wood was plentiful and he soon had a roaring fire. As readers well know, in a wild country where the lead animal has gone ahead, the rest are eager to follow, regardless of danger, and the General and his guide, after breaking the ice, had no difficulty in persuading their horses and pack-mules to make the plunge into the icy flood. They all landed in safety and spent the day in thoroughly drying out.

"Is the route passable?" asked Napoleon of his engineer. "Barely possible, sire," replied the engineer. "Then let the column move at once," said the Great Commander. The reader, in the incident of the Grand and on the mountains, sees the same hero who refused to believe the "impossible" of Captain Grant, at Fort Hall, and took that "historic wagon" to Oregon. It looked like a small event to take a wagon to Oregon, shattered and battered by the rocks and besetments of the long three thousand mile journey. The good wife many times mourned that the doctor should "Wear himself out in getting that wagon through." "Yesterday," she says, "it was overset in the river and he was wet from head to foot getting it out; to-day it was upset on the mountain side, and it was hard work to save it." The dear woman did not know it was an inspired wagon, the very implement upon which the fate of Oregon would turn. Small events are sometimes portentous, and the wagon that Whitman wheeled into Oregon, as we shall soon see, was of this character.

One of the Providential events was, that the little company had been turned aside from the attempt to make the journey over the direct route and sent over this unexplored course, fully one thousand miles longer. The winter of 1842-43 was very cold, and the snow throughout the West was heavy. From many of these storms they were protected by the ranges of high mountains, and what was of great value, had plenty of firewood; while on the other route for a thousand miles they would have had to depend mainly upon buffalo chips for fire, which it would have been impossible to find when the ground was covered with snow. To the traveler good fires in camp are a great comfort.

Even as it was, they suffered from the cold, all of them being severely frosted. Dr. Whitman, when he reached Washington, was suffering from frozen feet, hands and ears, although he had taken every precaution to protect himself and his companions.

The many vexatious delays had caused not only the loss of valuable time, but they had run out of provisions. A dog had accompanied the party and they ate him; a mule came next, and that kept them until they came to Santa Fe, where there was plenty. Santa Fe is one of the oldest cities upon the continent occupied by English-speaking people. The doctor, anxious for news, could find little there, and only stopped long enough to recruit his supplies. He was in no mood to enjoy the antiquities of this favorite resort of all the heroes of the plains.

74

Pushing on over the treeless prairies, they made good headway toward Bent's Fort on the headwaters of the Arkansas. The grass for the horses was plentiful. That is one of the prime requisites of the campaigner upon the plains. Had there been time for hunting, all along their route they could have captured any amount of wild game, but as it was, they attempted nothing except it came directly in the way. They even went hungry rather than lose an hour in the chase.

There was one little incident which may seem very small, but the old campaigner will see that it was big with importance. They lost their axe. It was after a long tedious day crossing a bleak prairie, when they reached one of the tributaries of the Arkansas River. On the opposite side was wood in great plenty. On their side there was none. The river was frozen over with smooth, clear ice, scarcely thick enough to bear a man. They must have wood.

The doctor seized the axe, lay down on the ice and snaked himself across on the thin crust. He cut loads of wood and pushed it before him or skated it across and returned in safety; but unfortunately split the axe helve. This they soon remedied by binding it with a fresh deer skin thong. But as it lay in the edge of the tent that night, a thieving wolf wanting the deer skin, took the axe and all, and they could find no trace of it. The great good fortune was, that such a catastrophe did not occur a thousand miles back. It is barely possible it might have defeated the enterprise.

"When within about four days' journey of Bent's Fort," says Gen. Lovejoy, "we met George Bent, a brother of Gen. Bent, with a caravan on his way to Taos. He told us that a party of mountain men would leave Bent's Fort in a few days for St. Louis, but said we could not reach the fort with our pack animals in time to join the party.

"The doctor being very anxious to join it, and push on to Washington, concluded to leave myself and guide with the packs, and he himself taking the best animal, with some bedding and a small allowance of provisions, started on alone, hoping by rapid traveling to reach the fort before the party left. But to do so he would have to travel upon the Sabbath, something we had not done before.

"Myself and guide traveled slowly and reached the fort in four days, but imagine my astonishment when told the doctor had not arrived nor been heard from. As this portion of the journey was infested by gangs of gray wolves, that had been half starved during the snows and cold weather, our anxiety for the doctor's safety was greatly increased. Every night our camp would be surrounded by them coming even to the door of the tent, and everything eatable had to be carefully stored and our animals picketed where we could defend them with our rifles; when a wolf fell he would instantly be devoured by his fellows.

"If not killed we knew the doctor was lost. Being furnished by the gentlemen of the fort with a good guide I started to search for him and traveled up the river about one hundred miles. I learned by the Indians that a man who was lost had been there and he was trying to find Bent's Fort. They said they had directed him down the river and how to find the fort. I knew from their description that it was the doctor, and I returned as rapidly as possible; but he had not arrived.

"Late in the afternoon he came in much fatigued and almost desponding. He said that God had hindered him for traveling on the Holy Sabbath." Says General Lovejoy: "This was the only time I ever knew him to travel on Sunday."

The party which the doctor was to accompany to St. Louis had already started, but was kindly stopped by a runner, and it was in camp waiting his coming. Tired as he was, he tarried but a single night at Fort Bent, and again with a guide hurried on to overtake the caravan. This was a dangerous part of the journey. Savage beasts and savage men were both to be feared.

In pioneer days the borders of civilization were always infested by the worst class of people, both whites and Indians. This made the doctor more anxious for an escort. Gen. Lovejoy remained at the fort until he entirely recovered from his fatigue, and went on with the next caravan passing eastward to St. Louis. In a letter to Dr. Atkinson, published in full in the appendix to this volume, Gen. Lovejoy recites many interesting incidents of this journey. Before reaching St. Louis, Gen. Lovejoy immediately began to advertise the emigration for the following May.

Dr. Barrows, in his fine volume, "Oregon—the Struggle for Possession," says: "Upon the arrival of Dr. Whitman in St. Louis it was my good fortune that he should be quartered as a guest under the same roof and at the same table with me. Those interested in the news from the plains, the trappers and traders in furs and Indian goods, gathered about him and beset him with a multitude of questions. Answering them courteously he in turn asked about Congress. Whether the Ashburton Treaty had been concluded? and whether it covered the Northwest Territory? The treaty he learned had been signed August 9th, long before he left Oregon, and had been confirmed by the Senate and signed by the President on November 10th, while he was floundering in the snow upon the mountains."

But the Oregon question was still open, and only the few acres up in Maine had been fixed. The question he was eager to have answered was: "Is the Oregon question still pending, and can I get there before Congress adjourns?" The river was frozen, and he had to depend upon the stage, and even from St. Louis a journey to Washington in midwinter at that time, was no small matter. But to a man like Whitman with muscles trained, and a brain which never seemed to tire, it was counted as nothing.

Dr. Barrows says: "Marcus Whitman once seen, and in our family circle, telling of his business, he had but one, was a man not to be forgotten by the writer. He was of medium height, more compact than spare, a stout shoulder, and large head not much above it, covered with stiff iron gray hair, while his face carried all the moustache and whiskers that four months had been able to put on it. He carried himself awkwardly, though perhaps courteously enough for trappers, Indians, mules and grizzlies, his principal company for six years. He seemed built as a man for whom more stock had been furnished than worked in symmetrically and gracefully.

"There was nothing quick in his motion or speech, and no trace of a fanatic; but under control of a thorough knowledge of his business, and with deep, ardent convictions about it, he was a profound enthusiast. A willful resolution and a tenacious earnestness would impress you as marking the man.

"He wore coarse fur garments with buckskin breeches. He had a buffalo overcoat, with a head hood for emergencies, with fur leggins and boot moccasins. His legs and feet fitted his Mexican stirrups. If my memory is not at fault his entire dress when on the street did not show one inch of woven fabric."

One can easily see that a dress of such kind and upon such a man would attract attention at the National Capital. But the history of the event nowhere hints that the old pioneer suffered in any quarter from his lack of fashionable garments. It was before the day of interviewing newspapers, but the men in authority in Washington soon learned of his coming and showed him every courtesy and kindness. He would have been lionized had he encouraged it. But he had not imperiled life for any such purpose. He was, after a four thousand miles ride, there upon a great mission and for business, and time was precious.

Almost in despair he had prayed that he might be enabled to reach the Capital of the Nation and make his plea for his land, Oregon, before it was too late. And here he was. Would he be given an audience? Would he be believed? Would he succeed? These were the questions uppermost in his mind.

CHAPTER VII.

WHITMAN IN THE PRESENCE OF PRESIDENT TYLER AND SECRETARY OF STATE DANIEL WEBSTER, AND THE RETURN TO OREGON.

It has been an American boast that the President of the United States is within the reach of the humblest subject. This was truer years ago than now, and possibly with some reason for it. Unfortunately the historian has no recorded account of the interview between the President, his Secretary of State and Whitman. Whitman worked for posterity, but did not write for it.

For his long journey over the plains in 1836 and the many entertaining and exciting events we are wholly dependent upon Mrs. Whitman, and for the narrative of the perilous ride to save Oregon, we are dependent upon the brief notes made by Gen. Lovejoy, and from personal talks with many friends. Whitman always seemed too busy to use pencil or pen, and yet when he did write, as a few recorded specimens show, he was remarkably clear, precise and forcible. But while we have no written statement of the celebrated interview, Dr. Whitman, in many private conversations with friends in Oregon said enough to give a fair and clear account of it.

It will require no stretch of imagination in any intelligent reader to suppose, that a man who had undergone the hardships and perils he had, would be at a loss how to present his case in the most forcible and best possible method. He was an educated man, a profound thinker; and he knew every phase of the questions he had to present, and no man of discernment could look into his honest eyes and upon his manly bearing, without acknowledging that they were in the presence of the very best specimen of American Christian manhood.

Both President Tyler and Secretary of State Daniel Webster, speedily granted him an audience. Some time in the future some great artist will paint a picture of this historic event. The old pioneer, in his leather breeches and worn and torn fur garments, and with frozen limbs, just in from a four thousand mile ride, is a picture by himself, but standing in the presence of the President and his great Secretary, to plead for Oregon and the old flag, the subject for a painter is second to none in American history.

Some writers have said that Whitman "had a chilling reception from Secretary Webster." Of this there is not a shadow of proof. It has also been asserted that Whitman assailed the Ashburton-Webster Treaty. This much only is true, that Whitman regarded the issues settled as comparatively insignificant to those involved in the possession and boundaries of Oregon; but he was profoundly grateful that in the treaty, Oregon had in no way been sacrificed, as he had feared.

Gen. Lovejoy says: "Dr. Whitman often related to me during our homeward journey the incidents of his reception by the President and his Secretary. He had several interviews with both of them, as well as with many of the leading senators and members of Congress." The burden of his speech in all these, says Gen. Lovejoy, was to "immediately terminate the treaty of 1818 and 1828, and extend the laws of the United States over Oregon." It takes a most credulous reader to doubt that.

For months prior to Whitman's visit to Washington in diplomatic circles it was well understood that there were negotiations on foot to trade American interests in Oregon for the fisheries of Newfoundland. Dr. Whitman soon heard of it, and heard it given as a reason why the boundary line between Oregon and the British possessions had been left open and only the little dispute in Maine adjusted.

According to all reports we can gather from the Doctor's conversations, there was only one time in the several conferences in which he and Secretary Webster got warm and crossed swords. Secretary Webster had received castigation from political leaders, and sharp criticism from his own party over the Ashburton Treaty, and was ready to resent every remote allusion to it, as a give-away of American interests. In defense of Secretary

Webster it has been asserted that "he had no intention of making such an exchange." But his well-known previous views, held in common by the leading statesmen of the day, already referred to, and openly expressed in Congress and upon the rostrum, that "Oregon was a barren worthless country, fit only for wild beasts and wild men, gave the air of truth to the reported negotiation." This he emphasized by the interruption of Whitman in one of his glowing descriptions of Oregon, by saying in effect that "Oregon was shut off by impassable mountains and a great desert, which made a wagon road impossible."

Then, says Whitman, I replied: "Mr. Secretary, that is the grand mistake that has been made by listening to the enemies of American interests in Oregon. Six years ago I was told there was no wagon road to Oregon, and it was impossible to take a wagon there, and yet in despite of pleadings and almost threats, I took a wagon over the road, and have it now." This was the historic wagon. It knocked all the argument out of the great Secretary. Facts are stubborn things to meet, and when told by a man like Whitman it is not difficult to imagine their effect.

He assured the Secretary that the possibilities of the territory beyond the Rockies were boundless, that under the poorest cultivation everything would grow; that he had tested a variety of crops and the soil made a wonderful yield. That not only is the soil fertile, the climate healthful and delightful, but there is every evidence of the hills and mountains being rich in ores; while the great forests are second to none in the world. But it was the battered old wagon that was the clinching argument that could not be overcome. No four-wheeled vehicle ever before in history performed such notable service. The real fact was, the Doctor took it into Oregon on two wheels, but he carefully hauled the other two wheels inside as precious treasures. He seems to have had a prophetic view of the value of the first incoming wagon from the United States. The events show his wisdom.

Proceeding with his argument, Dr. Whitman said: "Mr. Secretary, you had better give all New England for the cod and mackerel fisheries of New Foundland than to barter away Oregon."

WHITMAN PLEADING FOR OREGON BEFORE PRESIDENT TYLER AND SECRETARY WEBSTER.

From the outset, and at every audience granted, President Tyler treated Dr. Whitman with the greatest deference. He was a new character in the experience of both these polished and experienced politicians. Never before had they listened to a man who so eloquently plead for the cause of his country, with no selfish aim in sight. He asked for no money, or bonds, or land, or office, or anything, except that which would add to the nation's wealth, the glory and honor of the flag, and the benefit of the hardy pioneer of that far-off land, that the nation had for more than a third of the century wholly neglected. It was a powerful appeal to the manly heart of President Tyler, and as the facts show, was not lost on Secretary Webster.

The Rev. H. H. Spalding, Whitman's early associate in the Oregon work, had many conferences with Whitman after his return to Oregon. Spalding says, speaking of the conference: "Webster's interest lay too near to Cape Cod to see things as Whitman did, while he conceded sincerity to the missionary, but he was loth to admit that a six years' residence there gave Whitman a wider knowledge of the country than that possessed by Governor Simpson, who had explored every part of it and represented it as a sandy desert, cut off from the United States by impassable mountains, and fit only for wild animals and savage men."

With the light we now have upon the subject the greater wonder is that a brainy man like Webster could be so over-reached by an interested party such as Governor Simpson was; well knowing as he did, that he was the chief of the greatest monopoly existing upon either continent—the Hudson Bay Company. All Dr. Whitman demanded was that if it were true, as asserted by Mr. Webster himself, in his instructions to Edward Everett in 1840, then Minister to England, that "The ownership of Oregon is very likely to follow the greater settlement and larger amount of population;" then "All I ask is that you won't barter away Oregon, or allow English interference until

I can lead a band of stalwart American settlers across the plains: for this I will try to do."

President Tyler promptly and positively stated: "Dr. Whitman, your long ride and frozen limbs speak for your courage and patriotism; your missionary credentials are good vouchers for your character." And he promptly granted his request. Such promise was all that Whitman required. He firmly believed, as all the pioneers of Oregon at that time believed, that the treaty of 1818, while not saying in direct terms that the nationality settling the country should hold it, yet that that was the real meaning. Both countries claimed the territory, and England with the smallest rightful claim had, through the Hudson Bay Company, been the supreme autocratic ruler for a full third of a century.

More than half a dozen fur companies, attracted to Oregon by the wealth flowing into the coffers of the English company, had attempted, as we have before shown, to open up business on what they claimed was American soil; but, in every instance, they were starved out or bought out by the English company. The Indians obeyed its orders, and even the American missionaries settled in just the localities they were ordered to by the English monopoly. In another connection we have more fully explained this treaty of 1818, but, suffice it to say, these conditions led Whitman to believe that the only hope of saving Oregon was in American immigration. It was for this that he plead with President Tyler and Secretary Webster and the members of Congress he met.

From the President he went to the Hon. James M. Porter, Secretary of War, and by him was received with the greatest kindness, and he eagerly heard the whole story. He promised Dr. Whitman all the aid in his power in his scheme of immigration. He promised that Captain Fremont, with a company of troops, should act as escort to the caravan which Whitman was positive he could organize upon the frontier. The Secretary of War also inquired in what way he and the Government could aid the pioneers in the new country, and asked Dr. Whitman, at his leisure, to write out his views, and forward them to him. Dr. Whitman did this, and the State Historical

Society of Oregon did excellent service, recently, in publishing Whitman's proposed "Oregon Organization," found among the official papers of the War Department, a copy of which will be found in the appendix of this volume.

In a Senate document, December 31st, viz., the 41st Cong., February 9th, 1871, we read: "There is no doubt but that the arrival of Dr. Whitman, in 1843, was opportune. The President was satisfied that the territory was worth the effort to win it. The delay incident to a transfer of negotiations to London was fortunate, for there is reason to believe that if former negotiations had been renewed in Washington, and that, for the sake of a settlement of the protracted controversy and the only remaining unadjudicated cause of difference between the two Governments, the offer had been renewed of the 49th parallel to the Columbia and thence down the river to the Pacific Ocean, it would have been accepted. The visit of Whitman committed the President against any such action." This is a clear statement, summarizing the great historic event, and forever silencing effectually the slanderous tongues that have, in modern times, attempted to deprive the old Hero of his great and deserving tribute.

We will do Secretary Webster the justice to say here, that in his later years, he justly acknowledged the obligations of the nation to Dr. Whitman. In the New York Independent, for January, 1870, it is stated: "A personal friend of Mr. Webster, a legal gentleman, and with whom he conversed on the subject several times, remarked to the writer of this article: 'It is safe to assert that our country owes it to Dr. Whitman and his associate missionaries that all the territory west of the Rocky Mountains and south as far as the Columbia River, is not now owned by England and held by the Hudson Bay Company.'"

Having transacted his business and succeeded even beyond his expectations, Whitman hurried to Boston to report to the headquarters of the American Board. His enemies have often made sport over their version of his "cool reception by the American Board." If there was a severe reprimand, as reported, both the officers of the Board and Dr. Whitman failed to make record of it. But enough of the facts leaked out in the years after to show that it was not altogether a harmonious meeting. It is not to be wondered at.

The American Board was a religious organization working under fixed rules, and expected every member in every field to obey those rules. But here was a man, whose salary had been paid by the Board for special work, away from his field of labor without the consent from headquarters. It is not at all unlikely that he was severely reprimanded. The officers of the American Board had no reason to know, as Christian people can see now, that Whitman was an inspired man, and a man about his Father's business. It is even reported, but not vouched for, that they ordered him to promptly repair to his post of duty, and dismissed him with his pockets so empty, that, when starting upon his ever-memorable return journey across the plains, "He had but money enough to buy only a single ham for his supplies."

One of his old associates who had frequent conferences with Whitman—Dr. Gray—says: "Instead of being treated by the American Board as his labors justly deserved, he met the cold, calculating rebuke for unreasonable expenses, and for dangers incurred without orders or instructions or permission from headquarters. Thus, for economical, prudential reasons, the Board received him coldly, and rebuked him for his presence before them, causing a chill in his warm and generous heart, and a sense of unmerited rebuke from those who should have been most willing to listen to all his statements, and been most cordial and ready to sustain him in his herculean labors." We leave intelligent readers to answer for themselves, whether this attitude of this great and influential and excellent organization has not been, in a measure, responsible for the neglect of this Hero, who served it and the Christian world with all faithfulness and honesty, until he and his noble wife dropped into their martyr graves? If they say yea, we raise the question whether the time has not been reached to make amends?

Dr. Barrows says, in his "Oregon and the Struggle for Possession," "It should be said in apology for both parties at this late day that, at that time, the Oregon Mission and its managing board were widely asunder geographically, and as widely separated in knowledge of the condition of

85

affairs." Dr. Whitman seems to have assumed that his seven years' residence on the Northwest Coast would gain him a trustful hearing. But his knowledge gave him the disadvantage of a position and plans too advanced—not an uncommon mishap to eminent leaders. As said by Coleridge of Milton, "He strode so far before his contemporaries as to dwarf himself by the distance."

He adds that:

"Years after only, it was discovered by one of the officers of the American Board," that "It was not simply an American question then settled, but at the same time a Protestant question." He also refers to a recent work, "The Ely Volume," in which is discussed the question, "Instances where the direct influence of missionaries has controlled and hopefully shaped the destinies of communities and states," and illustrates by saying, "Perhaps no event in the history of missions will better illustrate this than the way in which Oregon and our whole Northwest Pacific Coast was saved to the United States."

This covered directly the Whitman idea. It was, as he before stated, a union of banners—the banner of the cross, and the banner of the country he loved. It took the spirit and love of both to sustain a man and to enable him to undergo the hardships and dangers and discouragements that he met, from the beginning to the end.

From Boston, with an aching heart, and yet doubtless serene over an accomplished duty, which he had faith to believe time would reveal in its real light, Dr. Whitman passed on to make a flying visit to his own and his wife's relations. From letters of Mrs. Whitman, it is easy to see that her prophecy was true; "He would be too full of his great work on hand, to tell much of the home in Oregon." His visit was hurried over and seemed more the necessity of a great duty than a pleasure.

But the Doctor's mind was westward. He had learned from Gen. Lovejoy that already there was gathering upon the frontier a goodly number of immigrants and the prospect was excellent for a large caravan. In the absence of Dr. Whitman, Gen. Lovejoy had neglected no opportunity to publish far and wide that Dr. Whitman and himself would, early in the Spring, pilot across the plains to Oregon, a body of immigrants. A rendezvous was appointed, not far from where Kansas City now stands, at the little town of Weston. But they were in various camps at Fort Leavenworth and other points, waiting both for their guide and for the growing spring grass—a necessity for the emigrant.

Certain modern historians have undertaken to rob Whitman of his great services in 1843, by gathering affidavits of people who emigrated to Oregon in that year, declaring, "We never saw Marcus Whitman," and "We were not persuaded to immigrate to Oregon by him," etc. Doubtless there were such upon the wide plains, scattered as they may have been, hundreds of miles apart. But it is just as certain that the large immigration to Oregon that year was incited by the movements of Whitman and Lovejoy, as any fact could be. There is no other method of explaining it. That he directly influenced every immigrant of that year, no one has claimed.

True, old Elijah White had paved the way, the year before, by leading in the first large band of agriculturist settlers; but men of families, undertaking a two thousand mile journey, with their families and their stock, were certainly desirous of an experienced guide. They may, as some of them say, never have met Whitman. He was not one of the free and easy kind that made himself popular with the masses.

Then, besides all that, fifty years ago plains life was an odd life. I have journeyed with men for weeks, and even after months of acquaintance have not known their names, except that of Buckeye, Sucker, Missouri, Cass County Bill, Bob, etc. Little bands would travel by themselves for days and weeks and then, under the sense of danger that would be passed along the line, and for defense against depredations of some dangerous tribe of Indians, they would gather into larger bands soon again to fall apart. Some of these would often follow many days behind the head of the column, but always have the benefit of its guidance.

That year grass was late, and they did not get fully under way until the first week in June. Whitman remained behind and did not overtake the advance of the column until it reached the Platte River. He knew the way, he had three times been over it. He was ahead arranging for camping places for those in his immediate company, or in the rear looking after the sick and discouraged. If some failed to know him by name, there were many who did, and all shared in all the knowledge of the country and road which he, better than any other, knew.

In answer to historical critics of modern times we quote Dr. H. H. Spalding, who says, in speaking of the immigration of 1843:

"And through that whole summer Dr. Whitman was everywhere present; the ministering angel to the sick, helping the weary, encouraging the wavering, cheering the tired mothers, setting broken bones and mending wagons. He was in the front, in the center and in the rear. He was in the river hunting out fords through the quicksand; in the desert places looking for water and grass; among the mountains hunting for passes, never before trodden by white men; at noontide and at midnight he was on the alert as if the whole line was his own family, and as if all the flocks and herds were his own. For all this he neither asked nor expected a dollar from any source, and especially did he feel repaid at the end, when, standing at his mission home, hundreds of his fellow pilgrims took him by the hand and thanked him with tears in their eyes for all that he had done."

The head of the column arrived at Fort Hall and there waited for the stragglers to come up. Dr. Whitman knew that here he would meet Captain Johnny Grant, and the old story, "You can't take a wagon into Oregon," would be dinned into the ears of the head of every family. He had heard it over and over again six years before. Fort Hall was thirteen hundred and twenty-three miles from the Missouri River at Kansas City. Here the Doctor expected trouble and found it. Johnny Grant was at Fort Hall to make trouble and discourage immigration. He was working under the pay of the Fur Company and earned his money. The Fur Company did not desire farmers in settlements in Oregon.

Captain Grant at once began to tell them the terrors of the mountain journey and the impossibility of hauling their wagons further. Then he showed them, to prove it, a corral full of fine wagons, with agricultural tools, and thousands of things greatly needed in Oregon, that immigrants had been forced to leave when they took to their pack-saddles. The men were ready, as had been others before, to give up and sacrifice the comforts of their families and rob themselves at the command of the oily advocate.

But here comes Whitman. Johnny Grant knows he now has his master. Dr. Whitman says: "Men, I have guided you thus far in safety. Believe nothing you hear about not being able to get your wagons through; every one of you stick to your wagons and your goods. They will be invaluable to you when you reach the end of your journey. I took a wagon through to Oregon six years ago." (Again we see the historic wagon.) The men believed him. They refused to obey Captain Grant's touching appeal and almost a command to leave their wagons behind. Never did an order, than the one Whitman made, add more to the comfort and actual value of a band of travelers.

One of a former company tells of a packing experience, after submitting to Captain Grant's orders. He says: "There were lively times around old Fort Hall when the patient old oxen and mules were taken from the wagons to be left behind and the loads of bedding, pots and pans were tied on to their backs. They were unused to such methods. There would first be a shying, then a fright and a stampede, and bellowing oxen and braying mules and the air would be full of flying kettles and camp fixtures, while women and children crying and the men swearing, made up a picture to live in the memory."

No one better than Whitman knew the toil and danger attending the last six hundred miles of the journey to Oregon. Col. George B. Curry, in an address before the Pioneer Society of Oregon in 1887, gives a graphic sketch, wonderfully realistic, of the immigrant train in 1853. He says: "From the South Pass the nature of our journeying changed, and assumed the character of a retreat, a disastrous, ruinous retreat. Oxen and horses began to perish in large numbers; often falling dead in their yokes in the road. The heat-dried wagon, striking on the rocks or banks would fall to pieces. As the beasts of burden grew weaker, and the wagon more rickety, teams began to be doubled and wagons abandoned. The approaching storms of autumn, which, on the high mountains at the last end of our journey, meant impassable snow, admitted of no delay. Whatever of strength remained of the jaded cattle must be forced out. Every thing of weight not absolutely necessary must be abandoned.

"There was no time to pause and recruit the hungry stock, nor dare we allow them much freedom to hunt the withered herbage, for a marauding enemy hung upon the rear, hovering on either flank, and skulked in ambuscade in the front, the horizon was a panorama of mountains, the grandest and most desolate on the continent. The road was strewn with dead cattle, abandoned wagons, discarded cooking utensils, ox-yokes, harness, chairs, mess chests, log chains, books, heirlooms, and family keepsakes. The inexorable surroundings of the struggling mass permitted no hesitation or sentiment.

"The failing strength of the team was a demand that must be complied with. Clothing not absolutely required at present was left on the bare rocks of the rugged canyons. Wagons were coupled shorter that a few extra pounds might be saved from the wagon beds. One set of wheels was left and a cart constructed. Men, women and children walked beside the enfeebled teams, ready to give an assisting push up a steep pitch.

"The fierce summer's heat beat upon this slow west rolling column. The herbage was dry and crisp, the rivulets had become but lines in the burning sand; the sun glared from a sky of brass; the stony mountain sides glared with the garnered heat of a cloudless Summer. The dusky brambles of the scraggy sage brush seemed to catch the fiery rays of heat and shiver them into choking dust, that rose like a tormenting plague and hung like a demon of destruction over the panting oxen and thirsty people.

"Thus day after day, for weeks and months, the slow but urgent retreat continued, each day demanding fresh sacrifices. An ox or a horse would fall, brave men would lift the useless yoke from his limp and lifeless neck in silence. If there was another to take his place he was brought from the loose band, yoked up and the journey resumed. When the stock of oxen became exhausted, cows were brought under the yoke, other wagons left, and the lessening store once more inspected; if possible, another pound would be dispensed with.

"Deeper and deeper into the flinty mountains the forlorn mass drives its weary way. Each morning the weakened team has to commence a struggle with yet greater difficulties. It is plain the journey will not be completed within the anticipated time, and the dread of hunger joins the ranks of the tormentors. The stench of carrion fills the air in many places; a watering place is reached to find the putrid carcass of a dead animal in the spring. The Indians hover in the rear, impatiently waiting for the train to move on that the abandoned trinkets may be gathered up. Whether these are gathering strength for a general attack we cannot tell. There is but one thing to do—press on. The retreat cannot hasten into rout, for the distance to safety is too great. Slower and slower is daily progress.

"I do not pretend to be versed in all the horrors that have made men groan on earth, but I have followed the "Flight of Tartar Tribes," under the focal light of DeQuincy's genius, the retreat of the ten thousand under Xenophon, but as far as I am able to judge, in heroism, endurance, patience, and suffering, the annual retreat of immigrants from the Black Hills to the Dalles surpasses either. The theater of their sufferings and success, for scenic grandeur, has no superior.

REV. H. H. SPALDING.

"The patient endurance of these men and women for sublime pathos may challenge the world. Men were impoverished and women reduced to beggary and absolute want, and no weakling's murmur of complaint escaped

91

their lips. It is true, when women saw their patient oxen or faithful horses fall by the roadside and die, they wept piteously, and men stood in all the 'silent manliness of grief' in the camp of their desolation, for the immigrants were men and women with hearts to feel and tears to flow."

This, it will be observed, was a train upon the road ten years later than Dr. Whitman's memorable journey. He was a wise guide, and his train met with fewer disasters. The Hon. S. A. Clarke in his address tells how Whitman moved his train across Snake River.

He says: "When the immigrants reached the Snake, Dr. Whitman proceeded to fasten wagons together in one long string, the strongest in the lead. As soon as the teams were in position, Dr. Whitman tied a rope around his waist and starting his horse into the current swam over. He called to others to follow him, and when they had force enough to pull at the rope the lead team was started in and all were drawn over in safety. As soon as the leading teams were able to get foothold on the bottom all was safe; as they, aided by the strong arms of the men pulling at the rope, pulled the weaker ones along."

The Snake River at the ford is divided into three rivers by islands, the last stream on the Oregon side is a deep and rapid current, and fully half a mile wide. To get so many wagons, pulled by jaded teams, and all the thousand men, women and children, and the loose stock across in safety showed wise generalship.

We here copy "A Day with the Cow Column in 1843," by the Hon Jesse Applegate, a late honored citizen of Oregon, who was one of Dr Whitman's company in 1843. It is a clear, graphic description of a sample day's journey on the famous trip, and was an address published in the transactions of the Pioneer Oregon Association in 1876.

The migration of a large body of men, women and children across the Continent to Oregon was, in the year 1843, strictly an experiment, not only in respect to the numbers, but to the outfit of the migrating party.

Before that date two or three missionaries had performed the journey on horseback, driving a few cows with them. Three or four wagons drawn by oxen had reached Fort Hall on Snake River, but it was the honest opinion of most of those who had traveled the route down Snake River that no large number of cattle could be subsisted on its scanty pasturage, or wagons taken over a route so rugged and mountainous.

The emigrants were also assured that the Sioux would be much opposed to the passage of so large a body through their country, and would probably resist it on account of the emigrants destroying and frightening away the buffaloes, which were then diminishing in numbers. The migrating body numbered over one thousand souls, with about one hundred and twenty wagons, drawn by ox teams, averaging about six yokes to the team, and several thousand loose horses and cattle.

The emigrants first organized and attempted to travel in one body, but it was soon found that no progress could be made with a body so cumbrous, and as yet, so averse to all discipline. And at the crossing of the "Big Blue," it divided into two columns, which traveled in supporting distance of each other as far as Independence Rock, on the Sweetwater.

From this point, all danger from Indians being over, the emigrants separated into small parties better suited to the narrow mountain paths and small pastures in their front.

Before the division on the Blue River there was some just cause for discontent in respect to loose cattle. Some of the emigrants had only their teams, while others had large herds in addition, which must share the pastures and be driven by the whole body.

This discontent had its effect in the division on the Blue, those not encumbered with or having but few loose cattle attached themselves to the light column, those having more than four or five cows had of necessity to join the heavy or cow column. Hence, the cow column, being much larger than the other and encumbered with its large herds, had to use greater exertion and observe a more rigid discipline to keep pace with the more agile consort.

It is with the cow or more clumsy column that I propose to journey with the reader for a single day.

It is four o'clock a. m., the sentinels on duty have discharged their rifles, the signal that the hours of sleep are over; and every wagon or tent is pouring forth its night tenants, and slow kindling smokes begin to rise and float away on the morning air. Sixty men start from the corral, spreading as they make through the vast herd of cattle and horses that form a semi-circle around the encampment, the most distant, perhaps, two miles away.

The herders pass to the extreme verge and carefully examine for trails beyond, to see that none of the animals have been stolen or strayed during the night. This morning no trails lead beyond the outside animals in sight, and by five o'clock the herders begin to contract the great moving circle, and the well-trained animals move slowly toward camp, clipping here and there a thistle or tempting bunch of grass on the way.

In about an hour 5,000 animals are close up to the encampment, and the teamsters are busy selecting their teams, and driving them inside the "corral" to be yoked. The corral is a circle one hundred yards deep, formed with wagons connected strongly with each other, the wagon in the rear being connected with the wagon in front by its tongue and ox chains. It is a strong barrier that the most vicious ox cannot break, and in case of an attack by the Sioux, would be no contemptible entrenchment.

From six to seven o'clock is a busy time; breakfast to be eaten, the tents struck, the wagons loaded, and the teams yoked and brought up in readiness to be attached to their respective wagons. All know, when at seven o'clock the signal to march sounds, that those not ready to take their proper places in the line of march must fall into the dusty rear for the day.

94

There are sixty wagons. They have been divided into sixteen divisions, or platoons of four wagons each, and each platoon is entitled to lead in its turn. The leading platoon of to-day will be the rear one to-morrow, and will bring up the rear, unless some teamster, through indolence or negligence, has lost his place in the line, and is condemned to that uncomfortable post. It is within ten minutes of seven; the corral, but now a strong barricade, is everywhere broken, the teams being attached to the wagons. The women and children have taken their places in them. The pilot (a borderer who has passed his life on the verge of civilization, and has been chosen to the post of leader from his knowledge of the savage and his experience in travel through roadless wastes) stands ready, in the midst of his pioneers and aides, to mount and lead the way.

Ten or fifteen young men, not to lead to-day, form another cluster. They are ready to start on a buffalo hunt, are well mounted and well armed, as they need to be, for the unfriendly Sioux have driven the buffalo out of the Platte, and the hunters must ride fifteen or twenty miles to reach them. The cow-drivers are hastening, as they get ready, to the rear of their charge, to collect and prepare them for the day's march.

It is on the stroke of seven; the rushing to and fro, the cracking of whips, the loud command to oxen, and what seemed to be the inextricable confusion of the last ten minutes has ceased. Fortunately, every one has been found, and every teamster is at his post. The clear notes of a trumpet sound in the front; the pilot and his guards mount their horses; the leading division of wagons move out of the encampment and take up the line of march; the rest fall into their places with the precision of clock-work, until the post, so lately full of life, sinks back into that solitude that seems to reign over the broad plain and rushing river, as the caravan draws its lazy length toward the distant El Dorado.

It is with the hunters we will briskly canter toward the bold but smooth and grassy bluffs that bound the broad valley, for we are not yet in sight of the grander, but less beautiful, scenery (of the Chimney Rock, Court House, and other bluffs so nearly resembling giant castles and palaces) made by the passage of the Platte through the Highlands near Laramie. We have been traveling briskly for more than an hour. We have reached the top of the bluff, and now have turned to view the wonderful panorama spread before us.

To those who have not been on the Platte, my powers of description are wholly inadequate to convey an idea of the vast extent and grandeur of the picture, and the rare beauty and distinctness of its detail. No haze or fog obscures objects in the pure and transparent atmosphere of this lofty region. To those accustomed to only the murky air of the sea-board, no correct judgment of distance can be formed by sight, and objects which they think they can reach in a two hours' walk, may be a day's travel away; and though the evening air is a better conductor of sound, on the high plain during the day the report of the loudest rifle sounds little louder than the bursting of a cap; and while the report can be heard but a few hundred yards, the smoke of the discharge may be seen for miles.

So extended is the view from the bluff on which the hunters stand, that the broad river, glowing under the morning sun like a sheet of silver, and the broader emerald valley that borders it, stretch away in the distance until they narrow at almost two points in the horizon, and when first seen, the vast pile of the Wind River mountains, though hundreds of miles away, looks clear and distinct as a white cottage on the plain.

We are full six miles away from the line of march; though everything is dwarfed by distance, it is seen distinctly. The caravan has been about two hours in motion, and is now extended as widely as a prudent regard for safety will permit. First, near the bank of the shining river, is a company of horsemen; they seem to have found an obstruction, for the main body has halted, while three or four ride rapidly along the bank of a creek or slough. They are hunting a favorable crossing for the wagons; while we look they have succeeded; it has apparently required no work to make it possible, while all but one of the party have passed on, and he has raised a flag, no doubt a signal to the wagons to steer their course to where he stands.

96

The leading teamster sees him, though he is yet two miles off, and steers his course directly towards him, all the wagons following in his track. They (the wagons) form a line three-quarters of a mile in length; some of the teamsters ride upon the front of their wagons, some march beside their teams; scattered along the line companies of women and children are taking exercise on foot; they gather bouquets of rare and beautiful flowers that line the way; near them stalks a stately greyhound or an Irish wolf dog, apparently proud of keeping watch and ward over his master's wife and children.

Next comes a band of horses; two or three men or boys follow them, the docile and sagacious animals scarcely needing this attention, for they have learned to follow in the rear of the wagons, and know that at noon they will be allowed to graze and rest. Their knowledge of time seems as accurate as of the place they are to occupy in the line, and even a full-blown thistle will scarce tempt them to straggle or halt until the dinner hour is arrived.

Not so with the large herd of horned beasts that bring up the rear; lazy, selfish and unsocial, it has been a task to get them in motion, the strong always ready to domineer over the weak, halt in the front and forbid the weaker to pass them. They seem to move only in fear of the driver's whip; though in the morning full to repletion, they have not been driven an hour, before their hunger and thirst seem to indicate a fast of days' duration. Through all the day long their greed is never sated nor their thirst quenched, nor is there a moment of relaxation of the tedious and vexatious labors of their drivers, although to all others the march furnishes some reason of relaxation or enjoyment. For the cow-drivers, there is none.

But from the standpoint of the hunters the vexations are not apparent; the crack of whip and loud objurgations are lost in the distance. Nothing of the moving panorama, smooth and orderly as it appears, has more attraction for the eye than that vast square column in which all colors are mingled, moving here slowly and there briskly as impelled by horsemen riding furiously in front and rear.

But the picture, in its grandeur, its wonderful mingling of colors and

97

distinctness of detail, is forgotten in contemplation of the singular people who give it life and animation. No other race of men, with the means at their command, would undertake so great a journey; none save these could successfully perform it, with no previous preparation, relying only on the fertility of their invention to devise the means to overcome each danger and difficulty as it arose.

They have undertaken to perform with slow-moving oxen, a journey of two thousand miles. The way lies over trackless wastes, wide and deep rivers, rugged and lofty mountains, and it is beset with hostile savages. Yet whether it were a deep river with no tree upon its banks, a rugged defile where even a loose horse could not pass, a hill too steep for him to climb, or a threatened attack of an enemy, they are always found ready and equal to the occasion, and always conquerors. May we not call them men of destiny? They are people changed in no essential particulars from their ancestors, who have followed closely on the footsteps of the receding savage, from the Atlantic sea-board to the great valley of the Mississippi.

But while we have been gazing at the picture in the valley, the hunters have been examining the high plain in the other direction. Some dark moving objects have been discovered in the distance, and all are closely watching them to discover what they are, for in the atmosphere of the plains a flock of crows marching miles away, or a band of buffaloes or Indians at ten times the distance look alike, and many ludicrous mistakes occur. But these are buffaloes, for two have struck their heads together, and are alternately pushing each other back. The hunters mount and away in pursuit, and I, a poor cow-driver, must hurry back to my daily toil, and take a scolding from my fellow-herders for so long playing truant.

The pilot, by measuring the ground and timing the speed of the wagons and the walk of his horses, has determined the rate of each, so as to enable him to select the nooning place, as nearly as the requisite grass and water can be had at the end of five hours' travel of the wagons. To-day, the ground being favorable, little time has been lost in preparing the road, so that he and his pioneers are at the nooning place an hour in advance of the

98

wagons, which time is spent in preparing convenient watering places for the animals, and digging little wells near the bank of the Platte.

As the teams are not unyoked, but simply turned loose from their wagons, a corral is not formed at noon, but the wagons are drawn up in columns, four abreast, the leading wagon of each platoon on the left—the platoons being formed with that view. This brings friends together at noon as well as at night.

To-day, an extra session of the Council is being held, to settle a dispute that does not admit of delay, between a proprietor and a young man who has undertaken to do a man's service on the journey for bed and board. Many such engagements exist, and much interest is taken in the manner this high court, from which there is no appeal, will define the rights of each party in such engagements.

The Council was a high court in a most exalted sense. It was a Senate, composed of the ablest and most respected fathers of the emigration. It exercised both legislative and judicial powers, and its laws and decisions proved it equal and worthy the high trust reposed in it. Its sessions were usually held on days when the caravan was not moving. It first took the state of the little commonwealth into consideration; revised or repealed rules defective or obsolete, and enacted such others as the exigencies seemed to require. The common weal being cared for, it next resolved itself into a court to hear and settle private disputes and grievances.

The offender and the aggrieved appeared before it; witnesses were examined and the parties were heard by themselves and sometimes by counsel. The judges thus being made fully acquainted with the case, and being in no way influenced or cramped by technicalities, decided all cases according to their merits. There was but little use for lawyers before this court, for no plea was entertained which was calculated to hinder or defeat the ends of justice.

Many of these Judges have since won honors in higher spheres. They have aided to establish on the broad basis of right and universal liberty two of the pillars of our Great Republic in the Occident. Some of the young men who appeared before them as advocates have themselves sat upon the highest judicial tribunal, commanded armies, been Governors of States, and taken high positions in the Senate of the Nation.

It is now one o'clock; the bugle has sounded, and the caravan has resumed its westward journey. It is in the same order, but the evening is far less animated than the morning march; a drowsiness has fallen apparently on man and beast; teamsters drop asleep on their perches and even when walking by their teams, and the words of command are now addressed to the slowly-creeping oxen in the softened tenor of a woman or the piping treble of children, while the snores of teamsters make a droning accompaniment.

But a little incident breaks the monotony of the march. An emigrant's wife, whose state of health has caused Dr. Whitman to travel near the wagon for the day, is now taken with violent illness. The Doctor has had the wagon driven out of the line, a tent pitched and a fire kindled. Many conjectures are hazarded in regard to this mysterious proceeding, and as to why this lone wagon is to be left behind.

And we, too, must leave it, hasten to the front and note the proceedings, for the sun is now getting low in the west, and at length the painstaking pilot is standing ready to conduct the train in the circle which he had previously measured and marked out, which is to form the invariable fortification for the night.

The leading wagons follow him so nearly round the circle, that but a wagon length separates them. Each wagon follows in its track, the rear closing on the front until its tongue and ox-chains will perfectly reach from one to the other, and so accurate the measurement and perfect the practice, that the hindmost wagon of the train always precisely closes the gateway. As each wagon is brought into position, it is dropped from its team (the teams being inside the circle), the team unyoked, and the yokes and chains are used to connect the wagon strongly with that in its front.

100

Within ten minutes from the time the leading wagon halted the barricade is formed, the teams unyoked and driven out to pasture. Every one is busy preparing fires of buffalo chips to cook the evening meal, pitching tents and otherwise preparing for the night.

There are anxious watchers for the absent wagon, for there are many matrons who may be afflicted like its inmate before the journey is over, and they fear the strange and startling practice of this Oregon doctor will be dangerous. But as the sun goes down, the absent wagon rolls into camp, the bright, speaking face and cheery look of the doctor, who rides in advance, declare without words that all is well, and that both mother and child are comfortable.

I would fain now and here pay a passing tribute to that noble and devoted man, Dr. Whitman. I will obtrude no other name upon the reader, nor would I his, were he of our party or even living, but his stay with us was transient, though the good he did was permanent, and he has long since died at his post.

From the time he joined us on the Platte, until he left us at Fort Hall, his great experience and indomitable energy was of priceless value to the migrating column. His constant advice, which we knew was based upon a knowledge of the road before us, was "travel, travel, travel—nothing else will take you to the end of your journey; nothing is wise that does not help you along; nothing is good for you that causes a moment's delay."

His great authority as a physician and complete success in the case above referred to, saved us many prolonged and perhaps ruinous delays from similar causes, and it is no disparagement to others to say that to no other individual are the immigrants of 1843 so much indebted for the successful conclusion of their journey, as to Dr. Marcus Whitman.

All able to bear arms in the party had been formed into three companies, and each of these into four watches; every third night it is the

101

duty of one of these companies to keep watch and ward over the camp, and it is so arranged that each watch takes its turn of guard duty through the different watches of the night. Those forming the first watch to-night, will be second on duty, then third and fourth, which brings them all through the watches of the night. They begin at eight o'clock p. m. and end at four o'clock a. m.

REV. CUSHING EELLS, D.D.
Founder of Whitman College.

It is not yet eight o'clock when the first watch is to be set; the evening meal is just over, and the corral now free from the intrusion of horses or cattle, groups of children are scattered over it. The larger are taking a game of romps; "the wee, toddling things" are being taught that great achievement which distinguishes men from the lower animals. Before a tent near the river, a violin makes lively music and some youths and maidens have improvised a dance upon the green; in another quarter a flute gives its mellow and melancholy notes to the still night air, which, as they float away over the quiet river, seem a lament for the past rather than for a hope of the future.

It has been a prosperous day; more than twenty miles have been accomplished of the great journey. The encampment is a good one; one of the causes that threatened much future delay has just been removed by the skill and energy of "that good angel" of the emigrants, Dr. Whitman, and it has lifted a load from the hearts of the elders. Many of these are assembled around the good doctor at the tent of the pilot (which is his home for the time being), and are giving grave attention to his wise and energetic counsel. The care-worn pilot sits aloof quietly smoking his pipe, for he knows the grave Doctor is "strength in his hands."

But time passes, the watch is set for the night, the council of good men has been broken up and each has returned to his own quarters. The flute has whispered its last lament to the deepening night. The violin is silent and the dancers have dispersed. Enamored youths have whispered a tender "good night" in the ear of blushing maidens, or stolen a kiss from the lips of some future bride; for Cupid, here as elsewhere, has been busy bringing together congenial hearts, and among these simple people, he alone is consulted in forming the marriage tie. Even the Doctor and the pilot have finished their confidential interview and have separated for the night. All is hushed and repose from the fatigues of the day, save the vigilant guard, and the wakeful leader who still has cares upon his mind that forbid sleep.

He hears the ten o'clock relief taking post, and the "all well" report of the returned guard; the night deepens, yet he seeks not the needed repose. At length a sentinel hurries to him with the welcome report that a party is approaching, as yet too far away for its character to be determined, and he instantly hurries out in the direction seen.

This he does both from inclination and duty, for, in times past, the camp has been unnecessarily alarmed by timid or inexperienced sentinels, causing much confusion and fright amongst women and children, and it had been made a rule that all extraordinary incidents of the night should be reported directly to the pilot, who alone had authority to call out the military strength of the column, or so much of it as was, in his judgment, necessary to prevent a stampede or repel an enemy.

To-night he is at no loss to determine that the approaching party are our missing hunters, and that they have met with success, and he only waits until, by some further signal, he can know that no ill has happened to them. This is not long wanting; he does not even wait their arrival, but the last care of the day being removed and the last duties performed, he, too, seeks the rest that will enable him to go through the same routine to-morrow. But here I leave him, for my task is also done, and, unlike his, it is to be repeated no more.

After passing through such trials and dangers, nothing could have been more cheering to these tired immigrants than the band of Cayuse and Nez Perces Indians, with pack mules loaded with supplies, meeting the Doctor upon the mountains with a glad welcome. From them he learned that in his absence his mill had been burned, but the Rev. H. H. Spalding, anticipating the needs of the caravan, had furnished flour from his mill, and nothing was ever more joyously received.

Dr. Whitman also received letters urging him to hurry on to his mission. He selected one of his most trusty Cayuse Indian guides, Istikus, and placed the company under his lead. He was no longer a necessity for it

104

comfort and safety. The most notable event in pioneer history is reaching its culmination. That long train of canvas-covered wagons moving across the plains, those two hundred campfires at night, with shouts and laughter and singing of children, were all new and strange to these solitudes. As simple facts in history, to an American they are profoundly interesting, but to the thoughtful student who views results, they assume proportions whose grandeur is not easily over-estimated.

But the little band has come safely across the Rockies; has forded and swam many intervening rivers; the dreary plains, with saleratus dust and buffalo gnats, had been left behind, and here they stand upon a slope of the farthest western range of mountains, with the fertile foot hills and beautiful green meadows reaching as far away as the eye can see. The wagons are well bunched. For weeks they have been eager to see the land of promise. It is a goodly sight to see, as they file down the mountain side, one hundred and twenty-five wagons, one thousand head of loose stock, cattle, horses and sheep, and about one thousand men, women and children, and Oregon is saved to the Union.

Who did it?

We leave every thoughtful, honest reader to answer the query.

CHAPTER VIII.

A BACKWARD LOOK AT RESULTS.

The reader of history is often moved to admiration at the dash and courage of some bold hero, even when he has failed in the work he set out to accomplish. The genius to invent, with the courage to prosecute, has often failed in reaching the hoped-for results. The pages of history of all time are burdened with the plaintive cry, "Oh, for night or Blucher." It is the timeliness of great events that marks real genius, and the largest wisdom.

Of Whitman it was a leading characteristic. He did the right thing just at the right time. His faith was equal to his courage and when his duty was made clear to his mind, there was no impediment that he would not attempt to overcome. Now we are to study the results of his heroic ride, and will see how dangerous would have been any delay.

We have noted Webster's letter to the English Minister, dated in 1840, in which he said, "The ownership of the whole country (referring to Oregon) will likely follow the greater settlement and larger amount of population," and this we may say was the common sentiment of our early statesmen, and not peculiar to Mr. Webster. But Whitman had started a new train of thought and given a new direction to the policy of the administration.

The President believed in the truthful report of the hero with his frozen limbs, who had ridden four thousand miles in midwinter without pay or hope of reward, to plead for Oregon. Immediately upon the close of the conference the record shows that Secretary Webster wrote to Minister Everett and said: "The Government of the United States has never offered any line south of forty-nine and never will, and England must not expect anything south of the forty-ninth degree."

That is a wonderful change. Upon receipt of the news that Dr. Whitman, in June, "Had started to Oregon with a great caravan numbering nearly one thousand souls," another letter was sent to the English Minister, still more pointed and impressive.

The President and his Secretary at once began to arrange terms for a treaty with England regarding the boundary line, and negotiations were speedily begun. It did not look to be a hopeful task when the Ashburton-Webster Treaty, just signed in 1842, had been a bone of contention for forty-eight years. Still more did it look discouraging from the fact that diplomats the year before had resolved to leave the Oregon boundary out of the case, as it was said, "Otherwise it would likely defeat the whole treaty."

But suddenly new blood had been injected into American veins in and about Washington. They saw a great fertile country, thirty times as large as Massachusetts, which was rightfully theirs and yet claimed by a power many thousand miles separated from it. The national blood was aroused. A great political party, not satisfied with Secretary Webster's modest "latitude of forty-nine degrees" emblazoned on its banners, "Oregon and fifty-four forty or fight."

The spirit of '76 and 1812 seemed to have suddenly been aroused throughout the Nation. People did not stop to ask, who has done it, or how it all happened; but no intelligent or thoughtful student of history can doubt how it all happened, or who was its author. It was also easy to see that it was to be no forty-eight year campaign before the question must be adjudicated.

The Hon. Elwood Evans, in a speech in 1871, well said: "The arrival of Dr. Whitman in 1843 was opportune. The President was satisfied the territory was worth preserving." He continues: "If the offer had been made in the Ashburton Treaty of the forty-ninth parallel to the Columbia River and thence down the Columbia to the Pacific Ocean, it would have been accepted, but the visit of Whitman committed the President against any such settlement."

The offer was not made by English diplomats, because they intended

107

to have a much larger slice. Captain Johnny Grant and the English Hudson Bay officials made their greatest blunder in allowing Whitman to make his perilous Winter ride. They were not prepared for the sudden change in American sentiment. In any enthusiasm for our hero, we would not willingly make any exaggerated claim for his services. Prior to the arrival of Whitman, President Tyler had shown thoughtful interest in the Oregon question, and in his message in 1842 he said: "In advance of the acquirement of individual rights to those lands, sound policy dictates that every effort should be resorted to by the two Governments to settle their respective claims."

Fifteen days before the arrival of Whitman, Senator Linn, always a firm friend of Oregon, in a resolution called for information, "Why Oregon was not included in the Ashburton-Webster Treaty." This resolution passed the Senate, but was defeated in the House. Neither the President, Senators, or Congressmen had the data upon which to base clear, intelligent action, and Whitman's arrival just when Congress was closing up its business gave no opportunity for the wider discussion which would have followed then and there. It was, however, another evidence of timeliness, which we wish to keep well to the front in all of Whitman's work.

All can see how fortunate it was that the Oregon boundary question was not included in the Ashburton Treaty in 1842, and that it had waited for later adjudication. During the summer of 1843 the people of the entire country had heard of the great overland emigration to Oregon, and on the 8th day of January, 1844, Congress was notified that the Whitman immigration to Oregon was a grand success, and upon the very day of the arrival of this news, a resolution was offered in the Senate which called for the instructions to our Minister in England, and all correspondence upon the subject. But the conservative Senate was not quite ready for such a move, and the resolution was defeated by a close vote. But two days after a similar resolution was passed by the House.

Urged to do so by Whitman, the Lees, Lovejoy, Spalding, Eells and others, scores of intelligent emigrants flooded their Congressmen with letters giving glowing descriptions of the beauty of the country, the fertility of the land, and the mildness and healthfulness of the climate. Even Senator Winthrop, who at one time declared that "Neither the West nor the country at large had any real interest in retaining Oregon; that we would not be straitened for elbow room in the West for a thousand years," was aroused to something of enthusiasm, and said in his place in the Senate: "For myself, certainly, I believe that we have a good title to the whole twelve degrees of latitude up to fifty-four, forty."

Senator Benton had long since materially changed his views from those he held when he had said that "The ridge of the Rocky Mountains may be named as the convenient, natural and everlasting boundary." Fremont, not Whitman, had converted him. Benton was aggressive and intelligent. In the discussion of 1844, he said: "Let the emigrants go on and carry their rifles. We want thirty thousand rifles in the valley of the Oregon. The war, if it come, will not be topical; it will not be confined to Oregon, but will embrace the possessions of the two powers throughout the Globe."

In the discussion, which took a wide turn, many of the eminent statesmen at that time took a part. Prominent among them was Calhoun, Linn, Benton, Choate, Berrien and Rives. Many of them tried the most persuasive words of peace, yet no one who reads the speeches and the proceedings, but will perceive the wonderful changes in public sentiment during a single year. The year 1844 ended with the struggle growing every day more intense. The English people had awakened to the fact that they had to meet the issue and there would not be any repetition of the old dallying with the Maine boundary. They sent to this country Minister Packenham as Minister Plenipotentiary to negotiate the treaty. Mr. Buchanan acted for the United States.

It was talk and counter-talk. Buchanan was one of the leading spirits in the demand for fifty-four forty, and his position was well understood both by the people of the United States and by England. President Tyler, in his final message, earnestly recommended the extension of the United States laws over the Territory of Oregon.

In this connection it will be remembered that Dr. Whitman, only a few months before the great massacre, in which he and his noble wife lost their lives, rode all the way to Oregon City to urge Judge Thornton to go to Washington and beg, on the part of the people of Oregon, for a "Provisional Government." Judge Thornton believed in Dr. Whitman's wisdom, and when the doctor declared that which seemed to be a prophecy, "Unless this is done nothing will save even my mission from murder," the Judge said, "If Governor Abernethy will furnish me a letter to the President, I will go." The Governor promptly furnished the required letter and Judge Thornton resigned his position as Supreme Judge. All know of the fatal events at the Whitman Mission in less than two months after Judge Thornton's departure.

But the boundary question lapped over into Mr. Polk's administration in 1845 with a promise of lively times. President Polk, in December, 1845 made it the leading question in his message. He covers the whole question in dispute and says: "The proposition of compromise which has been made and rejected, was by my order withdrawn, and our title to the whole of Oregon asserted, and, as it is believed, maintained by irrefragable facts and arguments." The President recommended that the joint occupation treaty of 1818-1828 be terminated by the stipulated notice, and that the civil and criminal laws of the United States be extended over the whole of Oregon and that a line of military posts be established along the route from the States to the Pacific.

If the reader will take the pains to read the paper which Dr. Whitman by request sent to the Secretary of War in 1843, republished in the appendix of this volume, he will find in it just the recommendations now two years later made by the President. The great misfortune was that it was not complied with promptly. War upon a grand scale seemed imminent. A leading Senator announced that "War may now be looked for almost inevitably."

The whole tone of public sentiment, in Congress and out, was that the United States owned Oregon, not only up to forty-nine degrees, but up to 54 degrees, 40 minutes. It was thought that the resolution of notice for the termination of the treaty would cause a declaration of war. For forty days the question was pending before the House and finally passed by the strong vote of 163 for to 54 against. In the Senate the resolution covered a still wider range and a longer time. But little else was thought or talked about. Business throughout the land was at a standstill in the suspense, or was hurrying to prepare for a great emergency. The wisest, coolest-headed Senators still regarded the question at issue open for peaceful settlement. They dwelt upon the horrors of a war, that would cost the Nation five hundred millions in treasure, besides the loss of life.

Webster, who had been so soundly abused for his Ashburton Treaty, had held aloof from this discussion. But there came a time when he could no longer remain silent, and he put himself on the record in a single sentence: "It is my opinion that it is not the judgment of this country, or that of the Senate, that the Government of the United States should run the hazard of a war for Oregon, by renouncing as no longer fit for consideration, the proposition of adjustment made by the Government thirty years ago, and repeated in the face of the world."

Calhoun, than whom no Senator was more influential, urged continued peaceful methods. He said: "A question of greater moment never has been presented to Congress." Others counseled a continuance of things as they were and letting immigration after the bold Whitman plan settle it.

Suffice it here to say that both Nations, after the wide discussion and threats, saw war as a costly experiment. In the last of April the terms of treaty were agreed upon, and on July 17th, 1846, both Governments had signed a treaty fixing the boundary line at forty-nine degrees.

Now here again comes in the timeliness of Whitman's memorable ride. It had taken every day of exciting contest in Congress since that event, up to April, 1846, to agree upon the boundary and for America to get her Oregon. On the 13th day of May, 1846, Congress declared war against Mexico, and California was at stake. Suppose England could have foreseen that event, would she not have declared in favor of a longer wait? Who that

111

knows England does not know that she would? With England still holding to her rights in Oregon how easy it would have been to take sides with Mexico and to have helped her hold California.

But we won not only California and New Mexico, but won riches. In the year 1848 gold was discovered in California. And now suppose England could have foreseen that, as she would have known it had she prolonged the negotiations, would she ever have signed away any possessions like that rolled in gold? When did the great and powerful Kingdom of Great Britain ever do anything of the kind?

It would not have done for Whitman to have waited for next year and warm weather as his friends demanded. "I must go," and "now," and at this day it is easy to see from the light of history how God rules in the minds and hearts of men, as he rules nations. They, as men and nations, turn aside from His commands, but a man like Marcus Whitman obeys.

Go still farther. From the time gold was discovered in California up to the outbreak of the War of the Rebellion, nine hundred millions of gold were dug from the mines of California and Oregon. Where did it go? The great bulk of it went into storehouses and manufactories and vaults of the North. The South was sparsely represented in California and Oregon in the early days. We repeat that when the war broke out, the great bulk of the yellow metal was behind the Union army. Who don't recognize that it was a great power? Even more than that, it was a controlling power. The Nation was to be tried as never before. Human slavery was the prize for which the South contended, while human freedom soon asserted itself, despite all opposition, as a contending force in the North. But the wisest were in doubt as to results. They could not see how it was possible that "the sum of all villainies" could be obliterated. In the East and the North and the West, the boys in blue flocked to the standard, and bayonets gleamed everywhere. The plow was left in the furrow, and the hum of the machine shop was not heard. The fires in the furnaces and forges went out, and multitudes were in despair over the mighty struggle at hand. The Union might have been saved without the wealth of gold of California and Oregon; it might have proved victorious, even if the two great loyal States of the Pacific had been in the hands of strangers or enemies, but they were behind the loyal Union army. And the men marched and fought and sung—

"In the beauty of the lilies, Christ was born across the sea,
With a glory in his bosom, that transfigures you and me;
As he died to make men holy, let us die to make men free,
While God is marching on,"

as they marched, leaving graves upon every mountain side and in every valley. Appomattox was reached, and lo, the chains dropped from the limbs of six million slaves, and "The flag of beauty and glory" floated from Lake to Gulf and from Ocean to Ocean, in truth as in song—

"O'er the land of the free,
And the home of the brave."

WHITMAN COLLEGE, WALLA WALLA, WASHINGTON.

Again, older readers will remember with what fear and trembling they opened their morning papers for many months, fearing to read that England had accorded "belligerent rights" to the Confederacy. They will have a vivid recollection of the eloquent orator, Henry Ward Beecher, as he plead, as no other man could, the cause of the Union in English cities. He was backed up by old John Bright, the descendants of Penn, Gurney and Wilberforce, and the old-time enemies of human slavery. But it took them all to stem the tide. At one time it even seemed that they had won over Gladstone to their interests.

While the great masses of the English people were in sympathy with the Union cause, the moneyed men and commerce sided with the Confederacy: "Cotton was King." They had been struck in a tender

113

place—their pockets and bank accounts. But suppose England had owned Oregon and its great interests, who don't see that all the danger would have been multiplied, and our interests endangered? There is in this no extravagant claim made that all this was done by Marcus Whitman. The Ruler of the Universe uses men, not a man, for its direction and government.

Going back upon the pages of history, the student sees Whittier in his study, and listens to his singing; he sees Mrs. Stowe educating with Uncle Tom in his cabin; he notes Garrison forging thunderbolts in his Liberator; he sees old Gamaliel Bailey with his National Era; he sees Sumner fall by a bludgeon in the Senate; he hears the eloquent thunderings of Hale and bluff old Ben Wade and Giddings and Julian and Chase; he sees Lovejoy fall by the hands of his assassin; he hears the guns of the old "fanatic" John Brown, as he began "marching on;" he sees a great army marshaled for the contest which led up to the election of the "Martyr President," and the crowning victories which redeemed the grandest nation upon which the sun shines from the curse of human slavery. Giving due credit to all, detracting no single honor from any one in all the distinguished galaxy of honored names, and yet the thoughtful student can reach but one conclusion, and that is, that in the timeliness of his acts, in the heroism with which they were carried out, in the unselfishness which marked every step of the way, and in the wide-reaching effects of his work, Dr. Marcus Whitman, as a man and patriot and national benefactor, was excelled by none.

Such unselfish devotion, such obedience to the call of duty, such love of "the flag that makes you free," such heroism, which never even once had an outcropping of personal benefit, will forever stand, when fully understood, as among the brightest and most inspiring pages of American history.

The young American loves to read of Paul Revere. He dwells with thrilling interest upon the ride of the boy Archie Gillespie, who saw the great dam breaking, and at the risk of his life rode down the valley of the Conemaugh to Johnstown, shouting, "Flee for your lives, the flood, the flood!" The people fled and two minutes behind the boy rolled the mighty flood of annihilation. How painter, and poet, and patriot, lingers over the ride of the gallant Sheridan "from Winchester, twenty miles away." All the honor is deserved; he saved an army and turned a defeat into victory.

But how do all these compare with the ride of Whitman? It, too, was a ride for life or death. Over snow-capped mountains, along ravines, traveled only by savage beasts and savage men. It was a plunge through icy rivers, tired, hungry, cold, and yet he rode on and on, until he stood before the President, four thousand miles away! Let us hope and believe that the time will come when Whitman, standing before President Tyler and Secretary Webster, in his buckskin breeches and a dress as we have shown, which was never woven in loom, will be the subject of some great painting. It would be grandly historical and tell a story that a patriotic people should never forget.

Alice Wellington Rollins wrote the following poem, which was published in the New York Independent, and widely copied. The Cassell Publishing Company made it one of their gems in their elegant volume, "Representative Poems of Living Poets," and kindly consent to its use in this volume:

WHITMAN'S RIDE.

Listen, my children, and you shall hear
Of a hero's ride that saved a State.
A midnight ride? Nay, child, for a year
He rode with a message that could not wait.
Eighteen hundred and forty-two;
No railroad then had gone crashing through
To the Western coast; not a telegraph wire
Had guided there the electric fire;
But a fire burned in one strong man's breast
For a beacon light. You shall hear the rest.
He said to his wife; "At the Fort to-day,
At Walla Walla, I heard them say
That a hundred British men had crossed
The mountains; and one young, ardent priest

Shouted, 'Hurrah for Oregon!
The Yankees are late by a year at least!'
They must know this at once at Washington.
Another year, and all would be lost.
Someone must ride, to give the alarm
Across the Continent; untold harm
In an hour's delay, and only I
Can make them understand how or why
The United States must keep Oregon!"
Twenty-four hours he stopped to think,
To think! Nay then, if he thought at all,
He thought as he tightened his saddle-girth.
One tried companion, who would not shrink
From the worst to come, with a mule or two
To carry arms and supplies, would do.
With a guide as far as Fort Bent. And she,
The woman of proud, heroic worth,
Who must part from him, if she wept at all,
Wept as she gathered whatever he
Might need for the outfit on his way.
Fame for the man who rode that day
Into the wilds at his Country's call;
And for her who waited for him a year
On that wild Pacific coast, a tear!
Then he said "Good-bye!" and with firm-set lips
Silently rode from his cabin door
Just as the sun rose over the tips
Of the phantom mountain that loomed before
The woman there in the cabin door,
With a dread at her heart she had not known
When she, with him, had dared to cross
The Great Divide. None better than she
Knew what the terrible ride would cost
As he rode, and she waited, each alone.
Whether all were gained or all were lost,

No message of either gain or loss
Could reach her; never a greeting stir
Her heart with sorrow or gladness; he
In another year would come back to her
If all went well; and if all went ill—
Ah, God! could even her courage still
The pain at her heart? If the blinding snow
Were his winding-sheet, she would never know;
If the Indian arrow pierced his side,
She would never know where he lay and died;
If the icy mountain torrents drowned
His cry for help, she would hear no sound!
Nay, none would hear, save God, who knew
What she had to bear, and he had to do.
The clattering hoof-beats died away
On the Walla Walla. Ah! had she known
They would echo in history still to-day
As they echoed then from her heart of stone!
He had left the valley. The mountains mock
His coming. Behind him, broad and deep,
The Columbia meets the Pacific tides;
Before him—four thousand miles before—
Four thousand miles from his cabin door,
The Potomac meets the Atlantic. On
Over the trail grown rough and steep,
Now soft on the snow, now loud on the rock,
Is heard the tramp of his steed as he rides.
The United States must keep Oregon.
It was October when he left
The Walla Walla, though little heed
Paid he to the season. Nay, indeed,
In the lonely canyons just ahead,
Little mattered it what the almanac said.
He heard the coyotes bark; but they
Are harmless creatures. No need to fear

117

A deadly rattlesnake coiled too near.
No rattlesnake ever was so bereft
Of sense as to creep out such a day
In the frost. Nay, scarce would a grizzly care
For a sniff at him. Only a man would dare
The bitter cold, in whose heart and brain
Burned the quenchless flame of a great desire;
A man with nothing himself to gain
From success, but whose heart-blood kept its fire
While with freezing face he rode on and on.
The United States must keep Oregon.
It was November when they came
To the icy stream. Would he hesitate?
Not he, the man who carried a State
At his saddle bow. They have made the leap;
Horse and rider have plunged below
The icy current that could not tame
Their proud life-current's fiercer flow.
They swim for it, reach it, clutch the shore,
Climb the river bank, cold and steep,
Mount, and ride the rest of that day,
Cased in an armor close and fine
As ever an ancient warrior wore;
Armor of ice that dared to shine
Back at a sunbeam's dazzling ray,
Fearless as plated steel of old
Before that slender lance of gold.
It is December as they ride
Slowly across the Great Divide;
The blinding storm turns day to night,
And clogs their feet; the snowflakes roll
The winding sheet about them; sight
Is darkened; faint the despairing soul.
No trail before or behind them. Spur
His horse? Nay, child, it were death to stir!

118

Motionless horse and rider stand,
Turning to stone; till one poor mule,
Pricking his ears as if to say
If they gave him rein he would find the way,
Found it and led them back, poor fool,
To last night's camp in that lonely land.
It was February when he rode
Into St. Louis. The gaping crowd
Gathered about him with questions loud
And eager. He raised one frozen hand
With a gesture of silent, proud command;
"I am here to ask, not answer! Tell
Me quick, is the Treaty signed?" "Why yes!
In August, six months ago or less!"
Six months ago! Two months before
The gay young priest at the fortress showed
The English hand! Two months before,
Four months ago at his cabin door,
He had saddled his horse! Too late then. "Well,
But Oregon? Have they signed the State
Away?" "Of course not. Nobody cares
About Oregon." He in silence bares
His head. "Thank God! I am not too late."
It was March when he rode at last
Into the streets of Washington.
The warning questions came thick and fast;
"Do you know that the British will colonize,
If you wait another year, Oregon
And the Northwest, thirty-six times the size
Of Massachusetts?" A courteous stare,
And the Government murmurs: "Ah, indeed!
Pray, why do you think that we should care?
With Indian arrows and mountain snow
Between us, we never can colonize
The wild Northwest from the East you know,

119

If you doubt it, why, we will let you read
The London Examiner; proofs enough
The Northwest is worth just a pinch of snuff."
And the Board of Missions that sent him out,
Gazed at the worn and weary man
With stern displeasure. "Pray, sir, who
Gave you orders to undertake
This journey hither, or to incur
Without due cause, such great expense
To the Board? Do you suppose we can
Overlook so grave an offense?
And the Indian converts? What about
The little flock, for whose precious sake
We sent you West? Can it be that you
Left them without a shepherd? Most
Extraordinary conduct, sir,
Thus to desert your chosen post."
Ah, well! What mattered it! He had dared
A hundred deaths, in his eager pride,
To bring to his Country at Washington
A message, for which, then, no one cared!
But Whitman could act as well as ride.
The United States must keep the Northwest.
He—whatever might say the rest—
Cared, and would colonize Oregon!
It was October, forty-two,
When the clattering hoof-beats died away
On the Walla Walla, that fateful day.
It was September, forty-three—
Little less than a year, you see—
When the woman who waited thought she heard
The clatter of foot-beats that she knew
On the Walla Walla again. "What word
From Whitman?" Whitman himself! And see!
What do her glad eyes look upon?

The first of two hundred wagons rolls
Into the valley before her. He
Who, a year ago, had left her side,
Had brought them over the Great Divide—
Men, women and children, a thousand souls—
The army to occupy Oregon.
You know the rest. In the books you have read
That the British were not a year ahead.
The United States have kept Oregon,
Because of one Marcus Whitman. He
Rode eight thousand miles, and was not too late!
In a single hand, not a Nation's fate,
Perhaps; but a gift for the Nation, she
Would hardly part with it to-day, if we
May believe what the papers say upon
This great Northwest, that was Oregon.
And Whitman? Ah! my children, he
And his wife sleep now in a martyr's grave!
Murdered! Murdered, both he and she,
By the Indian souls they went West to save!

CHAPTER IX.

THE CHANGE IN PUBLIC SENTIMENT.

The reader of history seldom sees a more notable instance of a changed public sentiment, than he can find in the authentic records dating from March, 1843, to July, 1846. If the epitome sketch made in another chapter has been studied the conditions now to be observed are phenomenal. Statesman after statesman puts himself on record. You hear no more of "No wagon road to Oregon," "That weary, desert road," those "Impassable mountains;" nor does Mr. McDuffie jump up to "Thank God for His mercy for the impassable barrier of the Rocky Mountains." No Mr. Benton arises and asks that "The statue of the fabled God Terminus should be erected or the highest peak, never to be thrown down." Nor does Mr. Jackson appear for "A compact Government."

Before the man clothed in buckskin left the National Capital, a message was on the way to our Minister to England proclaiming "The United States will consent to give nothing below the latitude of forty-nine degrees." When it was known that a great caravan of two hundred wagons and one thousand Americans had started for Oregon, a second message went to Minister Everett still more pointed and positive, "The United States will never consent that the boundary line to the Pacific Ocean shall move one foot below the latitude of forty-nine degrees." It is a historical fact that one hundred and twenty-five of the wagons went through.

The whole people began to talk, as well as to think and act. They had suddenly waked up to a great peril, and were casting about how to meet it. A political party painted upon its banners, "Oregon, fifty-four forty, or fight." Multitudes of those now living remember this great uprising of the people. How was it done? Who did it? Was it a spontaneous move without a reason. Intelligent readers can scan the facts of history and judge for themselves. But it is an historical fact there was a remarkably sudden change.

President Tyler, and his great Secretary, Webster, during the balance of his administration, used all the arts of diplomacy, and seemed to make but little progress, except a promise of a Minister Plenipotentiary to treat with the United States. At any time prior to the arrival of Marcus Whitman in Washington, or any time during the conference upon the Ashburton Treaty, had the English diplomats proposed to run the boundary line upon forty-nine degrees until it struck the Columbia River, and down that river to the ocean, there is multiplied evidence that the United States would have accepted it at once.

But England did not want a part, she wanted all. During the negotiations in 1827 as to the renewal of the Treaty of 1818, her commissioners stated the case diplomatically, thus: "Great Britain claims no exclusive sovereignty over any portion of that territory. Her present claim is not in respect to any part, but to the whole and is limited to a right of joint occupancy in common with other States, leaving the right of exclusive dominion in abeyance."

Some have urged that this was a give-away and a quit claim on the part of England, but at most, it is only the language of diplomacy, to be interpreted by the acts of the party in contest. Those who met and know the men in power in Oregon in those pioneer days, can fully attest the assertion of the Edinburgh Review in an article published in 1843, after Whitman's visit to Washington. It says: "They are chiefly Scotchmen, and a greater proportion of shrewdness, daring and commercial activity is probably not to be found in the same number of heads in the world." They made their grand mistake, however, that while being true Britons, they were Hudson Bay Company men first and foremost, and were anxious to keep out all immigration. None better knew the value of Oregon lands for the purposes of the agriculturist, than those "shrewd old Scotchmen" did.

About every trading post they had cleared farms, planted orchards and vineyards, and tested all kinds of grains. Mrs. Whitman, in her diary of September 14th, 1836, speaking of her visit to Fort Vancouver, says, "We were invited to see the farm. We rode for fifteen miles during the afternoon and visited the farms and stock, etc. They estimate their wheat crop this year at four thousand bushels, peas the same, oats and barley fifteen and seventeen hundred bushels each. The potato and turnip fields are large and fine. Their cattle are large and fine and estimated at one thousand head. They have swine in abundance, also sheep and goats, but the sheep are of an inferior quality. We also find hens, turkeys and pigeons, but no geese. Every day we have something new. The store-houses are filled from top to bottom with unbroken bales of goods, made up of every article of comfort."

She tells of "A new and improved method of raising cream" for butter-making, and "The abundant supply of the best cheese."

In another note she gives the menu for dinner. "First, we are treated to soup, which is very good, made of all kinds of vegetables, with a little rice. Tomatoes are a prominent vegetable. After soup the dishes are removed and roast duck, pork, tripe, fish, salmon or sturgeon, with other things too tedious to mention. When these are removed a rice pudding or apple pie is served with musk melons, cheese, biscuits and wine."

Shrewd Scotsmen! And yet this is the country which for years thereafter American statesmen declared "A desert waste," "Unfit for the habitation of civilized society," and from which our orators thanked Heaven they were "separated by insurmountable barriers of mountains," and "impassable deserts." We repeat, none better knew the value of Oregon soil for the purposes of agriculture, than did these princely retainers of England, and they well knew, that when agriculture and civilization gained a foothold, both they and their savage retainers would be compelled to move on. They held a bonanza of wealth in their hands, in a land of Arcadia, which they ruled to suit themselves.

It is not at all strange that they made the fight they did; they had in 1836 feared the advent of Dr. Whitman's old wagon, more than an army with banners. They had tried in every way in their power, except by absolute force, to arrest its progress. They foresaw that every turn of its wheels upon Oregon soil endangered fur. Those in command at Fort Hall and Fort Boise were warned to be more watchful. The consequence was that not another wheel was permitted to go beyond those forts, from 1836 to 1843. Dr. Edwards, however, reports that "Dr. Robert Newell brought three wagons through to Walla Walla in 1840."

But the fact remains that wagon after wagon was abandoned at those points and the things necessary for the comfort of the immigrant were sacrificed, and men, women and children were compelled to take to the pack-saddle, or journey the balance of the weary way on foot. Great stress was laid at these points of entrance, upon the dangers of the route to Oregon, and the comparative ease and comfort of the journey to California. Hundreds were thus induced to give up the journey to Oregon, in making which they would be forced to abandon their wagons and goods, and they turned their faces toward California.

General Palmer, in speaking of this, says: "While at Fort Hall in 1842, the perils of the way to Oregon were so magnified as to make us suppose the journey thither was impossible. They represented the dangers in passing over Snake River and the Columbia as very great. That but little stock had ever crossed those streams in safety. And more and worst of all, they represented that three or four tribes of Indians along the route had combined to resist all immigration." They represented that, "Famine and the snows of Winter would overtake all with destruction, before they could reach Oregon."

They did succeed in scaring this band of one hundred and thirty-seven men, women and children in 1842 into leaving all their wagons behind, but they went on to Oregon on pack-saddles.

In the meantime they ran a literary bureau for all it was worth, in the disparagement of Oregon for all purposes except those of the fur trader. The English press was mainly depended upon for this work, but the best means in reach were used that all these statements should reach the ruling powers and reading people of the United States.

The effect of this literary bureau upon American statesmen and the most intelligent class of readers prior to the Spring of 1843, is easily seen by the sentiments quoted, and by their published acts, in refusing to legislate for Oregon. Modern historians have said that, "The Hudson Bay Company and the English never at any time claimed anything south of the Columbia River." Such a statement can nowhere be proved from any official record; on the contrary, there are multiplied expressions and acts proving the opposite.

As early as the year 1828, the Hudson Bay Company saw the value of the Falls of the Willamette at Oregon City for manufacturing purposes, and took possession of the same; as Governor Simpson in command of the Company said, "To establish a British Colony of their retired servants." "Governor Simpson," says Dr. Eells in his "History of Indian Missions," "said in 1841 that the colonists in the Willamette Valley were British subjects, and that the English had no rivals on the coast but Russia, and that the United States will never possess more than a nominal jurisdiction, nor will long possess even that, on the west side of the Rocky Mountains." And he added, "Supposing the country to be divided to-morrow to the entire satisfaction of the most unscrupulous patriot in the Union, I challenge conquest to bring my prediction and its own power to the test by imposing the Atlantic tariff on the ports of the Pacific."

Such sentiments from the Governor, the man then in supreme power, who moulded and directed English sentiments, is of deep significance. A man only second in influence to Governor Simpson and even a much broader and brainier man, Dr. John McLoughlin, Factor of the Company, "said to me in 1842," says Dr. Eells, "that in fifty years the whole country will be filled with the descendants of the Hudson Bay Company." But while they believed, just as the American immigrants did, that as a result of the Treaty of 1818-28, the country would belong to the nationality settling it; yet they had so long held supreme power that they were slow to think that such power was soon to pass from them.

That the diplomacy of the home Government, the bold methods and "The shrewdness, daring and commercial activity in the heads" of the Rulers, that the Edinburgh Review pictures, were all to be thwarted and that speedily, had not entered into their calculations, and they did not awake to a sense of the real danger until those hundred and twenty-five wagons, loaded with live Americans and their household goods, rolled down the mountain sides and into the Valley of the Willamette on that memorable October day, 1843.

It was America's protest, made in an American fashion. It settled the question of American interests as far as Americans could settle it under the terms of the Treaty of 1818, as they understood it.

Under the full belief that Whitman would bring with him a large delegation, the Americans met and organized before he reached Oregon. And when the Whitman caravan arrived, they outnumbered the English and Canadian forces three to one; and the Stars and Stripes were run up, never again to be hauled down by any foreign power in all the wide domain of Oregon.

True, there was yet a battle to be fought. The interests at stake were too grand for the party who held supreme power so long to yield without a contest. But there were rugged, brave, intelligent American citizens now in Oregon, and there to stay. They had flooded home people with letters describing the salubrity of the climate and the fertility of the soil. Statesmen heard of it.

Sudden conversions sometimes make unreasonable converts. The very men who had rung the changes upon "worthless," "barren," "cut off by impassable deserts," now turned and not only claimed the legitimate territory up to forty-nine degrees, but made demands which were heard across the Atlantic. We will have "Oregon and fifty-four forty, or fight."

In a lengthy message in December, 1845, President Polk devotes nearly one-fifth of his space to the discussion of the Oregon question, and rehearses the discussion pro and con between the two governments and acknowledges, that thus far there has been absolute failure. He tells Congress that "The proposition of compromise, which was made and rejected, was, by my order, subsequently withdrawn, and our title up to 54 degrees 40 minutes

127

asserted, and, as it is believed, maintained by irrefragable facts and arguments." In that message, President Polk argued in favor of terminating the joint occupancy by giving the stipulated notice, and that the jurisdiction of the United States be extended over the entire territory, with a line of military posts along the entire frontier to the Pacific.

It all seemed warlike. The withdrawing of "the joint occupancy," many statesmen believed would precipitate a war. Senator Crittenden and others believed such to be the case. War seemed inevitable. Even Senator McDuffie, whom we have before quoted, as unwilling to "Give a pinch of snuff for all the territory beyond the Rockies," now is on record saying "Rather make that territory the grave of Americans, and color the soil with their blood, than to surrender one inch." While it was generally conceded that we would have a war, yet there were wise, cool-headed men in the Halls of National Legislation, determined to avert such disaster if possible, without sacrificing National honor.

The debate on giving legal notice to cancel the Treaty of 1818, as to joint occupancy, was the absorbing theme of Congress, and lasted for forty days before reaching a vote, and then passed by the great majority of 109.

But the Senate was more conservative, and continued the debate after the measure had passed the House by such an overwhelming majority. They saw the whole Country already in a half paralyzed condition. Its business had decreased, its capital was withdrawn from active participation in business, and its vessels stood empty at the wharves of ports of entry. Such statesmen a Crittenden and others who had not hurried to get in front of the excited people, now saw the necessity for decided action to avert war and secure peace. To brave public opinion and antagonize the Lower House of Congress required the largest courage.

Mr. Crittenden said, "I believe yet, a majority is still in favor of preserving the peace, if it can be done without dishonor. They favor the settling of the questions in dispute peaceably and honorably, to compromise by negotiations and arbitration, or some other mode known and recognized

128

among nations as suitable and proper and honorable."

Mr. Webster had been too severely chastised by both friends and enemies for his part in the Ashburton Treaty, to make him anxious to be prominent in the discussion in the earlier weeks, but when he did speak he pointed out the very road which the Nation would travel in its way for peace, viz.: a compromise upon latitude forty-nine.

Webster said, "In my opinion it is not the judgment of this country, nor the judgment of the Senate, that the Government of the United States should run the hazard of a war for Oregon by renouncing, as no longer fit for consideration, the proposition of adjustment made by this Government thirty years ago and repeated in the face of the world." His great speech, which extended through the sessions of two days, was a masterly defense and explanation of the Ashburton-Webster Treaty, which was signed three years before.

No American statesman of the time had so full and complete a knowledge of the questions at issue as had Webster. He had canvassed every one of them in all their bearings with the shrewdest English diplomats and had nothing to learn. His great speech can be marked as the turning point in the discussion, and the friends of peace took fresh courage.

The first and ablest aid Mr. Webster received was from Calhoun, then second to none in his influence. In his speech he said, "What has transpired here and in England within the last three months must, I think, show that the public opinion in both countries is coming to a conclusion that this controversy ought to be settled, and is not very diverse in the one country or the other, as to the general basis of such settlement. That basis is the offer made by the United States to England in 1826."

It may here be observed that President Monroe offered to compromise on forty-nine degrees. President Adams did the same in 1826, while President Tyler, in the year of Whitman's visit (1843), again offered the same compromise, and England had rejected each and all. She expected a much larger slice.

Gen. Cass followed Calhoun in a fiery war speech, which called out the applause of the multitude, in which he claimed that the United States owned the territory up to the Russian line of 54 degrees 40 minutes and he "Would press the claim at the peril of war."

Dayton and other Senators asked that present conditions be maintained, and that "The people of the United States meet Great Britain by a practical adoption of her own doctrine, that the title of the country should pass to those who occupied it."

This latter view was the pioneer view of the situation, and which was so fully believed as to cause the memorable ride of Whitman in mid-winter from Oregon to Washington. The resolution of notice to the English Government, as we have seen, passed the House Feb. 9, 1846, and came to a vote and passed the Senate April 23d, by 42 to 10. It, however, contained two important amendments to the House resolution, both suggestive of compromise. And as the President was allowed "At his discretion to serve the notice," the act was shorn of much of its warlike meaning.

When it is remembered that the President's message and recommendations were made on the 2d of December, 1845, and the question had absorbed the attention of Congress until April 23, 1846, before final action, it can be marked as one of the most memorable discussions that has ever occurred in our Halls of National Legislation.

It had now been three years since Whitman had made his protest to President Tyler and his Secretary; and while Congress had debated and the whole Nation was at a white heat of interest, the old pioneers had gone on settling the question in their own way by taking possession of the land, building themselves homes, erecting a State House, and, although four thousand miles distant from the National Capital, enacting laws, in keeping with American teachings, and demeaning themselves as became good citizens. Love of country, with sacrifices made to do honor to the flag, has seldom had a more beautiful and impressive illustration than that given by the old pioneers of Oregon during the years of their neglect by the home Government, which even seemed so far distant that it had lost all interest in their welfare.

CHAPTER X.

THE FAILURE OF MODERN HISTORY TO DO JUSTICE TO DR. WHITMAN.

Says an old author: "History is a river increasing in volume with every mile of its length, and the tributaries that join it nearer and nearer the sea are taken up and swept onward by a current that grows ever mightier." Napoleon said: "History is a fable agreed upon." If Napoleon could have looked downward to the closing years of this century and seen the genius of the literary world striving to do him honor, he would perhaps have modified the sentiment.

History, at its best, is a collection of biographies of the world's great leaders, and is best studied in biography. To be of value, it must be accurate. Scarcely has any great leader escaped from the stings of history, but it is well to know and believe that time will correct the wrong. The case of Dr. Whitman is peculiar in the fact that all his contemporaries united in doing him honor, save and except one, Bishop Brouillet. The men who knew the value of his work and his eminent services, such as Gray, Reed, Simpson, Barrows, and Parkman; the correspondence of Spalding, Lovejoy, Eells, and the Lees, have made the record clear.

It has been reserved for modern historians of that class who have just discovered the "Mistakes of Moses," and that Shakespeare never wrote Shakespeare's plays, to indulge in sneers and scoffs and to falsify the record. It is not the intention to attempt to reply to all these, but we shall notice the fallacies of two or three. In a recent edition of the history of the Lewis and Clarke Expedition, published by F. P. Harper, New York, and edited by Dr. Elliott Coues, a most entertaining volume, and yet wholly misleading as to the final issue which resulted in Oregon becoming a part of the Republic, Dr. Coues in his dedication of the volume says:

"To the people of the great West: Jefferson gave you the country.

132

Lewis and Clarke showed you the way. The rest is your own course of empire. Honor the statesman who foresaw your West. Honor the brave men who first saw your West. May the memory of their glorious achievement be your precious heritage. Accept from my heart this undying record of the beginning of all your greatness.

ELLIOTT COUES."

All honor to Jefferson, the far-sighted statesman; and a like honor to the courageous explorers, Lewis and Clarke; but the writer of history should be true to facts. Lewis and Clarke were not "The first men who saw your West." They were not the discoverers of Oregon. Old Captain Gray did that a dozen years prior to the visit of Lewis and Clarke. A writer of true history should not have blinded his eyes to that fact on his dedicatory page. Captain Gray sailed into the mouth of the Columbia River on his good ship Columbia, from Boston, on May 7th, 1792. The great river was named for his vessel. This, together with the title gained by the Louisiana purchase in 1803, and the treaty with Spain and Mexico, more fully recited in another chapter, made the claim of the United States to ownership in the soil of Oregon.

The mission of Lewis and Clarke was not that of discoverers, but to spy out and report upon the value of the discovery already made. Their work required rare courage, and was accomplished with such intelligence as to make them heroes, and both were rewarded with fat offices; one as the Governor of Louisiana, and the other as General Commissioner of Indian Affairs; and both were given large land grants. We have not been able to see in any of Dr. Coues' full notes any explanation of such facts, but even if he has given such explanation, he had no right, as a truthful chronicler of history, to mislead the reader by his highly ornate dedicatory: "Jefferson gave you the country, Lewis and Clarke showed you the way."

President Jefferson was much more of a seer and statesman than were his compeers. The Louisiana purchase, to him, was much more than gaining possession of the State at the mouth of the Mississippi River, with its rich acres for the use of slave-owners of the South. In his later years he said "I looked forward with gratification to the time when the descendants of the settlers of Oregon would spread themselves through the whole length of the coast, covering it with free, independent Americans, unconnected with us but by the ties of blood and interest, and enjoying, like us, the rights of self-government."

If the old statesman could view the scene and the condition now how much grander would be the view! It would be unjust to question the interest of President Jefferson in the Northwest Territory; the great misfortune was, that the statesmen of his day were almost wholly oblivious to his appeals. The report made by the Lewis and Clarke expedition was stuffed into a pigeon hole, and was not even published until eight years after the exploration, and after one of the explorers was dead. It was not received with a single ripple of enthusiasm by Congress or the people of the Nation. The Government, on the contrary, fourteen years after the advent of Lewis and Clarke in Oregon, entered into a treaty with England, which virtually gave the English people the control of the entire country for more than the first third of the century. The most that can be said of Lewis and Clarke is that they were faithful explorers, who blazed the way which Americans failed to travel until, in the fullness of time, a man appeared who led the way and millions followed.

Among the most pointed defamers of Dr. Whitman is Mrs. Frances F. Victor, of Oregon, author of "The River of the West," who seldom loses an opportunity to attempt to belittle the man and his work. In a communication to the Chicago Inter Ocean, she openly charges that his journey to Washington in the winter of 1842 and '43 was wholly for selfish interests. She charges that he was about to be removed from his Mission and wanted to present his case before the American Board. That he wanted his Mission as "A stopping place for immigrants." In other words, it was for personal and pecuniary gain that he made the perilous ride. We quote her exact language:

134

"That there was considerable practical self-interest in his desire to be left to manage the Mission as he thought best, there can be no question. It was not for the Indians, altogether, he wished to remain. He foresaw the wealth and importance of the country and that his place must become a supply station to the annual emigrations. Instead of making high-comedy speeches to the President and Secretary of State, he talked with them about the Indians, and what would, in his opinion, be the best thing to be done for them and for the white settlers. His visit was owing to the necessity that existed of explaining to the Board better than he could by letter, and more quickly, his reasons for wishing to remain at his station, and to convince them it was for the best." Says Mrs. Victor: "The Missionaries all believed that the United States would finally secure a title to at least that portion of Oregon south of the Columbia River, out of whose rich lands they would be given large tracts by the Government, and that was reason enough for the loyalty exhibited."

She openly charges that "Dr. Whitman acted deceitfully toward all the other members of the Mission." If such were true, is it not strange that in all the years that followed every man and woman among them were his staunchest and truest friends and most valiant defenders? She proceeds to call Whitman "Ignorant and conceited to believe that he influenced Secretary Webster." That the story of his suffering, frost-bitten condition was false. "He was not frost-bitten, or he would have been incapacitated to travel," etc. Mrs. Victor makes a grave charge against Whitman. She says: "He got well-to-do by selling flour and grain and vegetables to immigrants at high prices." Now, let us allow Dr. Spalding to answer this calumny. He knew Whitman and his work as well, or better than any other man. Dr. Spalding says:

"Immigrants, by hundreds and thousands, reached the Mission, way-worn, hungry, sick, and destitute, but he cared for all. Seven children of one family were left upon the hands of Dr. and Mrs. Whitman—one a babe four months old—and they cared for them all, giving food, clothing, and medicine without pay. Frequently, the Doctor would give away his entire food supply, and have to send to me for grain to get through the Winter."

135

She pointedly denies that Dr. Whitman went to Washington or the States with the expectation of bringing out settlers to Oregon.

The letters recently published by the State Historical Society of Oregon, quoted in another chapter, were written by Dr. Whitman the year following his famous journey. In them he clearly reveals the reasons for the ride to Washington. The reader can believe Dr. Whitman or believe Mrs. Victor, but both cannot be believed.

In addition to these letters, we have the clear testimony of General Lovejoy, who went with him; of Rev. Mr. Spalding, of Elkanah Walker, Dr. Gray, Rev. Cushing Eells, P. B. Whitman, who accompanied him on his return trip; Mr. Hinman, Dr. S. J. Parker, of Ithaca, N. Y., and the Rev. William Barrows, who had frequent conversations with him in St. Louis. In an interview with Dr. William Geiger, published in the New York Sun, January 17th, 1885, he says: "I was at Fort Walla Walla, and associated directly with Dr. Whitman when he started East to save Oregon. I was there when he returned, and I am, perhaps, the only living person who distinctly recollects all the facts. He left, not to go to St. Louis or to Boston, but for the distinct purpose of going to Washington to save Oregon; and yet he had to be very discreet about it."

Will the honest reader of history reject such testimony as worthless, and mark that of these modern skeptics valuable?

Mrs. Victor's charges, that selfishness and personal aggrandizement accounted for all the sacrifices made by Whitman, are preposterous in the light of testimony, and made utterly untenable by the environments of the Missionary. There was no time in all the years that Dr. and Mrs. Whitman lived in Oregon that they could not have packed all their worldly goods upon the backs of two mules. The American Board made no bribe of money to the men and women they sent out to Oregon and elsewhere. If the great farm he opened at Waiilatpui, and the buildings he erected by his patient toil, had grown to be worth a million, it would not have added a single dollar to

136

Whitman's wealth. Even the physician's fees given him by grateful sufferers, under the rules of the Board, were reported and counted as a part of his meager salary.

The idea that a man should leave wife and home, and endure the perils of a mid-winter journey to the States, to persuade Congress "To buy sheep" and "make his Mission a stopping place," or the American Board to allow him to work sixteen hours a day for the Cayuse Indians, is a heavy task on credulity, and is so far-fetched as to make Whitman's maligners only ridiculous.

But it is Hubert Howe Bancroft, the author of the thirty-eight volume History of the Pacific States, who is the offender-in-chief. As a collector and historian, Bancroft necessarily required many co-workers. It was in his failure to get them into harmony and tell the straight connected truth, in which he made his stupendous blunders. Chapter is arrayed against chapter, and volume against volume. One tells history, and another denies it. In Volume I, page 379, he refers to the incident, already fully recited in another chapter, of the visit of the Flathead Indians to St. Louis, and does not once doubt its historic accuracy; but in Volume XXIII, another of his literary army works up the same historic incident, and says:

"The Presbyterians were never very expert in improvising Providences. Therefore, when Gray, the great Untruthful, and whilom Christian Mission builder, undertakes to appropriate to the Unseen Powers of his sect the sending of four native delegates to St. Louis in 1832, begging saviors for transmontain castaways, it is, as most of Gray's affairs are, a failure. The Catholics manage such things better."

On page 584, Volume I, "Chronicles of the Builders," Mr. Bancroft says: "The Missionaries and Pioneers of Oregon did much to assure the country to the United States. Had there been no movement of the kind, England would have extended her claim over the whole territory, with a fair prospect of making it her own."

In another place says Mr. Bancroft: "The Missionary, Dr. Whitman, was no ordinary man. I do not know which to admire most in him, his coolness or his courage. His nerves were of steel, his patience was excelled only by his fearlessness. In the mighty calm of his nature he was a Caesar for Christ."

In the same volume another of his literary co-workers proceeds to glorify John Jacob Astor, and to give him all the honors for saving Oregon to the Union. Mr. Bancroft says:

"The American flag was raised none too soon at Fort Astoria to secure the great Oregon country to the United States, for already the men of Montreal were hastening thither to seize the prize; but they were too late. It is safe to say that had not Mr. Astor moved in this matter as he did, had his plans been frustrated or his purposes delayed, the northern boundary of the United States might to-day be the 42d parallel of latitude. Thus we see the momentous significance of the movement."

The author proceeds to picture Astor and make him the hero in saving Oregon. In another chapter we have given the full force and effect of Mr. Astor's settlement at Astoria. A careful reading will only show the exaggerated importance of the act, when compared with other acts which the historian only passes with a sneer or in silence. John Jacob Astor was in Oregon to make money and for no other purpose.

In Volume I, page 579, "Chronicle of the Builders," Mr. Bancroft allows Mrs. Victor, his authority, to dip her pen deep in slander. He refers to both the Methodist Missions on the Willamette and the Congregational and Presbyterian Missions of the Walla Walla, and writes:

"But missionary work did not pay, however, either with the white men or the red, whereupon the apostles of this region began to attend more to their own affairs than to the saving of savage souls. They broke up their establishments in 1844, and thenceforth became a political clique, whose chief aim was to acquire other men's property."

Please note the charges. Here are Christian men and women who have for years deprived themselves of all the benefits of civilization, and endured the hardships and dangers of frontier life, professedly that they might preach the gospel to savage people, but says Mr. Bancroft:

"Missionary work did not pay." In the sense of money making, when did Missionary work ever pay? This history of the Pacific States is a history for the generations to come. It is to go into Christian homes and upon the shelves of Christian libraries. If it is true, Christianity stands disgraced and Christian Missionaries stand dishonored.

Mr. Bancroft says: "They broke up their establishments in 1844 and became a political clique, whose chief aim was to acquire other men's property." As usual, another one of the historian's valuable aides comes upon the stage in the succeeding volume, and gives a horrifying account of "The great massacre at Dr. Whitman's Mission, on Nov. 29th, 1847." He tells us "There were at the time seventy souls at the Mission" and "Fourteen persons were killed and forty-seven taken captives." Does this prove the historian's truthfulness who had before told his readers that "They broke up their establishments in 1844 and thenceforth became a political clique, whose aim was to acquire other men's property?" There is no possible excuse for the historian to allow his aides to lead him into such blunders as we have pointed out.

The real facts were in reach. Here were men and women educated, cultivated, exiles from home, engaged in the great work of civilizing and Christianizing savages, and without a fact to sustain the charge, it is openly asserted that they gave up their work and entered upon the race for political power and for wealth. Instead of the Missions of the American Board being "closed in 1844," they were at no time in a more prosperous condition; as the record of Dr. Eells, Dr. Spalding and Dr. Whitman all show.

There is not a particle of evidence that Dr. Whitman ever took any part in any political movement in Oregon; save and except as his great effort

139

to bring in settlers to secure the country to the United States may be called political. As soon as he could leave the emigrants, he hurried home to his Mission, and at once took up his heavy work which he had laid aside eleven months before. He went on building and planting, and sowing and teaching the busiest of busy men up to the very date of the massacre. In his young manhood he sacrificed ease in a civilized home, and he and his equally noble wife dedicated themselves and their lives to the Missionary service. At all times they were the same patient, quiet, uncomplaining toilers.

Why should the great historian of the Pacific States stand above their martyr graves and attempt to discredit their lives and dishonor their memories? Dr. Whitman exhibited as much patriotism and performed as grand an act of heroism as any man of this century, and yet, Mr. Bancroft devotes half a dozen volumes to "The Chronicle of the Builders," in which he presents handsome photographs and clear, well-written sketches of hundreds of men, but they are mainly millionaires and politicians. The historian seems to have had no room for a Missionary or a poor Doctor. They were only pretending "to save savage souls." And that "did not pay," and "they broke up their settlements in 1844 and thenceforth became a political clique" whose "chief aim was to acquire other men's property."

It is a slander of the basest class, not backed up by a single credible fact, wholly dishonorable to the author, and discredits his entire history. An old poet says:

"And ever the right comes uppermost,
And ever is justice done!"

The Christian and patriotic people who believe in honest dealing will, in the years to come, compel all such histories to be re-written and their malice expunged, or they will cease to find an honored place in the best libraries.

It is by such history that the modern public has been blinded, and the real heroes relegated to the rear to make room for favorites. But facts are stubborn things, "The truth is mighty and will prevail." The great public is honest and loves justice and honesty; and it will not permit such a record to stand. The awakening has already begun. The time is coming when the martyred heroes in their unhonored graves at Waiilatpui, will receive the reward due for their patriotic and heroic service.

It is also gratifying to be able to observe that this malevolence is limited to narrow bounds. It has originated and has lived only in the fertile brains of two or three boasters of historic knowledge, who have made up in noise for all lack of principle and justice. They seem to have desired to gain notoriety for themselves and imagined that the world would admire their courage. It was Mr. Bancroft's great misfortune that this little coterie in Oregon were entrusted with the task of writing the most notable history of modern times, and his great work and his honored name will have to bear the odium of it until his volumes are called in and the grievous wrong is righted. It will be done. Mr. E. C. Ross, of Prescott, says in the Oregonian in 1884:

"Time will vindicate Dr. Whitman, and when all calumnies, and their inventors, shall have been forgotten, his name, and that of his devoted, noble wife, will stand forth in history as martyrs to the cause of God and their Country."

Let the loyal, patriotic men and women of America resolve that the time to do this is now.

CHAPTER XI.

THE MASSACRE AT WAIILATPUI.

In all the years since the terrible tragedy at Waiilatpui, historians have been seeking to find the cause of that great crime.

Some have traced it to religious jealousies, but have, in a great measure, failed to back such charges with substantial facts. It seems rather to have been a combination of causes working together for a common purpose.

For nearly half a century, as we have seen in the history of Oregon, the Indians and the Hudson Bay Company had been working harmoniously together. It was a case in which civilization had accommodated itself to the desires of savage life. The Company plainly showed the Indians that they did not wish their lands, or to deprive them of their homes. It only wanted their labor, and in return it would pay the Indians in many luxuries and comforts. The Indians were averse to manual labor, and the great Company had not seen fit to encourage it. They did not desire to see them plant or sow, raise cattle, or build houses for themselves and their families. That would directly interfere with their work as fur gatherers, and break in upon the source of wealth to the Company. To keep them at the steel trap, and in the chase, was the aim of the Hudson Bay policy, and such was congenial to the Indian, and just what he desired.

The Jesuit priests who were attached to the Hudson Bay Company, seconded the interest of the Company, and attempted to teach religion to the Indian and still leave him a savage. Upon the coming of the Protestant Missionaries, the Indians welcomed them and expressed great delight at the prospect of being taught. They gave their choice locations to the Missions, and most solemn promise to co-operate in the work. But neither they nor their fathers had used the hoe or the plow, or built permanent houses in which to live. They were by nature opposed to manual labor. Squaws were made to do all the work, while Indian men hunted and did the fighting. The

143

Missionaries could see but little hope of Christianizing, unless they could induce them to adopt civilized customs.

It was right there that the breach between the Indians and the Missionaries began to widen. They were willing to accept a religion which did not interfere with savage customs, which had become a part of their lives. It was the custom of the Hudson Bay Company, by giving modest bribes, to win over any unruly chief. It was the best way to hold power; but the Missionaries held the tribes which they served up to a higher standard of morals.

The Cayuse Indians made a foray upon a weaker tribe, and levied on their stock in payment for some imaginary debt. Dr. Whitman gave the Chiefs a reprimand, and called it thieving, and demanded that they send back everything they had taken. The Indians grew very angry in being thus reminded of their sins.

We mention these little incidents as illustrations of the strained conditions which speedily made their appearance in the government of the Indians, and made it easy work for the mischief-makers and criminals, later on. It was the boast of English authors that "The English people got along with Indians much better than Americans." This seems to be true, and it comes from the fact that they did not antagonize savage customs. As long as their savage subjects filled the treasury of the Hudson Bay Company, they cared little for aught else. As a matter of policy and self defense, they treated them honestly and fairly in all business transactions. They were in full sympathy with the Indians in their demand to keep out white immigration, and keep the entire land for fur-bearing animals and savage life.

Dr. Whitman's famous ride to the States in the Winter of 1842-43, and his piloting the large immigration of American settlers in 1843, made him a marked man, both with the Indians and the Hudson Bay Company. When the Treaty was signed in 1846, and England lost Oregon, Whitman was doubtless from that hour a doomed man. Both the Hudson Bay Company and the Indians well knew who was responsible.

First, "The great white-haired Chief," Dr. McLoughlin, was sacrificed because he was a friend of Whitman and the Missionaries. There was no other reason. If Dr. McLoughlin could have been induced to treat the Protestant Missionaries as he treated the American fur traders, his English Company would have been delighted to have retained him as Chief Factor for life. But with them it was a crime to show kindness to a Protestant Missionary, and thus foster American interests. If McLoughlin had not resigned and got out of the way, he would doubtless have lost his life by the hands of an assassin.

The Treaty was signed and proclaimed August 6th, 1846, and the massacre did not occur until the 29th of November, 1847. In those days the news moved slowly and the results, and the knowledge that England and the Hudson Bay Company had lost all, did not reach the outposts along the Columbia until late in the Spring of 1847. If the English and Hudson Bay Company had nothing to do in fanning the flame of Indian anger, it was because they had changed and reformed their methods. How much or how little they worked through the cunning and duplicity of Jesuit priests has never been demonstrated. After the Revolutionary War, England never lost an opportunity to incite the Indians upon our Northern frontier to make savage assaults. Her humane statesmen denounced her work as uncivilized and unchristian.

General Washington, in a published letter to John Jay, in 1794, said: "There does not remain a doubt in the mind of any well-informed person in this country, not shut against conviction, that all the difficulties we encounter with the Indians, their hostilities, the murders of helpless women and children along our frontiers, result from the conduct of the agents of Great Britain in this country."

At no time then had the English as much reason for anger at American success and prosperity as in the case of Oregon, where a great organization, which has been for well-nigh half a century in supreme control, was now compelled to move on. To have shown no resentment would have been unlike the representatives of England in the days of Washington.

Undoubtedly the sickness of the Indians, that year, and the charge that the Americans had introduced the disease to kill the Indians off and get their land, was a powerful agent in winning over to the murderers many who were still friendly to the Missionaries. The Indians had fallen from their high mark of honesty of which Mrs. Whitman in her diary, years before, boasted and had invaded the melon patch and stolen melons, so that the Indians who ate them were temporarily made sick. With their superstitious ideas they called it "conjuring the melon," and the incident was used effectually to excite hostilities.

There is no evidence that white men directly instigated the massacre or took a part in its horrors. While there is evidence of a bitter animosity existing among the Jesuit priests toward the Protestant Missionaries, and their defense of the open charges made against them is lame; yet the historical facts are not sufficient to lay the blame upon them.

Nor is it necessary to hold the leading officials of the Hudson Bay Company responsible for the crime as co-conspirators. There are always hangers-on and irresponsible parties who stand ready to do the villain's work.

The leader of the massacre was the half-breed, Joe Lewis, whose greatest accomplishment was lying. He seems to have brought the conspiracy up to the killing point by his falsehoods. He was a half Canadian and came to Oregon in company with a band of priests, and strangely enough, dropped down upon Dr. Whitman and by him was clothed and fed for many months. The Doctor soon learned his real character and how he was trying to breed distrust among the Indians. Dr. Whitman got him the position of teamster in a wagon train for the Willamette, and expressed a hope that he was clear of him. But Joe deserted his post and returned to Waiilatpui, and as events showed, was guided by some unseen power in the carrying out of the plans of the murderers.

To believe that he conceived it, or that the incentives to the execution

146

of the diabolism rested alone with the Indians, is to tax even the credulous. They were simply the direct agents, and were, doubtless, as has been said, wrought up to the crime through superstitions in regard to Dr. Whitman's responsibility for the prevailing sickness, which had caused many deaths among the Indians. For all the years to come, the readers of history will weigh the facts for themselves, and continue to place the responsibility upon this and that cause; but, for a safe standing point, will always have to drop back upon the fact that it was the "irrepressible conflict" between civilization and savagery, between Christianity and heathenism, backed up by national antagonisms, which had many times before engendered bad spirit.

It has been the history of the first settlement of every State of the Union, more or less, from the landing upon Plymouth Rock up to the tragedy at Waiilatpui. Only it seems in the case of the massacre at the Whitman Mission, to be more coldblooded and atrocious, in the fact that those killed had spent the best years of their lives in the service of the murderers.

Those who had received the largest favors and the most kindness from the Doctor and his good wife, were active leaders in the great crime. The Rev. H. H. Spalding, in a letter to the parents of Mrs. Whitman, dated April 6, 1848, gives a clear, concise account of the great tragedy.

He says: "They were inhumanly butchered by their own, up to the last moment, beloved Indians, for whom their warm Christian hearts had prayed for eleven years, and their unwearied hands had administered to their every want in sickness and distress, and had bestowed unnumbered blessings; who claimed to be, and were considered, in a high state of civilization and Christianity. Some of them were members of our Church; others, candidates for admission; some of them adherents of the Catholic Church; all praying Indians.

"They were, doubtless, urged on to the dreadful deed by foreign influences, which we have felt coming in upon us like a devastating flood for the last three or four years; and we have begged the authors, with tears in our eyes, to desist, not so much on account of our own lives and property, but for the sake of those coming, and the safety of those already in the country. But the authors thought none would be injured but the hated Missionaries—the devoted heretics; and the work of Hell was urged on, and has ended, not only in the death of three Missionaries, the ruin of our Mission, but in a bloody war with the settlements, which may end in the massacre of every adult.

"The massacre took place on the fatal 29th of November last, commencing at half-past one. Fourteen persons were murdered first and last; nine the first day. Five men escaped from the Station, three in a most wonderful manner, one of whom was the trembling writer, with whom, I know, you will unite in praising God for delivering even one.

"The names and places of the slain are as follows: The two precious names already given—my hand refuses to write them again; Mr. Rogers, young man, teacher of our Mission School in the Winter of '46, who since then has been aiding us in our Mission work, and studying for the ministry, with a view to be ordained and join our Mission; John and Francis Sager, the two eldest of the orphan family, ages 17 and 15; Mr. Kimball, of Laporte, Indiana, killed the second day, left a widow and five children; Mr. Saunders, of Oskaloosa, Iowa, left a widow and five children; Mr. Hall, of Missouri, escaped to Fort Walla Walla, was refused protection, put over the Columbia River, killed by the Walla Wallas, left a widow and five children; Mr. Marsh, of Missouri, left a son grown and young daughter; Mr. Hoffman, of Elmira, New York; Mr. Gillan, of Oskaloosa, Iowa; Mr. Sails, of the latter place; Mr. Bewley, of Missouri. The two last were dragged from their sickbeds, eight days after the first massacre, and butchered; Mr. Young, killed the second day. The last five were unmarried men.

"Forty women and children fell captives into the hands of the murderers, among them my own beloved daughter, Eliza, ten years old. Three of the captive children soon died, left without parental care, two of them your dear Narcissa's adopted children. The young women were dragged from the house by night, and beastly treated. Three of them were forced to become wives of the murderers of their parents, who often boasted of the

148

deed, to taunt their victims."

WHITMAN'S GRAVE.

Continuing the narrative Mr. Spalding says:

"Monday morning the Doctor assisted in burying an Indian; returned to the house and was reading; several Indians, as usual, were in the house; one sat down by him to attract his attention by asking for medicine; another came behind him with a tomahawk concealed under his blanket and with two blows in the back of the head, brought him to the floor senseless, probably, but not lifeless; soon after Telaukaikt, a candidate for admission in our Church, and who was receiving unnumbered favors every day from Brother and Sister Whitman, came in and took particular pains to cut and beat his face and cut his throat; but he still lingered till near night.

"As soon as the firing commenced at the different places, Mrs. Hayes ran in and assisted Sister Whitman in taking the Doctor from the kitchen to the sitting-room and placed him upon the settee. This was before his face was cut. His dear wife bent over him and mingled her flowing tears with his precious blood. It was all she could do. They were her last tears. To whatever she said, he would reply 'no' in a whisper, probably not sensible.

"John Sager, who was sitting by the Doctor when he received the first blow, drew his pistol, but his arm was seized, the room filling with Indians, and his head was cut to pieces. He lingered till near night. Mr. Rogers, attacked at the water, escaped with a broken arm and wound in the head, and rushing into the house, shut the door. The Indians seemed to have left the house now to assist in murdering others. Mr. Kimball, with a broken arm, rushed in; both secreted themselves upstairs.

"Sister Whitman in anguish, now bending over her dying husband and now over the sick; now comforting the flying, screaming children, was passing by the window, when she received the first shot in her right breast, and fell to the floor. She immediately arose and kneeled by the settee on which lay her bleeding husband, and in humble prayer commended her soul to God, and prayed for her dear children who were about to be made a second time orphans and to fall into the hands of her direct murderers. I am certain she prayed for her murderers, too. She now went into the chamber with Mrs. Hayes, Miss Bewley, Catharine, and the sick children. They remained till near night.

"In the meantime the doors and windows were broken in and the Indians entered and commenced plundering, but they feared to go into the chamber. They called for Sister Whitman and Brother Rogers to come down and promised they should not be hurt. This promise was often repeated, and they came down. Mrs. Whitman, faint with the loss of blood, was carried on a settee to the door by Brother Rogers and Miss Bewley.

"Every corner of the room was crowded with Indians having their guns ready to fire. The children had been brought down and huddled together to be shot. Eliza was one. Here they had stood for a long time surrounded by guns pointed at their breasts. She often heard the cry, "Shall we shoot?" and her blood became cold, she says, and she fell upon the floor. But now the order was given, "Do not shoot the children," as the settee passed by the children, over the bleeding, dying body of John.

"Fatal moment! The settee advanced about its length from the door, when the guns were discharged from without and within, the powder actually burning the faces of the children. Brother Rogers raised his hand and cried, "My God," and fell upon his face, pierced with many balls. But he fell not alone. An equal number of the deadly weapons were leveled at the settee and the discharge had been deadly. She groaned, and lingered for some time in great agony.

"Two of the humane Indians threw their blankets over the little children huddled together in the corner of the room, and shut out the sight as they beat their dying victims with whips, and cut their faces with knives. It was Joe Lewis, the Canadian half-breed, that first shot Mrs. Whitman, but it

150

was Tamtsaky who took her scalp as a trophy."

An old Oregon friend of the author, Samuel Campbell, now living in Moscow, Idaho, spent the Winter of '46 and '47 at the Whitman Mission, and never wearied in telling of the grandly Christian character of Mrs. Whitman, of her kindness and patience to all, whites and Indians alike. Every evening she delighted all with her singing. Her voice, after all her hard life, had lost none of its sweetness, nor had her environments in any sense soured her toward any of the little pleasantries of every-day life.

Says Mr. Campbell, "You can imagine my horror in 1849, when at Grand Ronde, old Tamtsaky acknowledged to me that he scalped Mrs. Whitman and told of her long, beautiful, silky hair." Soon after the United States Government, by order of General Lane, sent officers to arrest the murderers. Old Tamtsaky was killed at the time of the arrest and escaped the hangman's rope, which was given to five of the leaders, after trial in Oregon City, May, 1850. The names of the murderers hanged were Tilwkait, Tahamas, Quiahmarsum, Klvakamus and Siahsalucus.

The Rev. Cushing Eells says, "The day before the massacre, Istikus, a firm friend of Dr. Whitman, told him of the threats against his life, and advised him to 'go away until my people have better hearts.' He reached home from the lodge of Istikus late in the night, but visited his sick before retiring. Then he told Mrs. Whitman the words of Istikus. Knowing how true a friend Istikus was, and his great courage, the situation became more perilous in the estimation of both, than ever before. Mrs. Whitman was so affected by it that she remained in her room, and one of the children, who took her breakfast up to her room, found her weeping. The Doctor went about his work as usual, but told some of his associates that if it were possible to do so, he would remove all the family to a place of safety. It is the first time he ever seems to have been alarmed, or thought it possible that his Indians would attempt such a crime."

Rev. Mr. Eells gives a detailed account of the massacre and its horrors, but in this connection we only desire to give the reader a clear view

151

without dwelling upon its atrocities. "The tomahawk with which Dr Whitman was killed, was presented to the Cayuse Indians by the Blackfeet upon some great occasion, and was preserved by the Cayuse as a memorable relic long after the hanging of the Chiefs. In the Yakima War it passed to another tribe, and the Chief who owned it was killed; an Indian agent, Logan got possession of it and presented it to the Sanitary Society during the Civil War. A subscription of one hundred dollars was raised and it was presented to the Legislature of Oregon, and is preserved among the archives of the State."

This narrative would be incomplete without recording the prompt action of the Hudson Bay Company officers in coming to the relief of the captive women and children. As soon as Chief Factor Ogden heard of it, he lost no time in repairing to the scene, reaching Walla Walla December 12th. In about two weeks he succeeded in ransoming all the captives for blankets, shirts, guns, ammunition and tobacco, and at an expense of $500. No other man in the Territory, and no army that could have been mustered could have done it.

The Americans in Oregon promptly mustered and attacked the Indians, who retreated to the territory of a different tribe. But the murderers and leaders among the Indians were not arrested until nearly two years after the crime.

While some have charged that the officials of the Hudson Bay Company could have averted the massacre, this is only an opinion. Their humane and prompt act in releasing the captive women and children from worse than death, was worthy of it, and has received the strongest words of praise.

Thus was ended disastrously the work of the American Board which had given such large promise for eleven years. While its greatest achievement was not in saving savage souls, but in being largely instrumental in peacefully saving three great States to the American Union, yet there is good evidence years after the massacre, that the labors of the Missionaries had not been in vain. After the Treaty of 1855, seven years after the massacre, General Joel Palmer, who was one of the Council, says, "Forty-five Cayuse and one thousand Nez Perces have kept up regular family and public worship, singing from the Nez Perces Hymn Book and reading the Gospel of Matthew, translated into Nez Perces, the work of Dr. and Mrs. Spalding."

Says General Barloe, "Many of them showed surprising evidences of piety, especially Timothy, who was their regular and faithful preacher during all these years. Among the Cayuse, old Istikus, as long as he lived, rang his bell every Sabbath and called his little band together for worship."

Twelve years after leaving his Mission, Rev. Mr. Spalding returned to his people and found the Tribe had kept up the form of worship all the years since. Upon opening a school, it was at once crowded with children, and even old men and women, with failing eyesight, insisted upon being taught; and the interest did not flag until the failing health of Mr. Spalding forced him to give up his work. The Rev. Dr. Eells' experience was much the same; all going to prove that the early work of the American Board was not fruitless in good, and emphasizing the fact that good words and work are never wholly lost, and their power only will be known when the final summing up is made.

There have been few great men that have not felt the stings of criticism and misrepresentation. The wholly unselfish life of Dr. Marcus Whitman, from his young manhood to the day of his death, it would seem, ought to have shielded him from this class, but it did not. In justice to his contemporaries, however, it is due to say, every one of them, of all denominations except one, was his friend and defender.

That one man was a French Jesuit priest, by the name of J. B. A. Brouillett. He was Acting Bishop among the Indians, of a tribe near to the Cayuse, where Dr. Whitman had labored for eleven years, and where he perished in 1847. After the massacre, there were some grave charges made against Brouillett, and in 1853 he wrote a pamphlet, entitled, "Protestantism in Oregon," in which he made a vicious attack upon the dead Whitman, and the living Dr. Spalding, and the other Protestant Missionaries of the

American Board.

It naturally called out some very pointed rejoinders, yet attracted but little attention from the Christian world. Patriotic American Catholics took but little stock in the clamor of the French priest, and the matter was in a fair way to be forgotten, when interest was suddenly renewed in the subject by the appearance of an executive document, No. 38, 35th Congress, 1st Session, signed J. Ross Browne, Commissioner of Indian Affairs, and dated at San Francisco, December 4, 1867, which contained a few sentences from J. Ross Browne and all of the Brouillett pamphlet.

The idea of getting so slanderous a paper published as an official public document by the United States Congress, was an unheard-of challenge that called for a reply. And it came promptly and pointedly. From all parts of the country, Members of Congress were flooded with letters to find out how such a thing could be accomplished. None of them seemed able to answer. But the mischief was done and many of them expressed a willingness to help undo it.

The Old School and New School, and the United Presbyterians in their Presbyteries, resented the outrage, both in the Far West and in the East, and none more vigorously than did that of the Illinois Presbytery at the meeting in Chicago in 1871. The Methodists and Baptists and Congregational Conferences in Oregon and Washington, cordially united in the work, and demanded that an address, defending the Missionaries and the American Board, should be printed just as conspicuously to the World as had been the falsehoods of Brouillett.

The Presbyterian General Assembly at Chicago, May 18, 1871, led by the Rev. F. A. Noble, summed up the case under seven different counts of falsehoods, and demanded that Congress should, in simple justice, publish them in vindication of the Protestant Church. The Oregon Presbytery was still more positive and aggressive and made their specifications under twelve heads. The Congregationalists and the Methodists in Oregon were equally pointed and positive. It resulted in "A Committee on Protestantism in

154

Oregon," drawing up a reply.

In this they say: "The object of Brouillett's pamphlet appears to be to exculpate the real instigators of that terrible tragedy, the massacre at Waiilatpui, and to cast the blame upon the Protestant Missionaries who were the victims." They go on to declare that the paper "Is full of glaring and infamous falsehoods," and give their reasons concisely, and wholly exonerate Dr. Whitman from all blame.

They close their address thus: "With these facts before us, we would unite with all lovers of truth and justice, in earnestly petitioning Congress, as far as possible, to rectify the evils which have resulted from the publication, as a Congressional Document, of the slanders of J. Ross Browne, and thus lift the cloud of darkness that 'Hangs over the memory of the righteous dead and extend equal justice to those who survive.'" The Rev. Dr. Spalding prepared the matter and it was introduced through Secretary Columbus Delano, and the Indian Agent, N. B. Meacham, and passed Congress as "Ex-Document No. 37 of the 41st Congress."

Forty thousand copies were ordered printed, the same as of Brouillett's pamphlet. It is reported that less than fifty copies ever reached the public. They mysteriously disappeared, and no one ever learned and made public the manner in which it was done.

But the incident developed the fact, that the whole patriotic Christian people unitedly defended Whitman from the charges made.

CHAPTER XII.

BIOGRAPHICAL.—DR. MARCUS WHITMAN AND DR. JOHN McLOUGHLIN.

Dr. Marcus Whitman was a direct descendant of John Whitman of Weymouth, who came from England in the ship Confidence, December, 1638. Of him it is recorded that he feared God, hated covetousness and did good continually all the days of a long life.

Of the parents of Dr. Whitman, but little has been written. His father, Beza Whitman, was born in Bridgewater, Connecticut, May 13, 1775. In March, 1797, he married Alice Green, of Mumford, Connecticut. Two years later, with all of their worldly goods packed in an ox-cart, they moved to Rushville, New York, Mrs. Whitman making a large part of the tedious journey on foot, carrying her one-year-old babe in her arms.

Settled in their new home, with Indians for near neighbors and wilderness all about them, they began the struggle for life, and though no great success rewarded their efforts, it is known that their doors always swung open to the needy and their hands ministered to the sick.

Mr. Whitman died April 7, 1810, at the early age of 35 years, leaving his young wife to rear their family of four sons and one daughter. Mrs. Whitman, though not a professing Christian, was a woman of much energy and great endurance which, combined with strong Christian principle, enabled her to look well to the ways of her household. She lived to see every member of it an active Christian. She died September 6th, 1857, aged 79, and was buried beside her husband near Rushville, New York.

Dr. Marcus was her second son, and inherited from her a strong frame and great endurance. After his father's death he was sent to his paternal grandfather, Samuel Whitman, of Plainfield, Massachusetts, where he remained ten years for training and education. There he received a liberal

156

training in the best schools the place afforded, supplemented by a thorough course in Latin, and more advanced studies under the minister of the place.

We know little of the boyhood spent there, as we should know little of the whole life of Whitman, had not others lived to tell it, for he neither told or wrote of it; he was too modest and too busy for that. But we know it was the usual life of the Yankee boy, to bring the cows and milk them, to cut the wood, and later to plow and sow the fields, as we afterward find he knew how to do all these things. The strong, sturdy boy of ceaseless activity and indomitable will who loved hunting and exploring, and a touch of wild life, must have sometimes given his old grandfather a trial of his mettle, but on the whole, no doubt, he was a great comfort and help to his declining years.

After the death of his grandfather, he returned to the home of his mother in Rushville. There he became a member of the Congregational Church at the age of nineteen, and it is said was very desirous of studying for the ministry, but by a long illness, and the persuasion of friends, was turned from his purpose to the study of medicine.

He took a three years' course, and graduated at Fairfield, in 1824. He first went to Canada, where he practiced his profession for four years, then came back to his home, determined again to take up the study for the ministry, but was again frustrated in his design, and practiced his profession four years more in Wheeler, N. Y., where he was a member and an elder in the Presbyterian Church. He and a brother also owned a saw-mill near there, where he assisted in his spare hours, and so learned another trade that was most useful to him in later life. In fact, as we see his environments in his Mission Station in Oregon, these hard lessons of his earlier years seem to have been, in the best sense of the word, educational.

With but little help, he opened up and cultivated a great farm, and built a grist-mill and a saw-mill, and when his grist-mill was burned, built another, and, at the same time, attended to his professional duties that covered a wide district. It was the wonder of every visitor to the Mission how one man, with so few helpers, accomplished so much. At the time of the

157

massacre, the main building of the Mission was one hundred feet in the front with an L running back seventy feet, and part of it two stories high. Every visitor remarked on the cleanliness and comfort and thrift which everywhere appeared.

There are men who, with great incentives, have accomplished great things, but were utter failures when it came to practical, every-day duties. Dr Whitman, with a genius to conceive, and the will and energy to carry out the most difficult and daring undertaking, was just as faithful and efficient in the little things that made up the comforts of his wilderness home. Seeing these grand results—the commodious house, the increase in the herds and the stacks of grain—seems to have only angered his lazy, thriftless Indians, and they began to make demands for a division of his wealth.

Dr. Whitman has been accused of holding his Indians to a too strict moral accountability; that it would have been wiser to have been more lenient, and winked at, rather than denounced, some of their savage ways Those who have carefully studied the man, know how impossible it would have been for him, in any seeming way, to condone a crime, or to purchase peace with the criminal by a bribe. This was the method of the Hudson Bay Company, and was doubtless the cheap way.

By a series of events and environments, he seems to have been trained much as Moses was, but with wholly different surroundings from those of the great Lawgiver, whose first training was in the Royal Court and the schools of Egypt; then in its army; then an outcast, and as a shepherd guiding his flocks, and finding springs and pasturage in the land where, one day, he was to lead his people.

King David is another man made strong in the school of preparation As he watched his flocks on the Judean hills, he fought the lion and the bear and so was not afraid to meet and fight a giant, who defied the armies of the living God. It was there, under the stars, that he practiced music to quiet mad king, and was educated into a fitness to organize the great choirs, and furnish the grand anthems for the temple worship. After this, in self-defense

158

he became the commander of lawless bands of men, and so was trained to command the armies of Israel.

So it has been in our own Nation, with Washington and Lincoln, and Grant and Garfield; they had to pass through many hardships, and receive a many-sided training before they were fitted for the greater work to which they were called. So it was, this strong, conscientious, somewhat restless young man was being trained for the life that was to follow. The farmer boy, planting and reaping, the millwright planning and building, the country doctor on his long, lonely rides, the religious teacher who must oversee the physical and spiritual wants of his fellow church members, all were needed in the larger life for which he was longing and looking, when the sad appeal for the "Book of Life" came from the Indian Chiefs who had come so far, and failed to find it. His immediate and hearty response was, "Here am I, send me!"

Dr. Marcus Whitman, judged by his life as a Missionary, must ever be given due credit; for no man ever gave evidence of greater devotion to the work he found to do. He was doubtless excelled as a teacher of the Indians by many of his co-laborers. He was not, perhaps, even eminent as a teacher. His great reputation and the honor due him, does not rest upon such a claim, but upon his wisdom in seeing the future of the Great West, and his heroic rescue of the land from a foreign rule. That he heard a call to the duty from a higher source than any earthly potentate, none but the skeptic will doubt. The act stands out clear and bold and strong, as one of the finest instances of unselfish patriotism recorded in all history.

DR. JOHN McLOUGHLIN.

Any sketch of pioneer Oregon would be incomplete without an honorable mention of Dr. John McLoughlin. He was the Chief Factor of the Hudson Bay Company, an organization inimical to American interests, both for pecuniary and political reasons, and like Whitman, has been maligned and misunderstood. As the leading spirit, during all the stages of pioneer life, his life and acts have an importance second to none. Nothing could have been more important for the comfort and peace of the Missionaries than to have had a man as Supreme Ruler of Oregon, with so keen a sense of justice, as had Dr. McLoughlin.

Physically he was a fine specimen of a man. He was six feet, four inches, and well-proportioned. His bushy white hair and massive beard, caused the Indians everywhere to call him, the "Great White Head Chief."

He was born in 1784, and was eighteen years older than Dr. Whitman. He entered the Northwestern Fur Company's service in 1800. He afterward studied medicine, and for a time practiced his profession, but his fine business abilities were so apparent, that in 1824 we find him at the head of affairs in Oregon. His power over the rough men in the employ of the Company, and the savage tribes who filled their coffers with wealth, was so complete as to be phenomenal.

In many of the sketches we have shown that his kindness to the pioneer Missionaries in another and a higher sense, proved his manhood. To obey the orders of his company, and still remain a humane man, was something that required tact that few men could have brought to bear as well as Dr. McLoughlin. While he did slaughter, financially speaking, traders and fur gatherers right and left, and did his best to serve the pecuniary interests of his great monopoly, he drew the line there, and was the friend and the helper of the missionaries.

If the reader could glance through Mrs. Whitman's diary upon the very opening week of her arrival in Oregon, there would not be found anything but words of kindness and gratitude to Dr. McLoughlin. In justice to his company, to which he was always loyal, he pushed the Methodist missions far up the Willamette, and those of the American Board three hundred miles in another direction. But at the same time he was a friend and brother and adviser, and anything he had was at their service, whether they had money or not.

After the immigration in 1842, and the larger immigration led by

Whitman in 1843, the company in England became alarmed and sent out spies—Messrs. Park, Vavasaur and Peel, who were enjoined to find out whether McLoughlin was loyal to British interests. After many months spent in studying the situation, their adverse report is easily inferred from the fact that Dr. McLoughlin was ordered to report to headquarters. The full history of that secret investigation has never yet been revealed, but when it is, the whole blame will be found resting upon Whitman and his missionary co-workers, who wrested the land from English rule, and that Dr. McLoughlin aided them to success.

When the charge of "Friendship to the missionaries," was made, the old doctor flared up and replied: "What would you have? Would you have me turn the cold shoulder on the men of God who came to do that for the Indians which this company has neglected to do? If we had not helped the immigrants in '42 and '43 and '44, and relieved their necessities, Fort Vancouver would have been destroyed and the world would have treated us as our inhuman conduct deserved; every officer of the Company, from Governor down, would have been covered with obloquy, and the Company's business ruined!"

But it all resulted in the resignation of Dr. McLoughlin. The injustice he received at the hands of Americans afterward, is deeply to be regretted, and it is greatly to the credit of the thinking people of the State of Oregon that they have done their best to remedy the wrong. At many times, and in a multitude of ways, Dr. McLoughlin, by his kindness to the missionaries, won for himself the gratitude of thinking Americans in all the years to come. With a bad man in his place as Chief Factor, the old missionaries would have found life in Oregon well-nigh unbearable. While true to the exclusive and selfish interests of the great monopoly he served, he yet refused to resort to any form of unmanliness.

After his abuse by the English company and his severance of all connection with it, he settled at Oregon City and lived and died an American citizen. The tongue of slander was freely wagged against him, and his declining years were made miserable by unthinking Americans and revengeful

Englishmen. His property, of which he had been deprived, was returned to his heirs, and to-day his memory is cherished as among Oregon's benefactors. A fine oil painting of Dr. McLoughlin was secured and paid for by the old pioneers and presented to the State.

The Hon. John Minto, in making the address at the hanging of the picture, closed with these words:

"In this sad summary of such a life as Dr. McLoughlin's, there is a statement that merits our attention, which, if ever proven true, and no man who ever knew Dr. McLoughlin will doubt that he believed it true, namely, that he prevented war between Great Britain and the United States, will show that two of the greatest nations on this earth owe him a debt of gratitude, and that Oregon, in particular, is doubly bound to him as a public benefactor. British state papers may some day prove all this.

"It is now twenty-six years since the Legislative Assembly of the State of Oregon, so far as restoration of property to Dr. McLouglin's family could undo the wrong of Oregon's Land Bill, gave gladness to the heart of every Oregon pioneer worthy of the name. All of them yet living, now know that, good man as they believed him, he was better than they knew. They see him now, after the strife and jealousies of race, national, business, and sectarian interests are allayed, standing in the center of all these causes of contention—a position in which to please all parties was impossible, to 'Maintain which, only a good man could bear with patience'—and they have adopted this means of conveying their appreciation of this great forbearance and patient endurance, combined with his generous conduct.

"Looking, then, at this line of action in the light of the merest glimpses of history, known to be true by witnesses living, can any honest man wonder that the pioneers of Oregon, who have eaten the salt of this man's hospitality, who have been the eye-witnesses to his brave care for humanity, and participators in his generous aid, are unwilling to go to their graves in silence—which would imply base ingratitude—a silence which would be eloquent with falsehood?

"Governor and Representatives of Oregon: In recognition of the worthy manner in which Dr. John McLoughlin filled his trying and responsible position, in the heartfelt glow of a grateful remembrance of his humane and noble conduct to them, the Oregon pioneers leave this portrait with you, hoping that their descendants will not forget the friend of their fathers, and trusting that this gift of the men and women who led the advance which has planted thirty thousand rifles in the Valley of the Columbia, and three hundred thousand, when needed, in the National Domain facing the Pacific Ocean, will be deemed worthy of a place in your halls."

DR. JOHN MCLOUGHLIN,
Chief Factor of Hudson Bay Co., at Fort Walla Walla.

CHAPTER XIII.

WHITMAN SEMINARY AND COLLEGE.

Many institutions of learning have been erected and endowed by the generosity of the rich, but Whitman Seminary and College had its foundation laid in faith and prayer. Viewed from a worldly standpoint, backed only by a poor missionary, whose possessions could be packed upon the back of a mule, the outlook did not seem promising. During all the years of his missionary service in Oregon, none knew better the value of the patriotic Christian service of Dr. and Mrs. Whitman, than did the Rev. Dr. Cushing Eells and his good wife. After the massacre, Dr. Eells, and all his co-workers were moved under military escort to the Willamette, but he writes:

"My eyes were constantly turned east of the Cascade Range, a region I have given the best years of my life to."

It was not until 1859 when the country was declared open, that he visited Walla Walla, and stood at the "Great grave of Dr. Whitman and his wife." Standing there upon the consecrated spot, he says:

"I believe that the power of the Highest came upon me." And there he solemnly vowed that he would do something to honor the Christian martyrs whose remains rested in that grave. He says: "I felt as though if Dr. Whitman were alive, he would prefer a high school for the benefit of both sexes, rather than a monument of marble."

He pondered the subject and upon reaching home, sought the advice of the Congregational Association. The subject was carefully canvassed by those who well knew all the sad history, and the following note was entered upon the record:

"In the judgment of this association, the contemplated purpose of Brother C. Eells to remove to Waiilatpui, to establish a Christian school at that place, to be called the Whitman Seminary, in memory of the noble deeds and great works and the fulfillment of the benevolent plans of the late lamented Dr. Whitman and his wife: And his further purpose to act as home missionary in the Walla Walla Valley, meets our cordial approbation and shall receive our earnest support."

Dr. Eells at once resigned from the Tualitin Academy, where he was then teaching, and in 1859 and '60 obtained the charter for the Whitman Seminary. Dr. Eells had hoped to be employed by the Home Missionary Society, but that organization declined, as its object was not to build seminaries and colleges, but to establish churches. He bought from the American Board for $1,000 the farm of 640 acres where Dr. Whitman had toiled for eleven years.

It was Dr. Eells' idea to build a seminary directly upon this consecrated ground, and gather a quiet settlement about the school. But he soon found that it would be better to locate the seminary in the village, at that time made up of five resident families and about one hundred men. It, however, was in sight of the "Great grave."

Here the Eells family settled down upon the farm for hard work to raise the funds necessary to erect the buildings necessary for the seminary. He preached without compensation up and down the valley upon the Sabbath, and like Paul, worked with his hands during the week. His first Summer's work on the farm brought in $700; enough nearly to pay three-fourths of its cost; thus year after year Dr. Eells and his faithful wife labored on and on. He plowed and reaped, and cut cord wood, while she made butter, and raised chickens and saved every dollar for the one grand purpose of doing honor to their noble friends in the "Great grave" always in sight.

Rarely in this world has there been a more beautiful demonstration of loyalty and friendship, than of Dr. and Mrs. Eells. They lived and labored on the farm for ten years, and endured all the privations and isolations common to such a life. An article in the "Congregationalist" says:

"Mother Eells' churn with which she made four hundred pounds of butter for sale, ought to be kept for an honored place in the cabinet of Whitman College."

It was by such sacrifices that the first $4,000 were raised to begin the buildings. Five years had passed after the charter was granted, before the seminary was located, and then only on paper. And this was seven years before the completion of the first school building; the dedication of which occurred on October 13, 1866.

The first principal was the Rev. P. B. Chamberlain, who also organized and was first pastor of the Congregational Church at Walla Walla. In 1880, under the new impulse given to the work by the Rev. Dr. G. H. Atkinson, of Portland, Whitman Seminary developed into Whitman College. This was finally accomplished in 1883. During that year, College Hall was erected at a cost of $16,000. During 1883 and 1884, in the same spirit he had at all times exhibited, Dr. Eells felt it his duty to visit New England in the interest of the institution. He says:

"It was the hardest year's work I ever did, to raise that sixteen thousand dollars."

The old pioneer would much rather have cut cord wood or plowed his fields, if that would have brought in the money for his loved college. The Christian who reads Dr. Eells' diary during the closing years of his life, will easily see how devoted he was to the work of honoring the memory of the occupants of the "Great grave." His diary of May 24, 1890, says:

"The needs of Whitman College cause serious thought. My convictions have been that my efforts in its behalf were in obedience to Divine Will."

June 11, 1890. "During intervals of the night I was exercised in prayer for Whitman College. I am persuaded that my prayers are prevailing. In agony I pray for Whitman College."

October 2d. "Dreamed of Whitman College and awoke with a prayer."

His last entry in his diary was: "I could die for Whitman College."

The grand old man went to his great reward in February, 1893. Will the Christian people of the land allow such a prayer to go unanswered?

In 1884 Mrs. N. F. Cobleigh did some very effective work in canvassing sections of New England in behalf of the college, succeeding in raising $8,000.

Dr. Anderson, after his efficient labors of nine years, with many discouragements, resigned the Presidency in 1891, and the Rev. James F. Eaton, another scholarly earnest man, assumed its duties. In the meantime the struggling village of Walla Walla had grown into the "Garden City," and the demands upon such an institution had increased a hundred fold in the rapid development of the country in every direction. The people began to see the wisdom of the founder, and cast about for means to make the college more efficient. The Union Journal of Walla Walla, said:

"It is our pride. It is the cap sheaf of the educational institutions of Walla Walla, and should be the pride and boast of every good Walla Wallan. It has a corps of exceptionally good instructors, under the guidance of a man possessing breadth of intellect, liberal education and an enthusiastic desire to be successful in his chosen field of labor, with students who rank in natural ability with the best product of any land. But it is deficient in facilities. It lacks room in which to grow. It lacks library and apparatus, the tools of education."

President Eaton and the faculty saw this need and the necessity of a great effort. It was under this pressure, and the united desire of the friends of the college that the Rev. Stephen B. L. Penrose, of the "Yale band" assumed the duties of President in 1894, and began his plans to raise an endowment fund and place the college upon a sound financial basis, as well as to increase its educational facilities and requirements.

It was the misfortune of these educators to enter the field for money at a time of great financial embarrassment, such as has not been experienced in many decades; but it was at the same time their good fortune to enlist the aid of Dr. D. K. Pearsons of Chicago in the grand work with a generous gift of $50,000, provided that others could be induced to add $150,000 to it.

With such a start and with such a man as Dr. Pearsons, there will be no such word as fail. He is a man of faith like Dr. Eells and has long been administering upon his own estate in wise and generous gifts to deserving institutions. With such a man to encourage other liberal givers, the endowment will not stop at $200,000. If Whitman College is to be the Yale and Harvard and Chicago University of the Far West, it must meet with a generous response from liberal givers. Its name alone ought to be worth a million in money. When the people are educated in Whitman history, the money will come and the prayers of Dr. Eells will be answered.

The millions of people love fair play and honest dealing and can appreciate solid work, and they will learn to love the memory of the modest hero, and will be glad to do him honor in so practical a method. It will soon be half a century since Dr. Whitman and his noble wife fell at their post of duty at Waiilatpui. Had Dr. Whitman been a millionaire, a man of noble birth, had he been a military man or a statesman, his praise would have been sung upon historic pages as the praise of others has. But he was only a poor missionary doctor, who lost his life in the vain effort to civilize and Christianize savages, and an army of modern historians seem to have thought, as we have shown in another chapter, that the world would sit quietly by and see and applaud while they robbed him of his richly won honors. In that they have over-reached themselves. The name of Dr. Marcus Whitman will be honored and revered long after the names of his traducers have been obliterated and forgotten.

It is a name with a history, which will grow in honor and importance as the great States he saved to the Union will grow into the grandeur they naturally assume. There is not a clearer page of history in all the books than that Dr. Whitman, under the leading of Providence, saved the States of Oregon, Washington and Idaho to the Union. There is a possibility that by a long and destructive war we might have held them as against the claims of England. There were just two men who prevented that war and those two men were Drs. Whitman and McLoughlin. The latter indirectly by his humane and civilized treatment of the missionaries when he might have crushed them, and the former by his unparalleled heroism in his mid-winter ride to Washington, and his wisdom in piloting the immigrations to Oregon just the year that he did.

History correctly written, will truthfully say, "When Whitman fell at Waiilatpui, one of the grandest heroes of this century went to his great reward." The State of Washington has done well to name a great county to perpetuate his memory; Dr. Eells did a noble act in founding Whitman Seminary, and the time is coming and is near at hand, when the young men and women of the country will prize a diploma inscribed with the magic name of Whitman. Endow the college and endow it generously. Make it worthy of the man whose love of country felt that no task was too difficult and no danger so great as to make him hesitate.

After the endowment is full and complete, a great College Hall should be erected from a patriotic fund, and upon the central pillar should be inscribed: "Sacred to the memory of Dr. Marcus and Narcissa Whitman. While lifting up the banner of the cross in one hand to redeem and save savage souls, they thought it no wrong to carry the flag of the country they loved in the other."

There is no such thing as dividing the honors. They are simply Whitman honors; they lived and labored and achieved together; the bride upon the plains and in the mission home was a heroine scarcely second to the hero who swam icy rivers and climbed the snow-covered mountains in 1842 and 1843, upon his patriotic mission. It is a work that may well engage the patriotic women of America; for true womanhood has never had a more beautiful setting than in the life of Narcissa Whitman. At the death, by drowning, of her only child, that she almost idolized, she bowed humbly and said: "Thy Will be done!" And upon the day of her death, she was mother to eleven helpless adopted children, for whose safety she prayed in her expiring moments.

What an unselfish life she led. In her diary she says, but in no complaining mood: "Situated as we are, our house is the Missionaries' tavern, and we must accommodate more or less all the time. We have no less than seven families in our two houses; we are in peculiar and somewhat trying circumstances; we cannot sell to them because we are missionaries and not traders."

And we see by the record that there were no less than seventy souls in the Whitman family the day of the massacre.

Emerson says: "Heroism is an obedience to a secret impulse of individual character, and the characteristics of genuine heroism is its persistency."

Where was it ever more strongly marked than in Dr. Whitman? We are told that "History repeats itself." Going back upon the historic pages, one can find the best illustration of Dr. Whitman in faithful old Caleb. Their lives seem to run along similar lines. Both were sent to spy out the land. Both returned and made true and faithful reports. Both were selected for their great physical fitness, and for their fine mental and moral worth; and both proved among the finest specimens of unselfish manhood ever recorded. Turning to the Sacred Record we read that a great honor was ordered for Caleb; not only that he was permitted to enter the promised land, but it was also understood by all, that he should have the choice of all the fair country they were to occupy. His associates sent with him forty years before were terribly afraid of "the giants," and now they had reached "The land of promise," and Joshua had assembled the leaders of Israel to assign them their places. Just notice old Caleb. Standing in view of the meadows and fields and orchards, loaded with their rich clusters of purple grapes, everybody expected

171

he would select the best, for they knew that it was both promised and he deserved it; but Caleb, lifting up his voice so that all could hear, said:

"Lo, I am this day four score and five years old. As yet I am as strong this day as I was in the day that Moses sent me; as my strength was then, even so is my strength now for war, both to go out and to come in. Now, therefore, give me this mountain whereof the Lord spoke in that day; for thou heardest in that day how the Anakims were there, and that the cities were great and fenced. If so be, the Lord will be with me, then I shall be able to drive them out as the Lord said."

Noble, unselfish old Caleb! And how wonderfully like him was our hero thirty-four and a half centuries later. It mattered not that he had saved a great country, twice as large as New York, Pennsylvania and Illinois combined, or thirty-two times as large as Massachusetts. It mattered not that it was accomplished through great peril and trials and sufferings that no man can over-estimate, he never once asked a reward. "Give me this mountain," and he went back to his mission, and resumed his heavy burden, and let others gather the harvest, and "the clusters of purple grapes." There he was found at his post of duty, and met death on that fatal November the 29th, 1847.

When a generous people have made the endowment complete, and built the grand Memorial Hall, they should build a monument at the "Great Grave" at Waiilatpui. Americans are patriotic. They build monuments to their men of science, to their statesmen and to their soldiers. It is right to do so. They are grand object lessons, educating the young in patriotism and virtue and right living. The monument at no grave in all the land will more surely teach all these, than will that at the neglected grave at Waiilatpui. Build the monument and tell your children's children to go and stand uncovered in its shadow, and receive its lessons and breathe in its inspirations of patriotism.

CHAPTER XIV.

OREGON THEN, AND OREGON, WASHINGTON AND IDAHO NOW.

The beginning of a People, a State or a Nation is always an interesting study, and when the beginning has resulted in a grand success, the interest increases. It is seldom that in the lifetime of the multitudes of living actors, so great a transformation can be seen as that to-day illustrated in the Pacific States. Fifty years ago, the immigrant, after his long journey over arid plains, after swimming rivers and climbing three ranges of mountains, stood upon the last slope, and beheld primeval beauty spread out before him. The millions of acres of green meadows had never been disturbed by a furrow, and in the great forest the sound of the woodman's ax had never been heard.

Coming by way of the great river, as it meets the incoming waves of the Pacific, the scene is still more one of grandeur. Astoria, at that time, had a few straggling huts, and Portland was a village, with its streets so full of stumps as to require a good driver to get through with safety, and was referred to as a town twelve miles below Oregon City.

To the writer nothing has left such an impression of wilderness and solitude as a journey up the Willamette, forty-five years ago, in a birch-bark canoe, paddled by two Indian guides. The wild ducks were scarcely disturbed, and dropped to the water a hundred yards away, and the three-pronged buck, browsing among the lily pads, stopped to look at the unusual invasion of his domain, and went on feeding.

The population of Oregon in that year, 1850, as shown by census, was 13,294, and that included all of Oregon, Washington, and Idaho, with a part of Wyoming and Montana.

After years of importunity, Congress had given Oregon a Territorial Government in 1849. Prior to that—from 1843 to 1849—it was an independent American government, for the people and by the people. Notwithstanding the neglect of Oregon by the General Government, and its entire failure to foster or protect, the old pioneers were true and loyal American citizens, and for six years took such care of themselves as they were able, and performed the task so well as to merit the best words of commendation.

REV. STEPHEN B. L. PENROSE,
President of Whitman College.

The commerce of the country, aside from its furs, was scarcely worth mentioning. The author, in 1851, bought what few salted salmon there were in the market, and shipped them to San Francisco, but wise and prudent advisers regarded it as a risky venture. He would have been considered a wild visionary, indeed, had he even hinted of the shipments of fish now annually made to all parts of the civilized world.

It was then known that the rivers were filled with fish. In the spring of the year, the smaller streams, leading away from the Columbia, were literally blocked with almost solid masses of fish on their way to their spawning grounds. The bears along the Columbia, as well as the Indians, had an unlimited supply of the finest fish in the world, with scarcely an effort to take them. An Indian on the Willamette, at the foot of the falls, could fill his boat in an hour with salmon weighing from twenty to forty pounds.

In the spring of the year, when the salmon are running up the Willamette, they begin to jump from the water a quarter of a mile before reaching the falls. One could sit in a boat and see hundreds of the great fish in the air constantly. Multitudes of them maimed and killed themselves jumping against the rocks at the falls.

The Indian did not wait for "a rise" or "a bite." He had a hook with an eye socket, and a pole ten feet or more long. The hook he fastened to a deer thong, about two feet long, attached to the lower end of the pole. When ready for fishing the pole was inserted into the socket of the hook, and he felt for his fish, and by a sudden jerk caught it in the belly. The hook was pulled from the pole, and the fish had a play of the two feet of deer thong. But the Indian never stops to experiment; he hauled in his prize.

The great forests and prairies were a very paradise for the hunters of large game. Up to the date of 1842-3, of Dr. Whitman's ride, but a single hundred Americans had settled in Oregon, and they seemed to be almost accidental guests. The immigration in 1842 swelled the list, and the caravan of 1843 started the tide, so that in 1850, as we have seen, the first census showed an American population of 13,294.

In 1890, in contrast, the population of Washington was 349,390; Oregon, 313,707; Idaho, 84,385, and five counties in Southwestern Montana and one in Wyoming, originally Oregon territory, had a population of 65,862, making a total of 813,404. Considering the difficulties of reaching these distant States for many years, this change, in less than half a century, is a wonderful transformation. The Indians had held undisputed possession of the land for generations, and yet, as careful a census as could be made, placed their number at below 75,000. In 1892 the Indian Commissioner marks the number at 21,057.

The great changes are seen in the fact that in 1838 there were but thirteen settlements by white men in Oregon, viz.: That at Waiilatpui, at Lapwai, at the Dalles and near Salem, and the Hudson Bay Forts at Walla Walla, Colville, Fort Hall, Boise, Vancouver, Nisqually, Umpqua, Okanogan and the settlement at Astoria. The old missionaries felt thankful when letters reached them within two years after they were written.

Mrs. Whitman's first letter from home was two years and six months reaching the mission. The most sure and safe route was by way of New York or Montreal to London, around the Horn to the Sandwich Islands, from which place a vessel sailed every year for Columbia. The wildest visionaries at that time had not dreamed of being bound to the East by bands of steel, as Senator McDuffie said: "The wealth of the Indies would be insufficient to connect by steam the Columbia River to the States of the East." Uncle Sam seems to have been taking a very sound and peaceful nap. He did not own California, and was even desirous of trading Oregon for the cod fisheries of Newfoundland.

The debt of gratitude the Americans owe to the men and women who endured the privations of that early day, and educated the Nation into the knowledge of its future glory and greatness, has not been fully appreciated. The settlers of no other States of the frontier encountered such severe tests of courage and loyalty. The Middle States of the Great West while they had their hardships and trials, were always within reach of the strong arm of the Government, and felt its fostering care, and had many comforts which were wholly beyond the reach of the Oregon pioneers.

Their window glass for years and years was dressed deer skin; their parlor chairs were square blocks of wood; their center tables were made by driving down four sticks and sawing boards by hand for top, the nearest saw mill being four hundred miles off. A ten-penny nail was prized as a jewel, and until Dr. Whitman built his mill, a barrel of flour cost him twenty-four dollars, and in those days that amount of money was equal to a hundred in our times of to-day.

The plows were all wood, and deer thongs took the place of iron in binding the parts together. It was ten years after they began to raise wheat before they had any other implement than the sickle, and for threshing, the wooden flail. It was in the year 1839 the first printing press reached Oregon. It may be marked as among the pioneer civilizers of this now great and prosperous Christian land.

That press has a notable history and is to-day preserved at the State Capital of Oregon as a relic of by-gone days in printing. Long before the civilization of Oregon had begun in 1819, the Congregational Missionaries to the Sandwich Islands had imported this press around the Horn from New England, and from that time up to 1839 it had served an excellent purpose in furnishing Christian literature to the Kanakas. But the Sandwich Islanders

176

had grown beyond it; and being presented with a finer outfit, the First Native Church at Honolulu made a present of the press, ink and paper to the Missions of Waiilatpui, Lapwai and Walker's Plains.

The whole was valued at $450 at that time. The press was located at Lapwai, and used to print portions of Scripture and hymn books in the Nez Perces language, which books were used in all the missions of the American Board. Visitors to these tribes of Indians twenty-five years after the missions had been broken up, and the Indians had been dispersed, found copies of those books still in use and prized as great treasures.

Another interesting event was the building of the first steamer, the Lot Whitcomb, in the Columbia River waters. This steamer was built of Oregon fir and spruce, and was launched December 26th, 1850, at Milwaukee, then a rival of Portland. It was a staunch, well-equipped vessel, one hundred and sixty feet in length; beam, twenty-four feet; depth of hold, six feet ten inches; breadth over all, forty-two feet seven inches; diameter of wheel, nineteen feet; length of bucket, seven feet; dip one foot eight inches, and draft three feet two inches. It was a staunch and elegantly-equipped little vessel; did good service in the early days, making three round trips each week, from Milwaukee to Astoria, touching at Portland and Vancouver, then the only stopping places. The Whitcomb was finally sent to California, made over, named Annie Abernethy, and was used upon the Sacramento River as a pleasure and passenger boat.

These two beginnings, of the printer's art and the steamer, are all the more interesting when compared with the richness and show in the same fields to-day. The palatial ocean traveling steamers and the power presses and papers, scarcely second to any in editorial and news-gathering ability, best tell the wonderful advance from comparatively nothing at that time.

The taxable property of Oregon in 1893 was $168,088,095; in Washington it was $283,110,032; in Idaho, $34,276,000. The manufactories of Oregon in 1893 turned out products to the value of $245,100,267, and Washington, on fisheries alone, yielded a product valued at $915,500. There has been a great falling off, both in Oregon and Washington, in this source of wealth, and the eager desire to make money will cause the annihilation of this great traffic, unless there is better legal protection. Washington, in 1893, reported 227 saw mills and 300 shingle mills and 73 sash and door mills, and a capital invested in the lumber trade of $25,000,000. A wonderful change since Dr. Whitman sawed his boards by hand as late as 1840.

The acres of forest yet undisturbed in Washington are put down at 23,588,512. During President Harrison's term a wooded tract in the Cascade Mountains, thirty-five by forty miles, including Mount Rainier, was withdrawn from entry, and it is expected that Congress will reserve it for a National Park. The statistics relating to wheat, wool and fruits of all kinds fully justify the claim made by Dr. Whitman to President Tyler and Secretary Webster—that "The United States had better by far give all New England for the cod fisheries of Newfoundland than to sacrifice Oregon."

Reading the statistics of wealth of the States comprising the original territory of Oregon, their fisheries, their farm products, their lumber, their mines, yet scarcely begun to be developed, one wonders at the blindness and ignorance of our statesmen fifty or more years ago, who came so near losing the whole great territory. If Secretary Daniel Webster could have stepped into the buildings of Washington, Oregon and Idaho that contained the wonderful exhibit at the World's Fair, he would doubtless have lifted his thoughts with profound gratitude that Dr. Whitman made his winter ride and saved him from making the blunder of all the century.

If old Senator McDuffie who averred that "The wealth of the Indies could not pay for connecting by steam the Columbia River with the States," could now take his place in a palace car of some one of the four great transcontinental lines, and be whirled over "the inaccessible mountains, and the intervening desert wastes," he, too, might be willing to give more than "A pinch of snuff" for our Pacific possessions.

The original boundaries of Oregon contained over 300,000 square miles, which included all the country above latitude 42 degrees and west of the Rocky Mountains. Its climate is mild and delightful, and in great variety, owing to the natural divisions of great ranges of mountains, and the warm ocean currents which impinge upon its shores, with a rapid current from the hot seas of Asia. This causes about seventy per cent of the winds to blow from the southwest, bringing the warmth of the tropics to a land many hundreds of miles north of New York and Boston. It is felt even at Sitka, nearly 2,000 miles further north than Boston, where ice cannot be gathered for summer use, and whose harbor has never yet been obstructed by ice.

DR. DANIEL K. PEARSONS.

The typical features of the climate of Western Oregon are the rains of Winter and a protracted rainless season in Summer. In other words, there are two distinct seasons in Oregon—wet and dry. Snows in Winter and rains in Summer are exceptional. In Eastern Oregon the climate more nearly approaches conditions in Eastern States. There are not the same extremes, but there are the same features of Winter snow, and, in places, of Summer heat. Southern Oregon is more like Eastern than Western Oregon.

In Eastern Oregon the temperature is lower in Winter and higher in Summer than in Western. The annual rainfall varies from seven to twenty inches.

The Springs in Oregon are delightful; the Summers very pleasant. They are practically rainless, and almost always without great extremes of heat.

Fall rains usually begin in October. It is a noteworthy feature of Oregon Summers, that nights are always cool and refreshing.

The common valley soil of the State is a rich loam, with a subsoil of clay. Along the streams it is alluvial. The "beaverdam lands" of this class are wonderfully fertile. This soil is made through the work of the beavers who dammed up streams and created lakes. When the water was drained away, the

179

detritus covered the ground. The soil of the uplands is less fertile than that of the bottoms and valleys, and is a red, brown and black loam. It produces an excellent quality of natural grass, and under careful cultivation, produces good crops of grain, fruits and vegetables. East of the Cascade Mountains the soil is a dark loam of great depth, composed of alluvial deposits and decomposed lava, overlying a clay subsoil. The constituents of this soil adapt the land peculiarly to the production of wheat.

All the mineral salts which are necessary to the perfect development of this cereal are abundant, reproducing themselves constantly as the gradual processes of decomposition in this soil of volcanic origin proceeds. The clods are easily broken by the plow, and the ground quickly crumbles on exposure to the atmosphere.

In Northwestern Oregon, adjacent to the Columbia River, although the dry season continues for months, this light porous land retains and absorbs enough moisture from the atmosphere, after the particles have been partly disintegrated, to insure perfect development and full harvests.

In Southeastern Oregon, especially in the vast areas of fertile lands in Malheur and Snake River Valleys, the soils are much like those of the Northeastern Oregon region, but there is less moisture. Except in a very small portion of this region, irrigation is necessary to successful agriculture. The water supply is abundant and easily applied.

We have made no attempt to write a complete history of this great section or its wealth, but only to outline such facts as will make more impressive the value to the whole people of the distinguished services of the pioneers who saved this garden spot of the world to the people of the United States. "The Flag of Beauty and Glory" waves over no fairer land, or over no more intelligent, prosperous and happy people. All this too has been reached within the memory of multitudes of living actors; in fact it can be said the glow of youth is yet upon the brow of the young States.

The lover of romance in reality will scarcely repress a sigh of regret,

180

that with Oregon and Washington, the western limit of pioneering has been reached, after the strides of six thousand years.

The circuit of the globe has been completed and the curtain dropped upon the farther shores of Oregon and Washington, with a history as profoundly interesting and dramatic as that written on any section of the world. "The Stars and Stripes" now wave from ocean to ocean, and from the Great Lakes to the Gulf. It is a nation of grand possibilities, whose history would have been marred for all time to come, had any foreign power, however good or great, held possession of the Pacific States. With China open to the world's commerce; with the young giant Japan inciting all the Far East to a new life and energy, the Pacific States of the Republic stand in the very gateway of the world's footsteps, and commerce and wealth. Only when measured in and by the light of such facts, can we fully estimate the value to the whole people of the Nation of the midwinter ride of our hero, and to the brave pioneers of Oregon.

CHAPTER XV.

LIFE ON THE GREAT PLAINS IN PIONEER DAYS.

Nothing better shows the rapid advance of civilization in thi country, than the fact that multitudes of the actors of those eventful years o pioneer life in Oregon and California yet live to see and enjoy the wonderfu transformation. In fact, the pioneer, most of all others, can, in its greates fullness, take in and grasp the luxuries of modern life.

Taking his section in a palace car in luxurious ease, he travels in si: days over the same road which he wearily traveled, forty-five and fifty year ago, in from one hundred and fifty to one hundred and ninety days. The fac is not without interest to him that for more than a thousand miles of the wa on the great central routes, he can throw a stone from the car window int< his old camping grounds.

The old plainsmen were not bad surveyors. They may not have bee advanced in trigonometry or logarithms, but they had keen eyes and rip practical judgment, which enabled them to master the situation. The trail marked and traveled by the old missionaries, nine times in every ten, prove< the best. Many a time did I, and others, by taking what seemed to be invitin "cutoffs," find out to our sorrow that the old trailers of ten years before u had been wiser.

I make this a chapter of personal experience, not for any person;< gratification, but because of the desire to make it real and true in ever particular, and because the data and incidents of travel of the old missionarie are meager and incomplete.

The experiences in 1836, 1843 and 1850, were much the same, sav and except that in 1850 the way was more plainly marked than in 1836, whic then was nothing more than an Indian trail, and even that often misleading Besides that, the pioneer corps had made passable many danger points, an had even left ferries over the most dangerous rivers.

From 1846 to 1856 were ten years of great activity upon the frontier. The starting points for the journey across the plains were many and scattered, from where Kansas City now stands to Fort Leavenworth.

The time of which I write was 1850. Our little company of seven chosen friends, all young and inexperienced in any form of wild life, resolved upon the journey, and began preparations in 1849 and were ready in March, 1850, to take a steamer at Cincinnati for Fort Leavenworth. We had consulted every authority within reach as to our outfit, both for our safety and comfort, and few voyagers ever started upon the long journey who had nearer the essential things, and so few that proved useless.

In one thing we violated the recommendations of all experienced plainsmen, and that was in the purchase of stock. We were advised to buy only mustangs and Mexican mules, but chose to buy in Ohio the largest and finest mules we could find. Our wagons were selected with great care as to every piece of timber and steel in their make-up, and every leather and buckle in the harness was scrutinized.

Instead of a trunk, each carried clothes and valuables in a two-bushel rubber bag, which could be made water-tight or air-tight, if required. Extra shoes were fitted to the feet of each mule and riding horse and one of the number proved to be an expert shoer. The supply of provisions was made a careful study, and we did not have the uncomfortable experience of Dr. and Mrs. Whitman, and run out of flour before the journey was half over.

There is nothing that develops the manhood of a man, or the lack of it, more quickly than life on the plains. There is many a man surrounded by the sustaining influence of the home and of refined society, who seems very much of a man; and yet when these influences are removed, he wilts and dwarfs. I have seen men who had been religious leaders and exemplary in their lives, come from under all such restraints, and, within two months, "swear like troopers."

Our little company was fortunate in being made up of a manly set of young men, who resolved to stand by each other and each do his part. We soon joined the Mt. Sterling Mining Company, led by Major Fellows and Dr. C. P. Schlater, from Mt. Sterling, Ills. They were an excellent set of men and our company was then large enough for protection from any danger in the Indian country, and we kept together without a jar of any kind.

In the year 1850, the Spring upon the frontier was backward. The grass, a necessity for the campaigner upon the plains, was too slow for us, so we bought an old Government wagon, in addition to our regular wagons, filled it with corn, and upon May 1st, struck out through Kansas. It was then unsettled by white people.

On the 5th day of May, we woke up to find the earth enveloped in five inches of snow, and matters looked discouraging, but the sun soon shone out and the snow disappeared and we began to enter into the spirit and enjoyment of the wild life before us.

THE LOG SCHOOL HOUSE ON THE WILLAMETTE.

The Indians were plentiful and visited us frequently, but they were all friendly that year with the whites throughout the border. A war party of the Cheyenne Indians visited us on their way to fight their enemy, the Pawnees. They were, physically, the finest body of men I ever saw. We treated them hospitably and they would have given up their fight and gone with us on a grand buffalo hunt, had we consented. The chief would hardly take no for an answer.

One of the great comforts of the plains traveling in those days, was order and system. Each man knew his duty each day and each night. One day a man would drive; another he would cook; another he would ride on horseback. When we reached the more dangerous Indian country, our camp was arranged for defense in case of an attack, but we always left our mules

184

picketed out to grass all night, and never left them without a guard.

About the most trying labor of that journey was picket duty over the mules at night, especially when the grass was a long distance from the camp, as it sometimes was. After a long day's travel it was a lonesome, tiresome task to keep up all night, or even half of it. The animals were tethered with a rope eighteen feet long buckled to the fore leg, and the other end attached to an iron pin twelve to eighteen inches long, securely driven into the ground. As the animals fed they were moved so as to keep them upon the best pasture. In spite of the best care they would occasionally cross and the mischief would be to pay, unless promptly relieved.

Our greatest fear was from the danger of a stampede, either from Indians or from wild animals. The Indian regards it as a great accomplishment to steal a horse from a white man. One day a well-dressed and very polite Indian came into camp where we were laying by for a rest. He could talk broken English and mapped out the country in the sand over the route we were to travel—told us all about good water and plenty of grass. He informed us that for some days we would go through the good Indian's country, but then we came to the mountains; and then he began to paw the air with his arms and snap an imaginary whip and shout, "Gee Buck—wo haw, damn ye!" Then says our good Indian, "Look out for hoss thieves." Then he got down in the grass and showed us how the Indian would wiggle along in the grass until he found the picket pin and lead his horse out so slowly that the guard would not notice the change, until he was outside the line, when he would mount and ride away.

That very night two of the best horses of the Mt. Sterling Mining Company were stolen in just that way, and to make the act more grievous, they were picketed so near to the tents as to seem to the guards to be perfectly safe. We may have misjudged our "good Indian" who came into camp, but we have always believed that he was there to see whether there were any horses worth stealing, and then did the stealing himself.

We can bear testimony also, that he was a good geographer. His map

185

made in the sand and transferred to paper was perfect, and when we came to the mountains, his "Gee Buck, wo haw, damn ye!" was heard all up and down that mountain. The Indian had evidently been there and knew what he was saying. They gave us but little trouble except to watch our live stock, as the Indian never takes equal chances. He wants always three chances to one, in his favor. To show you are afraid, is to lose the contest with an Indian. I have many times, by showing a brave front, saved my scalp.

Upon one occasion when I had several loose mules leading, I allowed myself unthinkingly to lag for two miles behind the company through a dangerous district. I was hurrying to amend the wrong by a fast trot, when upon a turn in the road a vicious-looking Indian, with his bow half bent and an arrow on the string, stepped from behind a sage bush to the middle of the road and signaled me to stop when twenty feet away.

I was unarmed and made up my mind at once to show no fear. Upon coming within six or eight feet of him, I drove the spurs into my horse and gave such a yell that the Indian had all he could do to dodge my horse's feet. He was evidently astonished and thought, from the boldness of the move, that I had others near by. My horse and mules went on a dead run and I expected, as I leaned forward, every moment to feel his arrow.

I glanced back when fifty yards away and he was anxiously looking back to see who else was coming and I was out of his reach before he had made up his mind. I was never worse frightened.

Upon another occasion I bluffed an Indian just as effectively. With two companions I went to a Sioux village to buy a pair of moccasins. They were at peace and we felt no danger. Most of the men were absent from the village, leaving only a small guard. I got separated from my companions, but found an Indian making moccasins, and I stood in the door and pointed to a new pair about the size I wanted, that hung on the ridge pole, and showed him a pair of handsome suspenders that I would give him for them. He assented by a nod and a grunt, came to the door, took the suspenders and hung them up, deliberately sat down on the floor and took off a dirty old pair he was wearing and threw them to me. I immediately threw them back, and stepping into the tepee, caught hold of the moccasins I had bought, but by a quick motion he snatched them from me.

I then caught hold of the suspenders and bounded out of the door. When fifty feet away I looked back and he had just emerged from his tepee and began loading his rifle. I had emptied both barrels of my shotgun at a plover just before reaching the village and my gun was fortunately unloaded. It gave us equal chances: I stopped still, threw my gun from the strap and began loading. In those days I was something of an expert and before the Indian withdrew his ramrod, I was putting caps on both barrels and he bounded inside his wigwam, and I lost no time in putting a tepee between us, and finding my friends, when we hastily took leave.

Our company took great comfort and pride in our big American mules, trained in civilized Ohio. A pair of the largest, the wheelers in the six-mule team, were as good as setter dogs at night. They neither liked Indians, wolves nor grizzlies; and their scent was so keen they could smell their enemies two hundred yards away, unless the wind was too strong.

When on guard, and in a lonesome, dangerous place, we generally kept close to our long-eared friends, and when they stopped eating and raised their heads and pointed those ponderous ears in any direction, we would drop in the grass and hold ourselves ready for any emergency. They would never resume their feeding until assured that the danger had passed.

And then what faithful fellows to pull! At a word they would plant their feet on a mountain side and never allow the wagon to give back a single foot, no matter how precipitous; and again at the word, they would pull with the precision of a machine.

The off-leader, "Manda," was the handsomest mule ever harnessed. As everybody remarked, "She was as beautiful as a picture." She would pull and stand and hold the wagon as obedient to command as an animal could be, but she was by nature wild and vicious. She was the worst kicker I ever saw. She allowed herself to be shod, seeming to understand that this was a necessity. But no man ever succeeded in riding her. She beat the trick mules in any circus in jumping and kicking.

One night we had a stampede, and one of the flying picket pins struck the mule between the bones of the hind leg, cutting a deep gash, four inches or more long; the swelling of the limb causing the wound to gape open fully two inches. She did not attempt to bear her weight upon the limb, barely touching it to the ground. The flies were very bad, and knowing the animal, and while prizing her so highly, we were all convinced that we must leave her. The train pulled out. It was my duty that morning to bring on the loose stock, and see that nothing of value was overlooked in camp. I was ready to leave, when I went up to the mule that had come with us all the way from home, nearly three thousand miles, and had been a faithful servant, and began petting her, expressing my pity and sorrow that we had to leave her here for the Indians and the wolves. As I rubbed her head and talked to her the poor dumb brute seemed to understand every word said.

Never before in all the long journey had the famous six-mule team gone without Manda prancing as off leader. She rubbed me with her nose and laid it upon my shoulder, and seemed to beg as eloquently as a dumb beast can, "Don't leave me behind." With it all, there was a kindly look in her eye, I never before had seen. I stood stroking her head for some time, then patted her neck and walked a little back, but constantly on guard. It was then the animal turned her head and looked at me, and at the same time held up the wounded leg. My friend Moore, who had staid back to assist, was a little distance off, and I called him.

As he came up, I said to him: "This mule has had a change of heart." He put a bridle upon her so that he could hold up her head, and rubbing her side, I finally ventured to take hold of the wounded leg. I rubbed it and fondled it without her showing any symptom of resentment.

I got out instruments, sewed the wound up, and sewed bandages tight about the leg, made a capital dressing and we started, leading Manda. She

188

soon began to bear weight upon the wounded limb, and had no difficulty in keeping up with the train. When the bandages would get misplaced, one could get down in the road with no one to assist, and adjust them. We took Manda all the way, and no handsomer animal ever journeyed across the plains. She was never known to kick afterward.

People call it "instinct in animals," but the more men know and study dumb life, the more they are impressed with their reasoning intelligence. Dr. Whitman's mule, finding camp in the blinding snow storm on the mountains, when the shrewd guide was hopelessly lost; my old horse leading me and my friend in safety through the Mississippi River back water in the great forest of Arkansas, as well as this, which I have told without an embellishment, all teach impressively the duty of kindness that we owe to our dumb friends.

In Mrs. Whitman's diary we frequently find allusion to her faithful pony, and her sympathy with him when the grass is scarce and the work hard, is but an evidence of true nobility in the woman. In a long journey like the one made from Ohio to the Pacific Coast, it is wonderful what an affection grows up between man and his dumb helpers. And there is no mistaking the fact that animals appreciate and reciprocate such kindness. Even our dog was no exception.

As I have started in to introduce my dumb associates, it would be a mistake, especially for my boy readers, to omit Rover. He was a young dog when we started, but he was a dog of thorough education and large experience before he reached the end of his journey. He was no dog with a long pedigree of illustrious ancestors, but was a mixed St. Bernard and Newfoundland, and grew up large, stately and dignified. He was petted, but never spoiled. When he was tired and wanted to ride, he knew how to tell the fact and was never told that he was nothing but a dog.

He was no shirk as a walker, but the hot saleratus dust and sand wore out his feet. We took the fresh skin of an antelope and made boots for him, but when no one was looking at him he would gnaw them off. When the company separated after reaching the coast, Rover, by unanimous consent, went with his favorite master, J. S. Niswander, now a gray-haired, honored citizen of Gilroy, Cal. A few years ago I visited Niswander and Dr. J. Doan, who, with myself, are the only living survivors of our company, and he gave me the history of Rover after I left for Oregon.

Niswander was a famous grizzly bear hunter, and with Rover as a companion, he made journeys prospecting for gold, and hunting, long distances from civilization. When night came the pack mule was picketed near by and a big fire built, with plenty of wood to keep it replenished during the night. Rover laid himself against his master's feet, and in case of danger he would always waken him with a low growl close to his ear, and when this was done, he would lope off in the dark and find out what it was, while Niswander held his gun and revolver ready for use. If the dog came back and lay down he knew at once it was a false alarm and dropped to sleep in perfect security.

At one time he brought among his provisions a small firkin of butter, a great luxury at that time. He took the firkin and set it in the shade of a great red-wood, tumbled off the rest of his goods, picketed his mule, and went off prospecting for gold, telling Rover to take care of the things until he returned. He was gone all day and returned late in the evening, and looking around could not see his firkin of butter. He told me he turned to the old dog and said: "Rover, I never knew you to do such a trick before and I am ashamed of you." The old fellow only hung his head upon being scolded. But soon after Mr. N. noticed a suspicious pile of leaves about the roots of the tree, and when he had turned them aside he found his firkin of butter untouched.

The high wind which had arisen had blown the paper cover from the butter and the dog knew it ought to be covered, and with his feet and nose had gathered the leaves for more than a rod around and covered it up.

The Indians finally poisoned the old dog for the purpose of robbing his master. Said he: "When Rover died I shed more tears than I had shed for years."

While reading, as I have, Mrs. Whitman's daily diary of her journey in 1836, I am most astonished at the lack of all complaints and murmurings. I know so well the perils and discomforts she met on the way and see her every day, cheerful and smiling and happy, and filled with thankfulness for blessings received, that she seems for the very absence of any repining, to be a woman of the most exalted character.

I have traveled for days and weeks through saleratus dust that made lips, face and eyes tormentingly sore, while the throat and air tubes seemed to be raw. She barely mentions them. I have camped many a time, as she doubtless did, where the water was poisonous with alkali, and unfit for man or beast. I have been stung by buffalo flies until the sting of a Jersey mosquito would be a positive luxury. She barely mentions the pests. She does once mildly say: "The mosquitoes were so thick that we could hardly breathe," and that "the fleas covered all our garments" and made life a burden until she could get clear of them.

Then there were snakes. As far as I know she never once complained of snakes. This makes it all the more necessary in giving a true picture of pioneering upon the plains, to give a real experience. There is nothing more hateful than a snake. We were introduced to the prairie rattler very early in the journey and some had sport over it. We all wore high, rattlesnake boots; they were heavy and hard on the feet that had been accustomed to softer covering.

One of our gallant boys had received a present of a pair of beautiful embroidered slippers from a loved friend, and after supper he threw off those high snake boots and put on his slippers. Just then he was reminded that it was his duty that night to assist in picketing the mules in fresh pasture. He got hold of two lariats and started off singing "The Girl I Left Behind Me." About one hundred and fifty yards off he heard that ominous rattle near by and he dropped those lariats and came into camp at a speed that elicited cheers from the entire crowd.

Early in the journey an old Indian told me how to keep the snakes from our beds, and that was to get a lariat made from the hair of a buffalo's neck and lay it entirely around the bed. I got the lariat and seldom went to sleep without being inside of its coil. It is a fact that a snake will not willingly crawl over such a rope. The sharp prickly bristles are either uncomfortable to them, or they expect there is danger.

One night of horrors never to be forgotten was when I did not have my Indian lariat. Who of my readers ever had a rattlesnake attempt to make a nest in his hair? The story may hardly be worth telling, but I will relate it just as it occurred.

We had camped on the St. Mary's River and had gone four miles off the road to find good grazing for our animals. Supper was over, our bugler had sounded his last note, and we were preparing for bed when a man came in from a camp a mile off and reported that they had found a man on a small island, who was very sick and they wanted a doctor.

Dr. Schlater, of the Mt. Sterling Mining Company, at once got ready and went with him. Dr. Schlater was one of the grand specimens of manhood. He worked with the sick man all night and at daylight came down and asked me to go up with him. While we were bathing him the company of Michigan packers, who had found the stranger, moved off, and left us alone with the sick man, who was delirious and could give no account of himself.

We found from papers in his pockets that his name was West Williams of Bloomington, Iowa, and he carried a card from the I. O. O. F. of that place. We made him as comfortable as possible and went back to our camp and reported his condition. We found the company all ready to move out, only waiting for us. The man was too sick to travel and it would not do to let him remain there alone, and it was decided that Dr. S. and I should remain with him and try and find his friends or hire some person to take care of him, and then, by forced marches, we could follow on and catch the company.

192

We raised a purse of one hundred dollars and with such medicines as we needed and other supplies, also kept back a light spring wagon, and brought the sick man to our camp. I suggested to the Doctor that he ride over to the road and put up some written notices, giving the man's name, etc. He wrote out several and posted them on the trees where they would attract attention from passers. While he was doing this, a man with an ox-team came along and proved to be an old friend of the sick man right from the same locality. His name was Van S. Israel. He at once came with the Doctor and took charge of Williams, greatly to our relief.

While the Doctor was upon the road he was called to prescribe for another sick man by the name of Mahan, from Missouri. Learning where we were located, the Mahans moved down to our camp. The sick man was accompanied by his brother, and they had a splendid outfit. We concluded to give the entire day to the sick men and ride across the small desert just ahead during the night. A tent was erected for Mahan, and he walked in and laid down.

An hour or so later I went to the tent door and looking in saw the man lying dead. I spoke to his brother, who went into the tent convulsed with grief. I had scarcely reached my tent before I heard a piercing scream and rushed back, and upon opening the tent flap was horrified to behold the largest rattlesnake I had ever seen, coiled on the opposite side of the dead body and the living brother crowding as far away as possible on the other side to be out of his reach.

As soon as I appeared the snake uncoiled and slipped under the edge of the tent. I caught up a green cottonwood stick and ran around and he at once coiled for a fight. I let him strike the stick. After striking each time he would try to retreat, but a gentle tap with the stick would arouse his anger and he would coil and strike again. At first a full drop of the yellow fluid appeared upon the stick. This gradually diminished, and with it the courage of the reptile, which seemed to lose all fighting propensity. I then killed him.

Just before sunset we were ready to leave our sad associates, and we

193

rode down to the river to give our mules a drink. The St. Mary's is a deep stream running through a level stretch with no banks. The mules had often been caved into the deep water and learned to get down on their knees to drink. For fear of an accident I got off and allowed my mule to kneel and drink. As he got upon his feet I swung into the saddle and started on. I had scarcely got firmly seated when, right under the mule, a rattler sang out. My double-barrel gun was hanging from my shoulder, muzzle down. As quick as a flash I slipped my arm through the strap, cocked the gun at the same time and the mule shying, brought his snakeship in range, and just as he was in the act of striking, I shot him dead. The only good thing about the rattler is that he always gives the alarm before striking.

A. J. ANDERSON, Ph.D., (left)
First President of Whitman College.

REV. JAMES F. EATON, D.D., (right)
Second President of Whitman College.

It was about three o'clock in the morning when we got through the desert and reached a cluster of trees, and resolved to stop and take a little sleep, and give our mules the feed of grass we had tied behind our saddles. We found a fallen tree and tied our animals to the boughs and fed them. A small company of packers were there asleep with their heads toward the fallen tree. We passed them to near the butt of the tree, threw aside some rotten chunks, spread a blanket, and each rolled up in another, lay down to rest. My snake-lariat was with the wagon, but I was too tired to think much of it. The Doctor being up all the night before, was asleep in two minutes. I was dozing off, with rattlesnakes and all the horrors of the past day running through my mind, when I was suddenly awakened by something pulling and working in my long, bushy hair. Barbers were not plentiful on the plains, and, besides, the plainsmen wear long hair as a protection. I suppose it was only a few minutes of suspense, and yet it seemed an hour, before I became wide awake, and reached at once the conclusion that I had poked my head near the log where his snakeship was sleeping, and the evening being cool, he was trying to secure warmer quarters. I knew it would not do to move my head. I quietly slipped my right arm from the blanket, and slowly moved my hand within six inches of my head. I felt the raking of a harder material, which seemed like a fang scraping the scalp. This made me almost frantic. Suddenly I grasped the offender by the head, jerking hair and all, and, jumping to my feet, yelled, so that every packer bounced to his feet, and seized his gun, thinking we were attacked by Indians. This is a round-about way to tell a snake story, but all the facts had to be recited to reveal the real conditions.

It was forty-five years ago, and the sensations of the time are vivid to this day; and it doesn't even matter that the offender was not a rattler, but only an honest, little, cold-footed tree-toad, trying to get warmed up. But he

195

frightened me as badly as the biggest rattler on the St. Mary's could, and I helped him to make a hop that beat the record of Mark Twain's jumping-frog in his best days.

But life on the plains was not a continued succession of discomforts. The dyspeptic could well afford to make such a journey to gain the appetite and the good digestion. The absence of annoying insect life during the night, and the pure, invigorating air, makes sleep refreshing and health-giving. For a month at a time we have lain down to sleep, looking up at the stars, without the fear of catching cold, or feeling a drop of dew. There are long dreary reaches of plains to pass that are wearisome to the eye and the body, but the mountain scenery is nowhere more picturesquely beautiful.

At that time the sportsman could have a surfeit in all kinds of game, by branching off from the lines of travel and taking the chances of losing his scalp. Herds of antelope were seen every day feeding in the valleys, while farther away there were buffalo by the hundred thousand. The great butchery of these noble animals had then but fairly begun. To-day, there still live but three small herds. Our company did not call it sport to kill buffalo for amusement. It was not sport, but butchery. A man could ride up by the side of his victim and kill him with a pistol.

It was among our rules to allow no team animal to be used in the chase. But I forgot myself once and violated the rule. We were resting that day in camp. In the distance I saw two hunters after a huge buffalo bull, coming toward our camp. I saw by the direction that one could ride around the spur of a high hill about a mile distant and intercept him. We had as a saddle horse of one team an old clay-bank, which was one of the most solemn horses I have ever seen. His beauty was in his great strength and his long mane and tail. But he carried his head on a straight level with his back and never was known to put on any airs. He stood picketed handy, and seizing a bridle and my gun I mounted without a saddle and urged the old horse into a lope.

As I turned the spur of the hill, the bull came meeting me fifty yards

196

away. He was a monster; his tongue protruded, and he was frothing at the mouth from his long run. He showed no signs of turning from his road because of my appearance. Just then, when not more than thirty yards away, my old horse saw him and turned so quickly as to nearly unseat me. He threw up his head until that great mane of his enveloped me; and he broke for the camp at a gait no one ever dreamed he possessed. I did no shooting, but I did the fastest riding I ever indulged in before or since. It is a fact, that a mad buffalo, plunging toward you is only pleasant when you can get out of his way.

The slaughter and annihilation of the buffalo is the most atrocious act ever classed under the head of sport. A few years ago, while traveling over the Great Northern Railway, I saw at different stations ricks of bones from a quarter to a third of a mile long, piled up as high as the tops of the cars, awaiting shipment. I asked one of the experienced and reliable railway officials of the traffic, and he informed me that "Not less than 26,000 car loads of buffalo bones had been shipped over the Great Northern Railroad to the bone factories; and not one in a thousand of the remains had ever been touched." The weight of a full-sized buffalo's bones is about sixty pounds. The traffic is still enormous along these northern lines. If the Indian had any sentiment it would likely be called out as he wanders over the plains and gathers up the dry bones of these well-nigh extinct wild herds, that fed and clothed his tribe through so many generations.

I have seen beautiful horses, but never saw any half so handsome as the wild horses upon the plains. The tame horse, however well groomed, is despoiled of his grandeur. He compares with his wild brother as the plebeian compares with royalty. I saw a beautiful race between two Greasers who were chasing a herd of wild horses. They were running parallel with the road I was traveling, and I spurred up and ran by their side some four hundred yards distant, and had a chance to study them for many miles.

I afterward saw a handsome stallion that had just been caught. He was tied and in a corral, but if one approached he would jump at him and strike and kick as savagely as possible. His back showed saddle marks, which

197

proved that he had not always been the wild savage he had then become. The mountains and hills where the wild horses were then most numerous were covered with wild oats, which gave the country the appearance of large cultivation.

Among the interesting facts which the traveler on the great plains learns, and often to his discomfort, is the deception as to distance. He sees something of interest and resolves "it is but two miles away," but the chances are that it will prove to be eight or ten miles. The country is made up of great waves. Looking off you see the top of a wave, and when you get there a valley that you did not see, stretches away for miles.

We always tried to treat our Indian guests courteously, but they were often voted a nuisance. While cooking our supper they would often form a circle, twenty or thirty of them sitting on the ground, and they looked so longingly at the bread and ham and coffee, that it almost took one's appetite away. We could only afford to give the squaws what was left. To fill up such a crowd would have soon ended our stock of supplies.

One of the things that made an Indian grunt, and even laugh, was to see our cook baking pancakes in a long-handled frying pan. To turn the cake over he tossed it in the air and caught it as it came down. A cook on the plains that could not do that was not up in his business.

Except upon the mountains and rocky canyons, the roads were as good as a turnpike; but some of the climbs and descents were fearful, while an occasional canyon, miles long, looked wholly impassable without breaking the legs of half the animals and smashing the wagons.

The old plainsmen had a way of setting tires upon a loose wheel that was novel. Our tires became very loose from the long dry reaches. We took off the tire, tacked a slip of fresh hide entirely around the rim, heated the tire, dropped it on the wheel and quickly chucked it into the water and had wheels as good as new.

Our company was three nights and two days and nearly a half in crossing the widest desert. It was a beautiful firm road until we struck deep sand, which extended out for eleven miles from Carson River into the desert. Before starting we emptied our rubber clothes sacks, filled them with water, hauled hay, which we had cured, to feed our mules, and made the trip as pleasantly as if upon green sod. The lack of water on this wide desert had left many thousand bones of dead animals bleaching upon its wastes. Many wells had been dug in various places and we tested the water in them and found it intensely salt. The entire space is evidently the bed of a salt sea.

In the long reaches where no trees of any kind grow, the entire dependence of the early pioneer for fire was upon buffalo chips, the animal charcoal of the plains. It makes a good fire and is in no way offensive. And if no iron horse had invaded the plains, buffalo chips would be selling all along the route to-day at forty dollars per ton.

One of the pleasant historical events in which our company naturally takes a pride is, that one night we camped upon a little mountain stream near where the city of Denver now stands; the whole land as wild as nature made it. Many years afterward one of the little band, Frank Denver, was elected Lieutenant-Governor of Colorado, and Gen. J. W. Denver was among the most prominent politicians of the coast, and the city of Denver was named in honor of them. I have thus, as concisely as I could, sketched life as it was in a wagon journey across the plains forty-five and fifty years ago. It was a memorable experience, and none who took it will fail to have of it a vivid remembrance as long as life lasts. If its annoyances were many, its novelties and pleasing remembrances were so numerous as to make it the notable journey of even the most adventurous life.

APPENDIX.

NARRATIVE OF THE WINTER TRIP ACROSS THE ROCKY MOUNTAINS OF DR. MARCUS WHITMAN AND HON. A. LAWRENCE LOVEJOY, IN 1842, FURNISHED BY REQUEST, FROM MR. LOVEJOY, THE SURVIVOR.

Oregon City, Feb. 14, 1876.

Dr. Atkinson—Dear Sir: In compliance with your request, I wil endeavor to give you some idea of the journey of the late Dr. Marcu Whitman from Oregon to Washington, in the winter of 1842 and '43. True, was the Doctor's traveling companion in that arduous and trying journey, bu it would take volumes to describe the many thrilling scenes and dangerou hair-breadth escapes we passed through, traveling, as we did, almost th entire route through a hostile Indian country, and enduring much sufferin from the intense cold and snow we had to encounter in passing over th Rocky Mountains in midwinter. I crossed the plains in company with D White and others, and arrived at Waiilatpui the last of September, 1842. M party camped some two miles below Dr. Whitman's place. The day after ou arrival Dr. Whitman called at our camp and asked me to accompany him t his house, as he wished me to draw up a memorial to Congress to prohib the sale of ardent spirits in this country. The Doctor was alive to the interest of this coast, and manifested a very warm desire to have it properl represented at Washington; and after numerous conversations with th Doctor touching the future prosperity of Oregon, he asked me one day in very anxious manner, if I thought it would be possible for him to cross th mountains at that time of the year. I told him I thought he could. He nex asked: "Will you accompany me?" After a little reflection, I told him I woul His arrangements were rapidly made. Through the kindness of Mr. McKinl then stationed at Fort Walla Walla, Mrs. Whitman was provided with suitabl escorts to the Willamette Valley, where she was to remain with her missionary friends until the Doctor's return. We left Waiilatpui, October 3, 1842, traveled rapidly, reached Fort Hall in eleven days, remained two days to recruit and make a few purchases. The Doctor engaged a guide and we left for Fort Uintah. We changed from a direct route to one more southern, through the Spanish country via Salt Lake, Taos and Santa Fe. On our way from Fort Hall to Fort Uintah, we had terribly severe weather. The snows retarded our progress and blinded the trail so we lost much time. After arriving at Fort Uintah and making some purchases for our trip, we took a new guide and started for Fort Uncompahgra, situated on the waters of Grand River, in the Spanish country. Here our stay was very short.

We took a new guide and started for Taos. After being out some four or five days we encountered a terrible snow storm, which forced us to seek shelter in a deep ravine, where we remained snowed in for four days, at which time the storm had somewhat abated, and we attempted to make our way out upon the high lands, but the snow was so deep and the winds so piercing and cold we were compelled to return to camp and wait a few days for a change of weather.

Our next effort to reach the high lands was more successful; but after spending several days wandering around in the snow without making much headway, our guide told us that the deep snow had so changed the face of the country that he was completely lost and could take us no farther. This was a terrible blow to the Doctor, but he was determined not to give it up without another effort. We at once agreed that the Doctor should take the guide and return to Fort Uncompahgra and get a new guide, and I remain in camp with the animals until he could return; which he did in seven days with our new guide, and we were now on our route again. Nothing of much importance occurred but hard and slow traveling through deep snow until we reached Grand River, which was frozen on either side about one-third across. Although so intensely cold, the current was so very rapid, about one-third of the river in the center was not frozen. Our guide thought it would be dangerous to attempt to cross the river in its present condition, but the Doctor, nothing daunted, was the first to take the water. He mounted his horse and the guide and myself shoved the Doctor and his horse off the ice into the foaming stream. Away he went completely under water, horse and all, but directly came up, and after buffeting the rapid, foaming current he reached the ice on the opposite shore a long way down the stream. He leaped from his horse upon the ice and soon had his noble animal by his side. The guide and myself forced in the pack animals and followed the Doctor's example, and were soon on the opposite shore drying our frozen clothes by a comfortable fire. We reached Taos in about thirty days, suffering greatly from cold and scarcity of provisions. We were compelled to use mule meat, dogs and such other animals as came in our reach. We remained at Taos a few days only, and started for Bent's and Savery's Fort, on the headwaters of the Arkansas River. When we had been out some fifteen or twenty days, we met George Bent, a brother of Gov. Bent, on his way to Taos. He told us that a party of mountain men would leave Bent's Fort in a few days for St. Louis, but said we would not reach the fort with our pack animals in time to join the party. The Doctor being very anxious to join the party so he could push on as rapidly as possible to Washington, concluded to leave myself and guide with the animals, and he himself, taking the best animal, with some bedding and a small allowance of provision, started alone, hoping by rapid travel to reach the fort in time to join the St. Louis party, but to do so he would have to travel on the Sabbath, something we had not done before. Myself and guide traveled on slowly and reached the fort in four days, but imagine our astonishment, when on making inquiry about the Doctor, we were told that he had not arrived nor had he been heard of.

I learned that the party for St. Louis was camped at the Big Cottonwood, forty miles from the fort, and at my request, Mr. Savery sent an express telling the party not to proceed any further until we learned something of Dr. Whitman's whereabouts, as he wished to accompany them to St. Louis. Being furnished by the gentlemen of the fort with a suitable guide, I started in search of the Doctor, and traveled up the river about one hundred miles. I learned from the Indians that a man had been there, who was lost, and was trying to find Bent's Fort. They said they had directed him to go down the river, and how to find the fort. I knew from their description it was the Doctor. I returned to the fort as rapidly as possible, but the Doctor had not arrived. We had all become very anxious about him.

Late in the afternoon he came in very much fatigued and desponding; said that he knew that God had bewildered him to punish him for traveling on the Sabbath. During the whole trip he was very regular in his morning and evening devotions, and that was the only time I ever knew him to travel on the Sabbath.

The Doctor remained all night at the fort, starting early on the following morning to join the St. Louis party. Here we parted. The Doctor proceeded to Washington. I remained at Bent's Fort until Spring, and joined the Doctor the following July, near Fort Laramie, on his way to Oregon, in company with a train of emigrants. He often expressed himself to me about the remainder of his journey, and the manner in which he was received at Washington, and by the Board for Foreign Missions at Boston. He had several interviews with President Tyler, Secretary Webster, and a good many members of Congress—Congress being in session at that time. He urged the immediate termination of the treaty with Great Britain relative to this country, and begged them to extend the laws of the United States over Oregon, and asked for liberal inducements to emigrants to come to this coast. He was very cordially and kindly received by the President and members of Congress, and, without doubt, the Doctor's interviews resulted greatly to the benefit of Oregon and to this coast. But his reception at the Board for Foreign Missions was not so cordial. The Board was inclined to censure him for leaving his post. The Doctor came to the frontier settlement, urging the citizens to emigrate to the Pacific. He left Independence, Mo., in the month of May, 1843, with an emigrant train of about one thousand souls for Oregon. With his energy and knowledge of the country, he rendered them great assistance in fording the many dangerous and rapid streams they had to cross, and in finding a wagon road through many of the narrow rugged passes of the mountains. He arrived at Waiilatpui about one year from the time he left, to find his home sadly dilapidated, his flouring mill burned. The Indians were very hostile to the Doctor for leaving them, and without doubt, owing to his absence, the seeds of assassination were sown by those haughty Cayuse Indians which resulted in his and Mrs. Whitman's death, with

203

many others, although it did not take place until four years later.

I remain with great respect,

A. LAWRENCE LOVEJOY.

HEE-OH-KS-TE-KIN.—The Rabbit's Skin Leggins. (Drawn by George Catlin.)

The only one of five Nez Perces Chiefs (some say there were only four) who visited St. Louis in 1832, that lived to return to his people to tell the story.

HCO-A-HCO-A-HCOTES-MIN.—No Horns on His Head.

This one died on his return journey near the mouth of Yellowstone River.

This is what Catlin says himself: "These two men when I painted them, were in beautiful Sioux dresses, which had been presented to them in a talk with the Sioux, who treated them very kindly, while passing through the Sioux country. These two men were part of a delegation that came across the Rocky Mountains to St. Louis, a few years since, to inquire for the truth of a representation which they said some white man had made among them, "That our religion was better than theirs, and that they would be all lost if they did not embrace it." Two old and venerable men of this party died in St. Louis, and I traveled two thousand miles, companions with these two fellows, toward their own country, and became much pleased with their manners and dispositions. When I first heard the report of the object of this extraordinary mission across the mountains, I could scarcely believe it; but, on conversing with Gen. Clark, on a future occasion, I was fully convinced of the fact."

See Catlin's Eight Years, and Smithsonian Report for 1885, 2nd part.

DR. WHITMAN'S LETTER.

TO THE HON. JAMES M. PORTER, SECRETARY OF WAR, WITH A BILL TO BE LAID BEFORE CONGRESS, FOR ORGANIZATION OF OREGON.

The Rev. Myron Eells obtained from the original files of the office of the Secretary of War two valuable papers. They bear this endorsement:

"Marcus Whitman inclosing synopsis of a bill, with his views in reference to importance of the Oregon Territory, War. 382—rec. June 22 1844.

To the Hon. James M. Porter, Secretary of War:

Sir—In compliance with the request you did me the honor to make last Winter, while in Washington, I herewith transmit to you the synopsis of a bill which, if it could be adopted, would, according to my experience and observation, prove highly conducive to the best interests of the United States generally, to Oregon, where I have resided for more than seven years as missionary, and to the Indian tribes that inhabit the immediate country. The Government will now doubtless for the first time be apprised through you or by means of this communication, of the immense immigration of families to Oregon which has taken place this year. I have, since our interview, been instrumental in piloting across the route described in the accompanying bill and which is the only eligible wagon road, no less than three hundred families, consisting of one thousand persons of both sexes, with their wagons, amounting to one hundred and twenty, six hundred and ninety-four oxen, and seven hundred and seventy-three loose cattle.

The emigrants are from different States, but principally from Missouri, Arkansas, Illinois and New York. The majority of them are farmers lured by the prospect of bounty in lands, by the reported fertility of the soil and by the desire to be first among those who are planting our institutions on the Pacific Coast. Among them are artisans of every trade, comprising, with farmers, the very best material for a new colony. As pioneers, these people have undergone incredible hardships, and having now safely passed the Blue Mountain Range with their wagons and effects, have established a durable road from Missouri to Oregon, which will serve to mark permanently the route for larger numbers, each succeeding year, while they have practically demonstrated that wagons drawn by horses or oxen can cross the Rocky Mountains to the Columbia River, contrary to all the sinister assertions of all those who pretended it to be impossible.

In their slow progress, these persons have encountered, as in all former instances, and as all succeeding emigrants must, if this or some similar bill be not passed by Congress, the continual fear of Indian aggression, the actual loss through them of horses, cattle and other property, and the great labor of transporting an adequate amount of provisions for so long a journey. The bill herewith proposed would, in a great measure, lessen these inconveniences by the establishment of posts, which, while having the possessed power to keep the Indians in check, thus doing away with the necessity of military vigilance on the part of the traveler by day and night, would be able to furnish them in transit with fresh supplies of provisions, diminishing the original burdens of the emigrants, and finding thus a ready and profitable market for their produce—a market that would, in my opinion, more than suffice to defray all the current expenses of such post. The present party is supposed to have expended no less than $2,000 at Laramie's and Bridger's Forts, and as much more at Fort Hall and Fort Boise, two of the Hudson Bay Company's stations. These are at present the only stopping places in a journey of 2,200 miles, and the only place where additional supplies can be obtained, even at the enormous rate of charge, called mountain prices, i. e., $50 the hundred for flour, and $50 the hundred for coffee; the same for sugar, powder, etc.

Many cases of sickness and some deaths took place among those who accomplished the journey this season, owing, in a great measure, to the uninterrupted use of meat, salt and fresh, with flour, which constitute the chief articles of food they are able to convey on their wagons, and this could be obviated by the vegetable productions which the posts in contemplation could very profitably afford them. Those who rely on hunting as an auxiliary support, are at present unable to have their arms repaired when out of order; horses and oxen become tender-footed and require to be shod on this long journey, sometimes repeatedly, and the wagons repaired in a variety of ways. I mention these as valuable incidents to the proposed measure, as it will also be found to tend in many other incidental ways to benefit the migratory population of the United States choosing to take this direction, and on these accounts, as well as for the immediate use of the posts themselves, they ought to be provided with the necessary shops and mechanics, which would at the same time exhibit the several branches of civilized art to the Indians.

The outlay in the first instance would be but trifling. Forts like those of the Hudson Bay Company's surrounded by walls enclosing all the buildings, and constructed almost entirely of adobe, or sun-dried bricks, with stone foundations only, can be easily and cheaply erected.

There are very eligible places for as many of these as the Government will find necessary, at suitable distances, not further than one or two hundred miles apart, at the main crossing of the principal streams that now form impediments to the journey, and consequently well supplied with water, having alluvial bottom lands of a rich quality, and generally well wooded. If I might be allowed to suggest, the best sites for said posts, my personal knowledge and observation enable me to recommend first, the main crossing of the Kansas River, where a ferry would be very convenient to the traveler, and profitable to the station having it in charge; next, and about eighty miles distant, the crossing of the Blue River, where in times of unusual freshet, a ferry would be in like manner useful; next and distant from one hundred to one hundred and fifty miles from the last mentioned, the Little Blue, or Republican Fork of the Kansas; next, and from sixty to one hundred miles distant from the last mentioned, the point of intersection of the Platte River; next, and from one hundred to one hundred and fifty miles distant from the last mentioned, crossing of the South Fork of the Platte River; next, and about one hundred and eighty or two hundred miles distant from the last mentioned, Horseshoe Creek, which is about forty miles west of Laramie's

Fork in the Black Hills. Here is a fine creek for mills and irrigation, good land for cultivation, fine pasturage, timber and stone for building. Other locations may be had along the Platte and Sweetwater, on the Green River, or Black's Forks of the Bear River, near the great Soda Springs, near Fort Hall, and at suitable places down to the Columbia. These localities are all of the best description, so situated as to hold a ready intercourse with the Indians in their passage to and from the ordinary buffalo hunting grounds, and in themselves so well situated in all other respects as to be desirable to private enterprise if the usual advantage of trade existed. Any of the farms above indicated would be deemed extremely valuable in the States.

The Government cannot long overlook the importance of superintending the savages that endanger this line of travel, and that are not yet in treaty with it. Some of these are already well known to be led by desperate white men and mongrels, who form bandits in the most difficult passes, and are at all times ready to cut off some lagging emigrant in the rear of the party, or some adventurous one who may proceed a few miles in advance, or at night to make a descent upon the sleeping camp and carry away or kill horses and cattle. This is the case even now in the commencement of our western immigration, and when it comes to be more generally known that large quantities of valuable property and considerable sums of money are yearly carried over this desolate region, it is feared that an organized banditti will be instituted. The posts in contemplation would effectually counteract this. For the purpose they need not, or ought not, to be military establishments. The trading posts in this country have never been of such a character, and yet with very few men in them, have for years kept the surrounding Indians in the most pacific disposition, so that the traveler feels secure from molestation upon approaching Fort Laramie, Bridger's Fort, Fort Hall, etc., etc. The same can be obtained without any considerable expenditure by the Government, while by investing the officers in charge with competent authority, all evil-disposed white men, refugees from justice, or discharged vagabonds from trading posts might be easily removed from among the Indians and sent to the appropriate States for trial. The Hudson Bay Company's system of rewards among the savages would soon enable the posts to root out these desperadoes. A direct and friendly intercourse with all the tribes, even to the Pacific, might be thus maintained; the Government would become more intimately acquainted with them, and they with the Government, and instead of sending to the State courts a manifestly guilty Indian to be arraigned before a distant tribunal and acquitted for the want of testimony, by the technicalities of lawyers and of the law unknown to them, and sent back into the wilderness loaded with presents as an inducement to further crime, the post should be enabled to execute summary justice, as if the criminal had been already condemned by his tribe, because the tribe will be sure to deliver up none but the party whom they know to be guilty. They will in that way receive the trial of their peers, and secure within themselves to all intents and purposes, if not technically the trial by jury, yet the spirit of that trial. There are many powers which ought to reside in some person on this extended route for the convenience and even necessity of the public.

In this the emigrant and the people of Oregon are no more interested than the resident inhabitants of the States. At present no person is authorized to administer an oath, or legally attest a fact, from the western line of Missouri to the Pacific. The immigrant cannot dispose of his property at home, although an opportunity ever so advantageous to him should occur after he passes the western border of Missouri. No one can here make a legal demand and protest of a promissory note or bill of exchange. No one can secure the valuable testimony of a mountaineer, or an immigrating witness after he has entered this, at present, lawless country. Causes do exist and will continually arise, in which the private rights of citizens are, and will be, seriously prejudiced by such an utter absence of legal authority. A contraband trade from Mexico, the introduction from that country of liquors to be sold among the Indians west of the Kansas River, is already carried on with the mountain trappers, and very soon the teas, silks, nankeens, spices, camphor and opium of the East Indies will find their way, duty free, through Oregon, across the mountains and into the States, unless Custom House officers along this line find an interest in intercepting them.

Your familiarity with the Government policy, duties and interest renders it unnecessary for me to more than hint at the several objects intended by the enclosed bill, and any enlargement upon the topics here suggested as inducements to its adoption would be quite superfluous, if not impertinent. The very existence of such a system as the one above recommended suggests the utility of postoffices and mail arrangements, which it is the wish of all who now live in Oregon to have granted them; and I need only add that contracts for this purpose will be readily taken at reasonable rates for transporting the mail across from Missouri to the mouth of the Columbia in forty days, with fresh horses at each of the contemplated posts. The ruling policy proposed regards the Indians as the police of the country, who are to be relied upon to keep the peace, not only for themselves, but to repel lawless white men and prevent banditti, under the solitary guidance of the superintendents of the several posts, aided by a well directed system to induce the punishment of crime. It will only be after the failure of these means to procure the delivery or punishment of violent, lawless and savage acts of aggression, that a band or tribe should be regarded as conspirators against the peace, or punished accordingly by force of arms.

Hoping that these suggestions may meet your approbation, and conduce to the future interest of our growing country, I have the honor to be, Honorable Sir,

Your obedient servant,
MARCUS WHITMAN.

COPY OF PROPOSED BILL PREPARED BY DR. MARCUS WHITMAN IN 1843 AND SENT TO THE SECRETARY OF WAR.

A bill to promote safe intercourse with the Territory of Oregon, to suppress violent acts of aggression on the part of certain Indian tribes west of the Indian Territory, Neocho, better protect the revenue, for the transportation of the mail and for other purposes.

SYNOPSIS OF THE ACT.

Section 1.—To be enacted by the Senate and House of Representatives of the United States of America, in Congress assembled, that from and after the passage of this act, there shall be established at suitable distances, and in convenient and proper places, to be selected by the President, a chain of agricultural posts or farming stations, extending at intervals from the present most usual crossing, of the Kansas River, west of the western boundary of the State of Missouri, thence ascending the Platte River on the southern border, thence through the valley of the Sweetwater River to Fort Hall, and thence to settlements of the Willamette in the Territory of Oregon. Which said posts will have for their object to set examples of civilized industry to the several Indian tribes, to keep them in proper subjection to the laws of the United States, to suppress violent and lawless acts along the said line of the frontier, to facilitate the passage of troops and munitions of war into and out of the said Territory of Oregon and the transportation of the mail as hereinafter provided.

Section 2.—And be it further enacted, that there shall reside at each of said posts, one superintendent having charge thereof, with full power to carry into effect the provisions of this act, subject always to such instructions as the President may impose; one deputy superintendent to act in like manner in case of death, removal or absence of the superintendent, and such artificers and laborers, not exceeding twenty in number, as the said superintendent may deem necessary for the conduct and safety of said posts.

212

all of whom shall be subject to appointment and liable to removal.

Section 3.—And be it further enacted, that it shall be the duty of the President to cause to be erected, at each of the said posts, buildings suitable for the purpose herein contemplated, to-wit, one main dwelling house, one storehouse, one blacksmith's and one gunsmith's shop, one carpenter shop, with such and so many other buildings, for storing the products and supplies of said posts as he from time to time may deem expedient. To supply the same with all necessary mechanical and agricultural implements, to perform the labor incident thereto, and with all other articles he may judge requisite and proper for the safety, comfort and defense thereof.

To cause said posts in his discretion to be visited by detachments of troops stationed on the western frontier, to suppress through said posts the sale of munitions of war to the Indian tribes in case of hostilities, and annually to lay before Congress, at its general session, full returns, verified by the oaths of the several superintendents, of the several acts by them performed and of the condition of said posts, with the income and expenditures growing out of the same respectively.

Section 4.—And be it further enacted, that the said superintendents shall be appointed by the President by and with the advice and consent of the Senate for the term of four years, with a salary of two hundred dollars payable out of any moneys in the treasury not otherwise appropriated; that they shall respectively take an oath before the District Judge of the United States for the Western District of Missouri, faithfully to discharge the duties imposed on them in and by the provisions of this act, and give a bond to the President of the United States and to his successors in office and assigns, and with sufficient security to be approved by the said judge in at least the penalty of twenty-five thousand dollars, to indemnify the President or his successors or assigns for any unlawful acts by them performed, or injuries committed by virtue of their offices, which said bonds may at any time be assigned for prosecution against the said respective superintendents and their sureties upon application to the said judge at the instance of the United States District Attorney or of any private party aggrieved.

Section 5.—And be it further enacted, that it shall be the duty of said superintendents to cause the soil adjacent to said posts, in extent not exceeding 640 acres, to be cultivated in a farmer-like manner and to produce such articles of culture as in their judgment shall be deemed the most profitable and available for the maintenance of said posts, for the supply of troops and other Government agents which may from time to time resort thereto, and to render the products aforesaid adequate to defraying all the expenses of labor in and about said posts, and the salary of the said deputy superintendent, without resort to the Treasury of the United States, remitting to the Secretary of the Treasury yearly a sworn statement of the same, with the surplus moneys, if any there shall be.

Section 6.—And be it further enacted, that the said several superintendents of posts shall, ex-officia, be Superintendents of Indian Affairs west of the Indian Territory, Neocho, subordinate to and under the full control of the Commissioner-General of Indian affairs at Washington. That they shall by virtue of their offices, be conservators of the peace, with full powers to the extent hereinafter prescribed, in all cases of crimes and misdemeanors, whether committed by citizens of the United States or by Indians within the frontier line aforesaid. That they shall have power to administer oaths, to be valid in the several courts of the United States, to perpetuate testimony to be used in said courts, to take acknowledgments of deeds and other specialties in writing, to take probate of wills and the testaments executed upon the said frontier, of which the testators shall have died in transit between the State of Missouri and the Territory of Oregon, and to do and certify all notarial acts, and to perform the ceremony of marriage, with as legal effect as if the said several acts above enumerated had been performed by the magistrates of any of the States having power to perform the service. That they shall have power to arrest and remove from the line aforesaid all disorderly white persons, and all persons exciting the Indians to hostilities, and to surrender up all fugitives from justice upon the requisition of the Governor of any of the States; that they shall have power to demand of the several tribes within the said frontier line, the surrender of any Indian or Indians committing acts in contradiction of the laws of the

214

United States, and in case of such surrender, to inflict punishment thereon according to the tenor and effect of said laws, without further trial, presuming such offending Indian or Indians to have received the trial and condemnation of the tribe to which he or they may belong; to intercept and seize all articles of contraband trade, whether introduced into their jurisdiction in violation of the acts imposing duties on imports, or of the acts to regulate trade and intercourse with the several Indian tribes, to transmit the same to the Marshal of the Western District of Missouri, together with the proofs necessary for the confiscation thereof, and in every such case the Superintendent shall be entitled to receive one-half the sale value of the said confiscated articles, and the other half be disposed of as in like cases arising under the existing revenue laws.

Section 7.—And be it further enacted, that the several Superintendents shall have and keep at their several Posts, seals of office for the legal authentication of their public acts herein enumerated, and that the said seals shall have as a device the spread-eagle, with the words, "U. S. Superintendency of the Frontier," engraved thereon.

Section 8.—And be it further enacted, that the said Superintendents shall be entitled, in addition to the salary hereinbefore granted, the following perquisites and fees of office, to-wit: For the acknowledgment of all deeds and specialties, the sum of one dollar; for the administration of all oaths, twenty-five cents; for the authentication of all copies of written instruments, one dollar; for the perpetuation of all testimony to be used in the United States courts, by the folio, fifty cents; for the probate of all wills and testaments, by the folio, fifty cents; for all other writing done, by the folio, fifty cents; for solemnizing marriages, two dollars, including the certificate to be given to the parties; for the surrender of fugitives from justice, in addition to the necessary costs and expenses of arrest and detention, which shall be verified to the demanding Governor by the affidavit of the Superintendent, ten dollars.

Section 9.—And be it further enacted, that the said Superintendents shall, by virtue of their offices, be postmasters at the several stations for which they were appointed, and as such, shall be required to facilitate the transportation of mail to and from the Territory of Oregon and the nearest postoffice within the State of Missouri, subject to all the regulations of the Postoffice Department, and with all the immunities and privileges of the postmasters in the several States, except that no additional compensation shall be allowed for such services; and it is hereby made the duty of the Postmaster General to cause proposals to be issued for the transportation of the mail along the line of said Posts to and from said Territory within six months after the passage of this Act.

Section 10.—And be it further enacted, that the sum of —— thousand dollars be, and the same is hereby appropriated out of any moneys in the treasury not otherwise appropriated, for the purpose of carrying into effect the several provisions of this act.

DR. WHITMAN'S SUGGESTIONS TO THE SECRETARY OF WAR, AND TO THE COMMISSIONERS ON INDIAN AFFAIRS AND OREGON, IN THE U. S. SENATE AND HOUSE OF REPRESENTATIVES, DATED OCTOBER 16, 1847.

Perhaps the last work or writing of a public character done by Dr. Whitman, bears the date of Waiilatpui, October 16th, 1847. It was only one month before the massacre, and addressed as follows:

To the Honorable the Secretary of War, to the Committees on Indian Affairs and Oregon, in the Senate and House of Representatives of the United States, the following suggestions are respectfully submitted:

1st. That all Stations of the United States for troops be kept upon the borders of some State or Territory, when designed for the protection and regulation of Indian territory.

2nd. That a line of Posts be established along the traveled route to Oregon, at a distance, so far as practicable, of not more than 50 miles. That these Posts be located so as to afford the best opportunity for agriculture and grazing, to facilitate the production of provisions, and the care of horses and cattle, for the use and support of said Posts, and to furnish supplies to all passers through Indian territory, especially to mail-carriers and troops.

These Posts should be placed wherever a bridge or ferry would be required to facilitate the transport of the mail, and travel of troops or immigrants through the country.

In all fertile places, these Posts would support themselves, and give facilities for the several objects just named in transit. The other Posts, situated where the soil would not admit of cultivation, would still be useful, as they would afford the means of taking care of horses, and other facilities of transporting the mails.

These Posts could be supplied with provisions from others in the vicinity. A few large Posts in the more fertile regions could supply those more in the mountains.

On the other hand, military Posts can only be well supplied when near the settlements. In this way all transports for the supply of interior military Posts would be superseded.

The number of men at these Posts might vary from five to twenty-five.

In the interior the buildings may be built with adobes, that is, large unburnt bricks; and in form and size should much resemble the common Indian Trading Posts, with outer walls and bastions.

They would thus afford the same protection in any part of the territory as the common Trading Posts.

If provided with a small amount of goods, such goods could be bartered with the Indians for necessary supplies, as well as, on proper occasions, given to chiefs as a reward for punishing those who disturb or offend against the peace of the territory.

By these means the Indians would become the protectors of those Stations.

At the same time by being under one General Superintendent, subject to the inspection of the Government, the Indians may be concentrated under one general influence.

By such a superintendence the Indians would be prevented from fleeing from one place to another to secrete themselves from justice. By this simple arrangement all the need of troops in the interior would be obviated unless in some instance when the Indians fail to co-operate with the Superintendent of the Post or Posts, for the promotion of peace.

When troops shall be called for, to visit the interior, the farming Posts will be able to furnish them with supplies in passing so as to make their movements speedy and efficient.

A code of laws for the Indian territory might constitute as civil magistrates the first, or second, in command of these Posts.

The same arrangement would be equally well adapted for the respective routes to California and New Mexico.

Many reasons may be urged for the establishment of these Posts, among which are the following:

1st. By means of such Posts, all acts of the Indians would be under a full and complete inspection. All cases of murder, theft, or other outrage would be brought to light and the proper punishment inflicted.

2nd. In most cases this may be done by giving the Chiefs a small fee that they may either punish the offenders themselves, or deliver them up to the commander of the Post. In such cases it should be held that their peers have adjudged them guilty before punishment is inflicted.

3rd. By means of these Posts it will become safe and easy for the smallest number to pass and repass from Oregon to the States; and with a civil magistrate at each Station, all idle wandering white men without passports can be sent out of the territory.

4th. In this way all banditti for robbing the mails or travelers would be prevented, as well as all vagabonds removed from among the Indians.

5th. Immigrants now lose horses and other stock by the Indians, commencing from the border of the States to the Willamette. It is much to the praise of our countrymen that they bear so long with the Indians when our Government has done so little to enable them to pass in safety.

For one man to lose five or six horses is not a rare occurrence, which loss is felt heavily, when most of the family are compelled to walk, to favor a reduced and failing team.

6th. The Indians along the line take courage from the forbearance of the immigrants. The timid Indians on the Columbia have this year in open day attacked several parties of wagons, numbering from two to seven, and robbed them, being armed with guns, bows and arrows, knives and axes. Mr. Glenday from St. Charles, Mo., the bearer of this communication to the States, with Mr. Bear, his companion, rescued seven wagons from being plundered, and the people from gross insults, rescuing one woman, when the Indians were in the act of taking all the clothes from her person. The men were mostly stripped of their shirts and pantaloons at the time.

7th. The occasional supplies to passing immigrants, as well as the aid which may be afforded to the sick and needy, are not the least of the important results to follow from these establishments.

A profitable exchange to the Posts and immigrants, as also to others journeying through the country, can be made by exchanging worn-out horses and cattle for fresh ones.

8th. It scarcely need be mentioned what advantage the Government will derive by a similar exchange for the transport of the mail, as also for the use of troops passing through.

9th. To suppress the use of ardent spirits among the Indians it will be requisite to regard the giving or furnishing of it in any manner as a breach of the laws and peace of the territory.

All Superintendents of Posts, traders, and responsible persons, should be charged on oath, that they will not sell, give or furnish in any manner, ardent spirits to the Indians.

10th. Traders should be regarded by reason of the license they have to trade in the territory, as receiving a privilege, and therefore should be required to give and maintain good credentials of character. For this reason they may be required to send in the testimony of all their clerks and assistants of all ranks, to show under the solemnity of an oath, that the laws in this respect have not been violated or evaded. If at any time it became apparent to the Superintendent of any Post that the laws have been violated, he might be required to make full inquiry of all in any way connected with or assisting in the trade, to ascertain whether the laws were broken or their breach connived at. This will avail for the regular licensed trader.

11th. For illicit traders and smugglers it will suffice to instruct Commanders of Posts to offer a reward to the Indians for the safe delivery of any and all such persons as bring liquors among them, together with the liquors thus brought.

It is only on the borders of the respective States and Territories that any interruption will be found in the operation of these principles.

12th. Here also a modification of the same principle enacted by the several States and Territories might produce equally happy results.

13th. The mail may, with a change of horses every fifty miles, be carried at the rate of one hundred to one hundred and fifty miles in twenty-four hours.

14th. The leading reason in favor of adopting the aforesaid regulations would be, that by this means the Indians would become our faithful allies. In fact, they will be the best possible police for such a territory. This police can safely be relied upon when under a good supervision. Troops will only be required to correct their faults in cases of extreme misconduct.

15th. In closing, I would remark that I have conversed with many of the principal fur-traders of the American and Hudson Bay Companies, all of whom agree that the several regulations suggested in this communication will accomplish the object proposed, were suitable men appointed for its management and execution.

Respectfully yours,
MARCUS WHITMAN.

Waiilatpui, Oct. 16th, 1847.

Made in the USA
Coppell, TX
27 June 2022

79305997R00125